QUESTIONS AND ANSWERS

Harriet was alone again with Tenby. She did not dare look at his unforgettably handsome face. Instead she directed her eyes at his impeccably knotted neckcloth.

"I do not know why you danced with me or brought me driving, your Grace, especially when you knew that I would have had another escort even if you had not asked," she said. "But I think you should be with Lady Phyllis Reeder or someone else eligible to be your bride."

"You know very well why, Harriet," he said. When her eyes slipped even lower, he set one hand beneath her chin and raised her face. He kissed her, parting his lips over hers so that he could both feel and taste her. Her own lips tightened and trembled and then pushed back against his. He lifted his head and released her chin.

"That is why," he said.

How could Harriet argue with what was so clearly the truth? It would have been as hard as arguing with what was just as certainly coming next . . .

Tempting Harriet

Tempting Harriet

by

Mary Balogh

A SIGNET BOOK

SIGNET
Published by the Penguin Group
Penguin Books USA Inc., 375 Hudson Street,
New York, New York 10014, U.S.A.
Penguin Books Ltd, 27 Wrights Lane,
London W8 5TZ, England
Penguin Books Australia Ltd, Ringwood,
Victoria, Australia
Penguin Books Canada Ltd, 10 Alcorn Avenue,
Toronto, Ontario, Canada M4V 3B2
Penguin Books (N.Z.) Ltd, 182–190 Wairau Road,
Auckland 10, New Zealand

Penguin Books Ltd, Registered Offices:
Harmondsworth, Middlesex, England

First published by Signet, an imprint of Dutton Signet,
a division of Penguin Books USA Inc.

First Printing, May, 1994
10 9 8 7 6 5 4 3 2 1

Copyright © Mary Balogh, 1994
All rights reserved

 REGISTERED TRADEMARK—MARCA REGISTRADA

Printed in the United States of America

1

"Harriet. My dear." Lady Forbes clasped her hands to her bosom and gazed admiringly at her younger friend. "You look quite delectable. You will be all the rage before the evening is out. Does she not, Clive? And will she not?"

Sir Clive Forbes turned from the sideboard at which he was pouring drinks and looked at the lady who had just entered his drawing room and was blushing rosily. "You look very handsome, Harriet," he said, smiling kindly and crossing the room toward her in order to hand her a glass. "But then I do not remember a time when you did not."

"Thank you." Harriet, Lady Wingham, laughed a little nervously and took the offered glass. "It still seems strange to be wearing light colors again after a year in black. It feels even stranger to be wearing something so—sparse." She glanced down at her almost bare bosom and arms. "But I was assured that this design is all the crack."

"If it were not," Sir Clive said gallantly, "then you would soon make it so, Harriet."

"You must trust me," Lady Forbes said. "Did I not promise when you were finally persuaded to come to town for the Season that I would bring you into fashion, my dear? Not that I was taking on an onerous task. You are still as lovely as a girl, even though you must be—?"

"Eight-and-twenty," Harriet said. She grimaced. "A ludicrous age at which to be making my entrée into polite society."

"But still beautiful," Lady Forbes said. "And widows are always intriguing. Especially young and lovely ones."

"And wealthy ones," Sir Clive added with a twinkle in his eye.

"It helps," Lady Forbes said. "Do sit down, dear. We are early. But Robin will be here soon. You will like him as an escort. He quite understands that you are new to London and to the Season and that you have come to meet gentlemen."

"Oh, I have not—" Harriet protested.

"It is as well to call a spade a spade," her friend said, holding up a staying hand. "Of course you have, my dear. You are young and have been widowed for well over a year. And Godfrey, rest his soul, was neither a young nor a robust man."

"I loved him," Harriet said quietly, seating herself carefully so as not to crease the delicate lace and satin of her ball gown.

"That was obvious," Sir Clive said kindly. "You were unfailingly good to him, Harriet. But he is gone. He would be the first to want you to go on enjoying life."

"Yes, he would," Harriet said. "But I am not desperately searching for his successor. I have Susan, after all."

"But daughters do not quite make up for the lack of a husband," Lady Forbes said. "Besides, Susan needs a father."

"There is someone at the door," Sir Clive said. "It will be Robin. Harriet, my dear, I can see we have been alarming you. You arrived in town only a week ago and are about to attend your first London ball and already we are talking about your finding a husband. What we should be advising you to do is enjoy yourself. But without a doubt you will do that. You will certainly not lack for partners."

The butler entered the drawing room at that moment to announce the arrival of Mr. Robin Hammond. Harriet rose and curtsied when he was presented to her. She had not met him before. He was an auburn-haired, fresh-faced gentleman of about her own age. His elegantly clad figure showed signs of portliness to come. He was a cousin of Amanda's and had kindly agreed to escort Harriet to Lady Avingleigh's ball. He bowed and gazed admiringly at the pale blue confection of a ball dress that had been made for the occasion.

"You see, Robin?" Lady Forbes said bluntly as her husband handed him a drink. "I told you she was a beauty, did I not?"

"You did indeed, Amanda," Mr. Hammond agreed, flushing.

Fifteen minutes later the four of them were in Sir Clive's carriage on the way to the Earl of Avingleigh's home on Berkeley Square. Harriet shivered beneath her wrap, partly from the slight chill of the evening air and partly from nervous apprehension. It was still hard to believe that her four-year marriage to Godfrey gave her entrance to *ton* events. They had lived so simply and so quietly in Bath that she had scarcely been aware of the significance of the fact that he was a baron. And until his death fifteen months before, she had been quite ignorant of the fact that he was a very wealthy man. Though of course he had always been generous to her. He had always insisted that she have pretty and fashionable clothes. He had left a generous portion to their daughter. Everything else he had left to Harriet.

Without even being quite aware of the fact, Harriet thought, she had been elevated socially. Although her father had been a gentleman, he had been a mere country parson. His early death had left her mother with only enough money on which to live very frugally in Bath. Harriet herself had been forced to take employment as a lady's companion, though she had been very fortunate in her employer. Clara had seemed more of a friend than an employer. But the association had ended eventually after Clara's marriage and a pregnancy had made Harriet's position redundant, though Clara had urged her to stay anyway. But there had been another reason for leaving. . . .

"We are arriving at the fashionable time, it seems," Mr. Hammond said, moving his head close to the window and gazing ahead. "There must be five carriages pulled up ahead of ours."

"We will have to be patient, then," Sir Clive said. "This ball is expected to be the greatest squeeze of the early part of the Season, I gather."

"It usually is," his wife agreed.

Harriet shivered again and had to make a conscious effort to stop her teeth from chattering. This was not the first time she had been in London. Mr. Sullivan, Clara's husband, had brought them there once for a brief visit and shown them all the famous sights. On one memorable occasion he had taken them to the theater. On most of those outings his friend had been Harriet's escort. Lord Archibald Vinney—tall, blond, handsome, charming. Harriet swallowed and remembered the pathetically naive girl she had been then, though she had been two-and-twenty at the time. Although she had thought herself on her guard, she had still believed when he began to propose to her that it was marriage he was offering. An aristocrat, heir to a dukedom, proposing marriage to a little mouse of a lady's companion! Harriet felt embarrassment for her former self. It was a very generous *carte blanche* he had been offering.

Finally their carriage drew level with the open doors into the Avingleigh mansion. They waited until a footman let down the steps. Sir Clive helped his wife to the pavement and then Mr. Hammond helped Harriet. She glanced up the shallow flight of steps into the brightly lit hall. It appeared to be milling with liveried servants and splendidly ·clad guests. Suddenly she no longer felt overdressed. She was not going to be conspicuous after all. But her stomach performed a giant somersault and she took Mr. Hammond's offered arm with gratitude. At the grand age of eight-and-twenty she was attending her first London ball and feeling as excited and nervous as a girl.

Lord Archibald Vinney, she thought, looking about her nervously as they entered the crowded hall and Lady Forbes whisked her off toward the ladies' withdrawing room. Was he in London? Would he be at Lady Avingleigh's ball? Was he married? She had heard nothing about him since Clara's return to London from her country home six years before had sent Harriet fleeing home to Bath lest she see him again and give in to the dreadful temptation to accept *carte blanche*. Clara knew of her infatuation and had never mentioned him, though she wrote frequently. And yet, Harriet had to admit, though it would have been easier to deny the truth, he was a large part of her reason for accepting Amanda's invitation to spend a few months in London for the Season now that her year of mourning for God-frey was over.

It sounded laughable. It *was* laughable. After six years she could still feel sick with longing at the mere thought of him. She had come to London to enjoy herself, to fulfill a girlhood dream that had seemed unrealizable until very recently. She had come to shop and to visit, to mingle and to dance. She had come to live out the youth that had passed her by in some dullness. She had come because she was a widow and had found that a dull widowhood did not have the sense of security or bring the contentment that a rather dull marriage had brought. She had come because Godfrey was dead and there was no bringing him back, though she had bitterly mourned his loss. She had come because Susan would enjoy a change of scenery and some of the pleasures of town. And because perhaps—though probably not—she would catch a glimpse of Lord Archibald Vinney again.

"No," Lady Forbes said with a sigh and a laugh, turning away from a looking glass at which she had adjusted her hair and the shoulders of her gown, "there is nothing you can possibly do to improve your appearance, Harriet, dear. One cannot improve upon perfection. Ah, to be young and lovely again. Though I was only ever one of the two." She chuckled. "Do you like Robin? He is rather dull, I must confess, but I am fond of the boy."

"He is kind," Harriet said. Mr. Hammond had made an effort to converse and set her at her ease both in Sir Clive's drawing room and in the carriage. "I feel like a gauche girl, Amanda."

"I will not argue with the one word," Lady Forbes said, "but I can assure you that you do not look gauche, Harriet. You will be well received, mark my words."

She was to be proved quite correct. Amanda Forbes was only a baronet's wife and as such was low on the social scale as far as the *ton* was concerned, but her father had been a viscount, a title that her brother now held, and she had been careful to cultivate influential connections. She and Sir Clive had visited Bath regularly each year and had been friends of Lord Wingham. Lady Forbes had grown fond of the baron's young and lovely wife and had now set herself to make his widow fashionable and to find her a husband of some position. She could not expect to attract anyone above the rank of baron as a husband, of course, since despite her wealth and her title she was not herself of noble birth. But there must be scores of unattached and perfectly eligible gentlemen who were not out of her reach and would be only too happy to attach themselves to such wealth and beauty and charm—even though there was a child who would come along with her.

And so Lady Forbes had been busy ensuring that there would be gentlemen ready to be presented to Harriet and to dance with her. And of course she must arrive with an escort since she was not an unmarried young girl but a woman and a widow. Lady Forbes, looking now with an almost envious approval at her young friend and protégée as they turned to leave the withdrawing room to join the receiving line with their men, was quite sure that Harriet would do very well indeed.

Before she danced the opening set of country dances with Mr. Hammond, Harriet was feeling flushed and happy. No fewer than four gentlemen had asked Amanda to present them, and three of them had engaged her to dance later in the evening. Even if no one else asked her, she had four dances to look forward to, with four different gentlemen. The fear she supposed all women experienced at their first ball that they would be wallflowers had been put to rest even before the dancing began.

Harriet smiled at Mr. Hammond as he led her onto the floor, and hoped that she would not forget the steps of the dance in her nervousness. But she would not think of such a thing. It was not as if she had never danced at all. Godfrey had often taken her to the assemblies in Bath and had always encouraged her to dance, though his weak heart had prevented him from ever dancing with her himself.

She was going to enjoy herself, she thought determinedly. From now until the end of the Season, when she would return home with Susan, she was going to give herself up to pleasure—even though several glances about the ballroom had revealed to her that *he* was not there. She had not expected him anyway. And it was as well he was absent. She could expect nothing but misery from seeing him again. Six years had passed. Doubtless he was married by now. The thought caused pain. Foolishly, after six years, she could still feel pain. Heavens, she had been married herself during that time and was now a mother. She would not think of him. She had trained herself over the years to remember him, if at all, only as a rather bittersweet memory. It would be as well to keep it that way.

The music began, and Harriet found that her feet moved gracefully and easily to the steps. She returned Mr. Hammond's smile. It was really a very pleasant smile, one that set her at her ease. Amanda had made a very good choice of escort.

"I cannot," the Duke of Tenby said with a sigh to his companion when the latter asked him if he would go straight to the card room. They were on their way up the stairs of Lord Avingleigh's mansion. Their path was clear since they had arrived deliberately late in order to avoid the crush. "I have decided to go shopping in earnest."

Lord Bruce Ingram looked at him with some interest and laughed. "You have been threatening to do so these four or five years, Archie," he said. "Has the time really come?"

"It has," the duke said. "At Christmas my grandmother made a point of informing the whole family that it could very well be her last Christmas, since she will turn eighty during August. She made a particular point of ensuring that I was present every time she broached the subject. Privately she reminded me of the vow she made on the death of my grandfather six years ago not to die herself until I was married and my wife safely delivered of our first boy."

Lord Bruce grimaced in sympathy.

"The only way I could have helped her keep her vow before next Christmas," the duke said, "was to have rushed some sweet thing to the altar with the aid of a special license and to have immediately set to work on her." He yawned behind one lace-edged hand.

"The idea has its appeal, one must admit," Lord Bruce said, turning with his friend at the top of the stairs in the direction of the ballroom. "There is less interesting work to be done in this world."

His grace frowned at him, not amused by his tone of levity. "It is not easy to rush a sweet young thing to the altar," he said, "since just any sweet young thing will not do, Bruce. It has been instilled in me since childhood that only females of suitably elevated rank will do as my duchess. Nothing below an earl's daughter, in other words. Why is it that daughters of viscounts and lower are often appealingly pretty while daughters of earls and upward are invariably antidotes?"

Lord Bruce laughed. "Ah," he said, "we have missed the receiving line. That, at least, is a blessing."

"And doubtless we have missed the first two or three sets too," the duke said with a sigh. "I made my grandmother a promise. I promised that I would be married before September and have my wife swelling with child before next Christmas. Under such circumstances, the old girl undertook to remain alive that long and probably until the birth to make sure I do not commit the unpardonable faux pas of begetting a daughter first."

"The Season swung to life a week or so ago," Lord Bruce said. "A trifle slow, are you not, Archie?"

"As you say." The duke spoke with haughty gloom. "I have procrastinated too long. But behold me tonight a serious shopper, Bruce. How long will it be before the fact becomes general knowledge, do you suppose?"

"Ten minutes?" his friend suggested with a grin. "It is not often you are seen in a ballroom, Archie. The cat will certainly be out of the bag as soon as you single someone out to dance with. All the mamas will turn ecstatic."

The duke frowned as the two of them stood in the doorway of the ballroom and glanced about them. Already he had been noticed. He could feel eyes on him, and met many of them as he looked around with a forced air of languidness. He fingered the ribbon of his quizzing glass, though he did not raise it to his eye. Of course, Bruce was doubtless receiving his share of looks too, as he was no small matrimonial prize and was an equally unfamiliar sight on the marriage mart. But his grace of Tenby did not for a moment believe that he himself was not the prime object of interest. His lip curled with distaste.

He had no wish to be married. Before succeeding to his title, he had persuaded himself that there was no need to think of marriage yet, since he was still only the heir to a dukedom. And then when his grandfather died, he had persuaded himself that six-and-twenty was too young to marry and that he would wait until he was thirty. He had turned thirty two years ago and had stopped making excuses. He had tried not to think of marriage. Or of that nasty duty of begetting heirs.

He had considered marriage only once in his life. Quite madly, the only reason having been that the girl was adamantly unwilling to be bedded as a mistress and he had very badly wanted to bed her. At the time he had described his feelings to himself as being in love. He had since realized that he had been merely in lust. But he had come perilously close. If his grandfather had not died when he had, it would have been too late. He had been preparing to go after the girl to offer her marriage when he had been summoned to what had turned out to be his grandfather's deathbed. By the time that was over and the funeral and all the business of mourning and getting himself acquainted with his new position as Duke of Tenby and head of the family, he had recovered from his madness. A good thing too. His grandmother and his mother and all his uncles and aunts and cousins would have had a collective heart seizure if he had married so far beneath him. And if he had done anything as plebeian as marry for love.

"There is Kingsley's daughter," Lord Bruce said. "Fresh from the schoolroom and a marquess's filly, Archie. What more could you ask for? It is hard to decide, though, which end of a horse she most resembles."

The duke allowed his eyes to rest for a moment on the young girl in question. "Unkind, Bruce," he said. "But frankly the mere thought of deflowering an infant makes me shudder. She must surely have left the schoolroom early."

"Barthorpe's girl, then," Lord Bruce said a short while later. "An earl's daughter. As low as you dare go, Archie.

She is in her third Season, of course. One does wonder what is wrong with the girl."

"Perhaps no more than the fact that she is discriminating," the duke said, turning his glance on Lady Phyllis Reeder, daughter of the Earl of Barthorpe. "Or perhaps she likes attention. She was apparently the toast of the last two Seasons."

"She had better marry this year, then, before she gets long in the tooth," Lord Bruce said. "She cannot expect to be the toast forever. She is not a bad looker, Archie."

"Hm," the duke said. "Good-natured too. I have been in company with her once or twice. I could do worse, I suppose. Grandmama would be ecstatic. Lady Phyllis is one of a list of ten females that have her unqualified approval."

"Well, then." His friend laughed heartily. "What are you waiting for, Arch? There is a distinct air of anticipation about us. Everyone is waiting to see if you will advance into the ballroom and perhaps even dance, or if you are merely teasing and will turn and disappear into the card room for the rest of the evening."

The duke fingered the ribbon of his quizzing glass and pursed his lips. "If life were only that easy," he said. "I shall make my bow to Lady Phyllis and the countess, then. And take the girl out for a dance if I am unfortunate enough to find that she has one free. In a moment, Bruce. Give me that moment to collect myself."

He looked about the ballroom again, reluctant to move. Once he stepped inside, and made his bow to any unmarried lady below the age of thirty, he believed, he would have taken an irrevocable step. Word that the Duke of Tenby was finally shopping for a duchess would be out almost before he had taken that step and made that bow. There were a few ladies present that he did not know. The new Season had brought some new faces to town as it always did. Some of them were even pretty. Perhaps he should find out who exactly was in town before embarking on anything that might be construed as a courtship of one particular lady.

That one, for example, he thought, his eyes coming to rest on a particular young lady who had just finished dancing with one partner and was smiling with engaging and unfashionable enthusiasm at two prospective ones who had converged on her at the same moment. Small, girlishly slim, dainty, blond-haired, exquisitely gowned in pale blue satin overlaid with lace. She reminded him . . .

The Duke of Tenby relinquished the ribbon of his quizzing glass in order to grasp its jeweled handle and raise it to his eye. The woman—or girl—had turned her head away, so that all he could see were the soft and shining ringlets at the back of her head, the creamy skin of her back above the low cut of her gown, and the suggestion of slim shapeliness beneath its loose folds. Delicious! He waited for her to turn her head, oblivious for the moment to the fact that he was still under close observation himself.

And then she did turn her head so that suddenly he saw her full face as she laughed at one of her would-be partners with upward-curving lips and sparkling eyes.

The duke lowered his glass hastily and turned without a word to hurry from the ballroom. Lord Bruce Ingram appeared at his side again after a few moments. He was laughing.

"You have turned craven already, Archie?" he said. "You know, I seem to remember having heard somewhere that it is permitted to dance with a lady without being obligated to offer for her the very next morning. Of course, you could just defy your grandmother and order her to live for another ten years or so if she wants to see your offspring. You are head of the family after all, Arch. It is your place to give orders, not hers." He laughed again.

"Do me a favor, Bruce, will you?" the duke said, his voice tight with some unexplained emotion. "Go and play cards. I'll see you later."

Lord Bruce threw back his head and roared with mirth, drawing the curious and rather disapproving stares of those people who were standing about on the landing outside the ballroom. "I am making you nervous, Arch," he said. "But I'll do as you ask, old chap. I must confess, standing in a ballroom like that makes me a trifle nervous too." He slapped his friend on the back. "Don't shop for too long. I have heard it gives one blisters on the feet." He disappeared in the direction of the card room.

His grace of Tenby did not even see him go. He must have been mistaken, he thought. She was very familiar. He had noticed that as soon as his eyes had alighted on her. The same coloring. The same small slimness. The same face, except that this woman's was laughing and animated. Not exactly flirtatious, perhaps, but definitely the face of a woman who knew herself beautiful and attractive to men. Harriet Pope had never looked like that. Quiet, sweet. The duke stopped his pacing and closed his eyes for a moment. She had blushed easily and very charmingly. He had delighted in making her blush.

No, of course the woman in the ballroom was not Harriet. Harriet had been a servant, a lady's companion. Freddie's wife's companion for a while until she had gone home to her mother in Bath. Six years ago. He had deliberately not asked either Freddie or Clara about her since then. He had not wanted to know. The woman in the ballroom was not anyone's paid companion. If she were, she would be dressed soberly and sitting demurely in the shadows with the other chaperons.

It was just that he was thinking of the wife he had promised Grandmama he would take within the next few months and had thought, very naturally, of the only woman he had ever seriously considered marrying.

Harriet! Seeing the woman in the ballroom had set him to fleeing like a boy and his heart to racing just as if he really had been in love with her all those years ago. Just as if it had not been the mere lust to put himself inside the girl's body. Though she had not been a girl even then. Six years later she could no longer possibly resemble that woman in the ballroom, whom he was going to have to force himself to look at once more. Harriet Pope must be close to thirty years of age. He strolled nonchalantly in the direction of the doors once more.

But this time he was not left to stand alone, observing those within the ballroom at his leisure. His hostess was at his side almost as soon as he made his appearance, smiling graciously and apologizing for not greeting him on his arrival.

"It was not that I did not see you, Tenby," she said. "Who could miss noticing such a blond god? Especially when he is looking so startlingly distinguished in black. And when he is a duke to boot." She tapped him on the arm with her fan. "Never say you are going to grace my ballroom by dancing in it. I would not be able to bear such success."

He smiled at her. "Am I such a hopeless case, Chloe?" he asked. "Who is the lady in pale blue, pray?" He made a slight gesture in the direction of the lady at whom he had had no chance to have a second look.

"Lady Wingham?" she said. "Baron Wingham's wife up for the Season. She is having some success tonight."

"Present me, Chloe, if you will," he said, "before the dancing starts again."

"There will just be time," she said, taking his arm. "I wonder if Lady Wingham realizes what a rare honor is about to be accorded her. Every other lady's eyes in the room will turn instantly and uniformly green, Tenby."

His grace was not listening. She had her head turned away again and was talking to a third gentleman. She looked very like indeed. And then she turned her head as he approached with Lady Avingleigh and the latter called her by name.

Harriet Pope glanced, smiling, into his eyes and then stared into them without smiling.

And then she blushed.

2

As a girl she had dreamed of dancing at a real ball, of being the focus of attention and admiration, of being whisked off to dance by dashing gentlemen. It was a typical girlish dream, even though her upbringing as a clergyman's daughter had taught her that it would be wicked to dwell on such dreams. For one thing, one did not waste one's time on dreams of the impossible. For another, it was wicked to hanker after frivolity and indulge personal vanity.

The dreams had not entirely died when she grew older, though they had been tempered by her knowledge that they were only dreams, that they could never become reality. When her father had died, her mother was poor. She herself had had to become a servant. But it had been there nevertheless, the dream of what might have been and of what might still be if only she were Cinderella, if only fairy tales could become reality. But she had been too sensible and too practical a young lady to believe that such a thing could really be possible. Except that once, of course, in London, when several times she had had a dizzyingly handsome escort and when for a brief moment—two brief moments—she had allowed her dreams to turn into painful hope. He had offered for her twice, once in London and once at Ebury Court, Clara's home in Kent. Twice he had offered to make her his mistress.

Dreams had become firmly anchored in reality when Godfrey offered her marriage after the death of her mother, whose friend he had been. She had married him without hesitation, even though he had been fifty-six to her twenty-three. He had been able to offer her security, emotional as well as financial. She had married him because she did not want to become someone else's paid companion or governess and because he had always been kind to her and because she would have thought her heart was dead if it had not pained her so much and so often. She had been unexpectedly happy with Godfrey. He had been good to her and she had tried her very best to be good to him. But dreams had died. This was reality, this marriage to an ailing man much older than herself, this life of rather dull routine in Bath.

But now the dream was back and it was becoming suddenly and stunningly real. Far from being a wallflower at Lady Avingleigh's ball, she had a partner for each set and a choice of partners for each one after the first. Gentlemen came to be presented to her, some of them taking even Amanda by surprise, Harriet suspected. She also suspected that some of the gentlemen came because Amanda and Clive had arranged that they would just in case she should be in danger of being a wallflower. All the gentlemen with whom she danced conversed politely with her. Some of them paid her compliments—about her hair, her gown, her dancing skills, her eyes, her smile. Two of them named other social events that would be happening in the coming weeks and asked her if she was to attend. One of them asked if he might call at Lady Forbes's the next day.

It was all wonderful beyond imagining. It was foolish to be so excited by it all, Harriet knew. It was only a ball, after all. Making polite conversation and paying compliments were part of what gentlemen did at balls. But sometimes, she decided very early in the evening, it was wonderful to give in to foolishness. There had been so little of it in her life. And so she did nothing to try to hide her enjoyment, though she knew that it was fashionable to appear bored in company. She knew that her cheeks must be flushed and that her eyes were probably bright and her lips smiling. She did not care.

She finished dancing a quadrille with Mr. Kershaw and smiled at both him and Mr. Hammond, to whose side he returned her. Mr. Hammond was waiting to present Sir Philip Grafton, who bowed gravely and requested the next set with her. She stood talking with the two of them during the

five or ten minutes between sets and then turned to greet
Mr. Selway, to whom Clive had presented her earlier.

It would be very easy to believe, Harriet thought, that she
was a great success, that she really was taking the *ton* by
storm, as the expression went. At the tender age of eight-
and-twenty. As a widow. As the mother of a four-year-old
daughter. The thought amused her and caused her to laugh
merrily at some witticism of Mr. Selway's. His look, focused on her mouth, became more appreciative. Godfrey
had always said she had lovely teeth.

Mr. Selway began to say something else. She guessed he
was about to ask her for the set following the next. But he
was interrupted by a woman's voice—Lady Avingleigh's—
calling her by name. A couple of times before their hostess
had presented a gentleman to her. Harriet turned with a
smile. Lady Avingleigh had a gentleman with her this time
too, a tall and wondrously elegant gentleman dressed very
differently from all the other men present in black coat and
knee breeches. Harriet glanced at his face before turning
politely to Lady Avingleigh. Though in fact she never did
turn.

He had very blond hair and plenty of it. His face was
handsome, aristocratic, thin-lipped. And he had silver eyes.
She had always been fascinated by them. They were, she
supposed whenever she was not looking into them, a light
gray. But when she did look into them she knew that they
could only be described as silver. Usually they looked back
into hers with amusement or irony. Now they were blank
but focused very fully on hers.

The last time she had seen him—the very last—he had
ridden all the way from London to Ebury Court in order to
make her his second offer. After her refusal he had kissed
her and taken his leave. She had stood where she was for
many long minutes, counting slowly and deliberately until
she could be sure that he had gone beyond recall and that
she would not go running after him, begging to be taken
with him to whatever love nest he had had prepared for her.

He bowed suddenly, leaving her feeling bewildered and
wondering for how long they had stared at each other. She

was aware that she had stopped smiling, but seemed incapable of putting her smile back on. Her cheeks felt hot.

"Ah, I was not mistaken, then," he said in a soft, pleasant voice that jolted her memory. "Lady Wingham and I have a former acquaintance, Chloe. She was Miss Harriet Pope when I last knew her."

Harriet curtsied on legs that felt as if they might give up supporting her at any moment. She was only just beginning to realize that it was happening. It was actually happening. She was seeing him again. And it could have been yesterday. He looked very little different. No older. No less handsome.

"My lord," she murmured.

"Come, Lady Wingham," he said, and his eyes were mocking her as they had always used to do, "that should be 'your grace,' you know. I suspect you have not been listening to Chloe." He was fingering the ribbon of his quizzing glass.

"His grace, the Duke of Tenby, Lady Wingham," Lady Avingleigh said, and Harriet became aware that the words were being said for the second time. She could feel her cheeks grow hot again.

"I beg your pardon, your grace," she said, grasping the fan that dangled from her wrist by a ribbon, opening it, and waving it before her face to cool herself. She smiled and tried to recapture the mood of exhilaration and wonder that had borne her through the evening thus far. She had a moment in which to collect herself. The Duke of Tenby was bowing and assuring Lady Avingleigh that yes, indeed, he was acquainted with the other gentlemen.

"Lady Wingham," he said then, "will you honor me by dancing a set with me?"

"The next is promised to Sir Philip Grafton," she said, seeing beyond his shoulder couples taking their places on the floor.

"And the one after to me, Tenby," Mr. Selway said. Harriet did not contradict him, though she had not, strictly speaking, promised any such thing.

The duke looked at Lady Avingleigh. "When is the next

waltz to be, Chloe?" he asked. "There are to be waltzes, I take it?"

"The supper dance, Tenby," she said. "If you are to dance it, it will be as well that everyone can sit and revive themselves afterward. The shock will be great."

The silver eyes turned on Harriet again as Sir Philip Grafton extended an arm for hers. "The supper waltz, Lady Wingham?" he said. "You will dance it with me?" It seemed more a command than a request.

"Thank you, your grace," she said and placed her arm along Sir Philip's and was led away into the dance. Her heart felt as if it had leapt right into her throat and was beating there at double time.

"My reputation will be made," Sir Philip said, laughing. "To have led a lady out right under the nose of Tenby is no mean feat."

"I did not know that he is a duke," Harriet said foolishly.

"The *ton* has been waiting with some impatience for several years for him to begin to show an interest in its daughters," Sir Philip said. "He avoids ballrooms as if the plague raged within their portals. He has never been known to dance. One wonders if he is able. Perhaps he will tread all over your feet, Lady Wingham." He was still laughing.

Or I all over his, Harriet thought. She looked swiftly about her, but the Duke of Tenby had disappeared. Just as if he had never been there. Just as if she had imagined it all, foolish woman. And imagined that he had singled her out and solicited a dance with her when he was reputed never to enter ballrooms or to dance in them. But she had not imagined it. Her heart would not be beating so wildly if she had. And Sir Philip would not be laughing and saying what he just had if it had all been imagination.

The Duke of Tenby. She had never known his grandfather's title. She had not known that his grandfather had died. His grace. It was strange to think of him by another name. As if it was not he after all. As if she had imagined that it was he. As if the duke to whom she had just been presented merely resembled him and her imagination had taken flight. Except that he had told Lady Avingleigh that they had a previous acquaintance, that he had known her as Harriet Pope.

"You will be the envy of every lady at the ball," Sir Philip was saying. "By this time tomorrow you will be the envy of every lady in London."

"How absurd," she said. "Merely because he is to dance with me? You are dancing with me, sir, and Mr. Kershaw and Mr. Hammond and other gentlemen have danced with me. What is the difference, pray?"

He laughed again. "None of us is the Duke of Tenby, ma'am," he said.

At first Harriet thought she imagined it. But as they danced on and began to converse on other topics, her eyes occasionally strayed to the other dancers and to those people, most notably older ladies, who did not dance but stood or sat about the perimeter of the ballroom. Wherever she looked she caught eyes or quizzing glasses or lorgnettes looking directly back at her. After a while she realized that it was not her imagination.

Lord Archibald Vinney had become the Duke of Tenby. Young, unmarried, elusive, he had become also a great matrimonial prize. And for the first time since he had succeeded to his title, apparently, he had stepped inside a ballroom and asked a lady to dance. Her. Harriet. She wondered how the people whose interest she seemed to have aroused would react if they knew that six years ago she might have left employment as a lady's companion for the far more lucrative post of mistress to Lord Archibald Vinney. She wondered how soon he would have tired of her, how generous a settlement he would have made on her when he discarded her.

She wondered if by any chance he would renew his offer, and her insides somersaulted at the thought.

When Sir Philip returned her to Amanda and Mr. Hammond at the end of the set, there were no fewer than four gentlemen waiting to be presented to her and two more strolled up within the following minutes, before Mr. Selway claimed his dance.

"You have been brought into fashion, my dear," Lady Forbes breathed in her ear when she could do so without being overheard, "quite brilliantly. Tenby has made his bow to you. It is a singular honor."

Damnation, but she was more beautiful than ever. She had no business still being beautiful at her age. The Duke of Tenby stood behind Lord Bruce Ingram's chair in the card room, his pose relaxed, his lips pursed. Bruce was about to make a stupid move—disastrous if the stakes had been higher. But there was nothing particularly unusual about that. One thing his grace always studiously avoided when playing cards himself was partnering Ingram.

He was still shaken from seeing her and realizing that it was indeed she. Like a little ghost out of his past. He had always assumed whenever he thought of her that she was living a life of quiet and blameless drudgery somewhere, resisting the advances of amorous employers as she had resisted him, making an armor of her virtue. She had wanted him. He knew that. She had even admitted as much on the last occasion he had seen her, but had added with that sweet gravity that had always been able to raise his temperature a few degrees that temptation was not sin, only the giving in to temptation.

He had been about to marry her when his grandfather became gravely ill. Or to offer her marriage, anyway. Perhaps she would have refused. He had been about to offer her marriage because a marriage bed had seemed the only one he had had a chance of coaxing her into. And because he had been in love with her—in lust with her.

He had marveled at himself over the years since, wondering what could possibly have tempted him to act so out of character and so contrary to all that his family and upbringing expected of him. As memory of her had faded, blurring about the edges, it had seemed to him that she was nothing so out of the ordinary. She was a quiet, sweet little blusher. None of those qualities was appealing to him in other women. It was just that he had expected an easy lay with Miss Harriet Pope, he had convinced himself, and had been piqued at being rejected by a mere servant.

But he had remembered wrongly. Harriet Pope had been all of those things he had remembered, but it was the sum total of all the qualities he usually found unappealing rather than each taken separately that had so affected him. And he really had been in love with her, he realized now in some surprise, wincing as Lord Bruce Ingram made the expected fatal move. It had not been just the desire to mount her body, though it had definitely been that too. It had been the need to possess her and to be possessed by her. The realization shook him. He had never felt that way about any other mistress, either before or after the start of a liaison. He did not feel it about Bridget, his current resident mistress. He visited Bridget in order to satisfy his lust. It was as simple as that. He cared not one fig for the person inside Bridget's body.

"The devil," Lord Bruce said, scraping back his chair and getting to his feet. "I can't think why I play, Tenby. I have no luck."

The duke forbore to comment on the fact that it was not always luck or the lack thereof that accounted for a loss at the tables. "You need to find a servant to refill your glass," he said.

Lord Bruce nodded and signaled a footman. "So you did not pluck up the courage to go shopping after all, Tenby?" he said. "Many a fluttering hope must have been dashed when you walked away from the ballroom doors. You care to play?"

"Do you know a Lord Wingham?" the duke asked abruptly.

Lord Bruce thought for a moment. "Can't say I do," he said. "What about him?"

"I am dancing the supper waltz with his wife," the duke said.

Lord Bruce grinned. "You made the supreme effort after all, old chap?" he said. "And found that the first woman you fancied is not a marketable commodity? Hard luck, Tenby. They should have to wear different-colored plumes in their hair or something, don't you agree? Yellow for married, red for single, pink for married yet available, blue for single but not interested. It would all give a man a sporting chance not to make an ass of himself."

The duke was not paying attention. He was wondering

who Wingham was, how long she had been married to him, how deeply she cared for him. Was he a handsome devil, damn him? The name made him sound dashing. Was he one of her former employers who had also discovered that it had to be a marriage bed at Miss Harriet Pope's back or none at all? Was that what she had always been in search of? A wedding ring in exchange for her virtue? Was that what she had hoped for from him? She had very nearly got her wish too, by Jove.

But there was no point in whipping up anger against her, he thought. That was all any woman was after, was it not? That was what virtue was—that marketable commodity which a woman of quality sold in exchange for a husband. Harriet had sold to Wingham, whoever the devil he was. He wondered if she was happy, if she considered she had made a fair exchange. She had looked happy enough until she had caught sight of him.

But damnation, she looked lovely when she blushed. He had not been able to resist falling into the old habit of trying to make her do so. It was no more difficult to do now than it had been six years ago. How much longer did he have to wait before the supper dance?

"You may wear a hole in it if you stare so fixedly and so ferociously at it, Arch," Lord Bruce said.

The duke looked up at him, frowning in incomprehension, and then back down to the carpet at which he had been staring.

"She must be a looker," Lord Bruce said. "But not a better looker than Bridget, surely? And certainly not better endowed by nature in her other parts? Impossible, Archie."

"You are referring to a lady," the duke said, his voice haughtily aristocratic, one hand playing with the handle of his quizzing glass. "And another man's wife, Bruce."

Lord Bruce chuckled, quite uncowed by the reprimand. "She is a looker," he said. "This I have to see, Arch, my boy, even at the expense of having to step into the lions' den for the second time in one evening. The supper waltz. And then supper. Someone had better warn Wingham, whoever he might be, poor devil. But he might be a ferocious giant who has no respect for ducal titles, you know.

You might be going into the lions' den in dead earnest, Archie."

"I am not planning to ravish the woman in the middle of the ballroom," the duke said with a hauteur that would have cowed most listeners.

His friend merely chuckled. "In some secluded corner, then?" he said. "Much more tasteful, Archie. You had better not be late. It must be approaching suppertime if my stomach is a reliable hourglass. It usually is."

Damnation, the duke thought, releasing his hold on his quizzing glass and turning to leave the card room and return to the ballroom, he was feeling nervous! Nervous of going back in there and dancing with her. With Harriet Pope, the little girl who had worked for Freddie's wife. With a woman who was now married to another man and of no possible interest to him except as a slightly nostalgic memory.

More likely, he thought, it was of entering the ballroom he was nervous. He had the feeling that doing so would change the whole comfortable and familiar pattern of his life. Though perhaps that was already an accomplished fact. He had already entered the ballroom and found Harriet there. Already he was uncomfortable and already he was on unfamiliar ground.

He squared his shoulders as he approached the ballroom, Bruce at his side, and concentrated on looking haughty and slightly bored. It was an effective mask and had served him well through the years. She was in the middle of a circle of admirers, he saw at once, flushed and laughing. Behaving quite unlike her former self.

"Which one?" Lord Bruce asked.

"In front of Lady Muir," the duke said, turning his eyes away from her. Obviously a set had just ended and the supper waltz was next. "Holding court."

Lord Bruce Ingram was silent for a few moments. "Yes, a looker," he said. "And more than that. Definitely more than that. Poor Bridget. I hear a death knell tolling. Do knells toll? Or is my lady a virtuous wife, do you suppose? What a bore for you if she is, Arch. My commiserations, old chap."

"I had better go and claim her," the duke said, strolling away, feeling again as he had felt earlier the attention he was drawing. Well, he would waltz with her and have supper with her, if the unknown Lord Wingham did not raise any objection. And then he would take himself off to Bridget's to give her an unexpected night of hard work and to proceed to lay the ghost that should have been laid six years ago.

She was aware of his approach. He could tell that, though she was half turned away from him. He watched her flush deepen and her smile become more fixed as she listened to what Robin Hammond was saying to her. He wondered how she had remembered him through the years, if she had remembered him at all. With shame? With indignation? With regret? With indifference? He wondered how she had been comparing her memories of him with her present feelings for her husband.

"Lady Wingham?" He bowed to her as she and her whole court turned to look at him. He had almost the feeling of being on the stage, of having the whole room watching the little drama unfold. "My set, I believe?"

"Thank you." Her eyes were green. Their color had been one detail of her appearance that he had not been able to recall. Though looking into them now, he could not understand how he could have forgotten. They were such a very distinctive shade of green. They were wide eyes, disturbingly and perhaps unwisely direct. Perhaps that was the reason for his forgetting their color. Somehow Harriet's eyes drew one beyond their color and their form into the woman herself. She appeared to have no defenses as almost all other people of his acquaintance did. Another of her undeniable attractions, perhaps. One felt immediately protective of her. At least he had. And did.

Her arm was light along the top of his. The tips of her fingers extended beyond the lace of the ruffles that partly covered his hands, and brushed against his bare flesh. There was something distinctly erotic about her touch, though he was sure it must have happened dozens of times before when other women had taken his arm. He led her out onto the dance floor. The top of her head reached barely to his chin. And yet in memory she had seemed even smaller. Perhaps it was the girlish slimness of her body that gave the impression of excessive smallness. She smelled of some appealing perfume, and yet when he tried to identify it to himself it seemed to him like nothing so much as clean soap.

She turned toward him when he stopped, and fixed her eyes on the neckcloth his valet had tied earlier in the evening with great artistry and greater pride. The music began almost immediately. She raised her arms and set one hand very lightly on his shoulder. He could feel it there like a lover's touch on bare skin. He raised his eyebrows at the fanciful thought. He set his hand behind her waist and felt its smallness, its warmth, the feminine arch of her back. Her palm touched his and he enclosed her hand in his own. They moved to the music.

"Well, Harriet," he said softly, "we meet again, my little blushing charmer." The old words that he had used to use. He had not intended to say them now.

Her eyelashes lifted and her eyes looked into his, almost setting him back on his heels. "Yes, my lord," she said. His heart did strange things as the predictable blush made its appearance. "Yes, your grace."

3

She felt like a girl fresh from the schoolroom, in the company of a young man for the first time, noticed by one for the first time. She felt weak-kneed and breathless and tongue-tied. She was a woman of eight-and-twenty, she reminded herself. She was a widow. She had known many men as friends and acquaintances. She had known one man as a lover. She raised her eyes to his again.

Silver. They were pure silver. And they were watching her, a mocking smile lurking somewhere not far from their surface.

"Is it so hard to realize that I have become such a grand personage?" he asked. "My grandfather died quite soon after you sent me away from Ebury Court."

"I am sorry," she said.

"That he died?" he asked. "Or that you sent me away?"

"That he died," she said. "Were you fond of him?"

"Ours has always been a close family," he said. "And now they are all mine. All my responsibility—a grandmother, a mother, uncles and aunts and cousins galore. Were you ever sorry that you sent me away?"

Yes. To her shame, yes. Sorry at the time and sorry for painful weeks and months afterward. Sorry even after she had married Godfrey and he had somewhat surprised her by making a real marriage of it and she had wondered what it would have been like . . .

"No, of course not," she said.

He was smiling at her. "You hesitated a little too long and have allowed a little too much color to flow into your cheeks," he said. "I have regretted it, Harriet. And I am ready to kill out of jealous rage. Where is he? Is he in the ballroom?"

"Who?" She looked at him blankly.

"Lord Wingham," he said. "Your husband."

He did not know. Obviously he knew as little about her as she knew about him. For the same reason? she wondered. But no, of course not. What reason would he have had to remember her and deliberately avoid pursuing any news of her?

"Godfrey," she said. "He died fifteen months ago."

"Ah," he said. "You are the merry widow, then. And you have come to take the *ton* by storm and to enjoy yourself quite ferociously until the Season's end."

He made the truth sound rather sordid and her rather heartless. "I loved him," she said.

His eyes roamed over her face. His voice was almost gentle when he spoke. "Did you, Harriet?" he asked. "Did some accident take him from you?"

"It was heart failure," she said. "We found him dead in his bed one morning." His valet and she. The valet had been alarmed by his stillness in bed and his lack of response to having the curtains drawn back from the window and to the man's discreet cough to announce the arrival of the baron's shaving water. The valet had come for her, afraid to check more closely for himself. Godfrey had been cold to her touch. He had been dead for several hours.

"Ah," the duke said.

She knew that he must be wondering. But of course he would not ask the question. "He was sixty years old," she said. "His heart had been weak for years."

It was only after she had spoken and he continued to look at her while she gazed beyond him that she heard the echo of what sounded like defiance in her voice. It would seem to him that she had married an older, ailing man for his money and for position. It would seem that she was conniving. Here she was little more than a year after his death in London enjoying herself at one of the grand balls of the Season. And there would be some truth in his assumption. But only some. She would not have married Godfrey if she had not liked him and if she had not believed in her heart that she could and would make him a good wife.

She looked back up into the Duke of Tenby's eyes, defiance in her own now as well as in her voice. "I loved him," she said again. "He was good to me."

"I am glad of both facts," he said softly. "I never said otherwise, Harriet."

"No," she said, "but you thought it. You thought I refused your very generous offer because it did not include respectability and then went and did better for myself in Bath by marrying a wealthy man who could not be expected to live long." Where were the words and the ideas coming from? She felt dismayed and mortified. She had no need whatsoever to be on the defensive with the Duke of Tenby.

"Did I think so?" His eyes were mocking again. "How very ungentlemanly of me. I am sorry for your loss, Harriet. It must have been painful. But I am glad you are beginning to put it behind you. You have come to enjoy the Season, I presume? And are enjoying it? You appeared to be doing so until you began to dance with me, anyway. Have I diminished your joy?"

"Of course not." Her eyes slipped to his neckcloth. He must have a very skilled valet. Godfrey had always worn his simply tied.

"The devil!" he said suddenly and his arm at her waist tightened and drew her right against him for the merest moment before loosening and setting her at the correct distance again. "An imminent collision avoided. Bixby is twirling his partner with wild enthusiasm."

Harriet glanced over her shoulder to find that it was indeed so. Her body and her mind reacted belatedly. She had felt him, every contour of his hard, muscled body, through the thin satin and lace of her gown. She raised her eyes unwillingly to his.

"Ah, Harriet," he said. "Harriet."

She lowered her eyes and was aware suddenly and for the first time of people around them—couples twirling on the dance floor, groups standing or sitting about its edges, either conversing or observing. They were being watched, she knew. He was being watched.

"Where are you staying?" he asked.

"I am a guest at Sir Clive Forbes's home."

"Forbes?" he said. "Ah, yes, I know. May I call on you there, Harriet?"

Why? To tease her? To renew his dalliance with her? But did it matter why? She had come to town in the conscious hope that she would see him again, had she not? Well, then, she was getting more than she had hoped for. She had seen him again on her first real appearance in public and he had singled her out for attention and wished to call on her at Amanda's. Why should she hesitate? For fear of getting hurt again? It was an absurd fear. She was a mature, experienced woman now. She would be hurt only if she chose to be hurt.

"You can do dreadful things to the esteem in which I hold myself, you know, Harriet," he said. "Are you about to reject me—again? And yet all I have asked for is permission to call on you."

"I would be happy to receive you, your grace," she said.

"Would you?" He smiled. "Happy, Harriet? You are not happy at all to see me, are you? Do you despise me? Because I am the sort of man who takes mistresses? You would scarce be able to find a man to respect in this ballroom if you have such high standards for everyone, my dear."

Harriet flushed and his smile deepened.

"I have never known any other woman blush as charmingly as you," he said. "Did my words outrage you? I am sorry. I am not, however, sorry that this is the supper dance. The music is coming to an end, but I may still have your company for supper. Come." He bowed to her when the music stopped and offered his arm. "Let me fill a plate for you and you shall tell me all about the excitement of living in Bath. That was where you lived with Lord Wingham?"

"Yes," she said and set her arm along his. "It was never exciting. But I have always been comfortable there."

He chuckled. "Comfortable!" he said. "Poor Harriet. I hope you feel more hungry than I do. It would suit my in-

clination far better to take you out onto the terrace and
draw nourishment from fresh air and moonlight and kisses,
but unfortunately we are being too closely observed. Did
you know that I rarely dance?"

His words were outrageous and were spoken aloud solely
to draw her blushes, Harriet supposed. But even so they
made her feel weak at the knees again. Moonlight and
kisses. She could remember his kiss. He parted his lips
when he did it. Godfrey had never done so, though he had
liked to kiss her frequently.

"Don't you?" she said. "Don't you enjoy dancing?"

"I enjoy it immensely when there is a lady I wish to get
close to," he said. "I even enjoy protecting her from wild
twirlers. What I do not like is being thought to be shopping
at the marriage mart. That is what balls of the Season are
all about, Harriet. Is that why you are here, by the way? But
don't answer. You could hardly admit it if it were true,
could you? I, on the other hand, will admit it. With dragging feet and the greatest reluctance I am bowing to my
family's anxieties this year. They believe that at the advanced age of two-and-thirty I really cannot wait any
longer to begin setting up my nursery and securing the succession. It is quite enough to make one wince, is it not?"

Harriet was blushing.

"And so," he said, "I made my appearance here tonight
to see what earls' or dukes' or marquesses' daughters are
available. I cannot go lower. My grandmother would not be
able to go contentedly to her grave if I did. But I was distracted by the sight of you. I suppose I should make a determined effort after supper to do what I came here to do. My
maternal relatives expect frequent letters and become depressed when I have nothing to report in the matrimonial
line. It would cheer them no end to know that I had danced
with an earl's daughter at Chloe's ball."

Harriet had got the message. She had learned a great deal
in six years. He did not have to put it into words. The interest was there as it had been before. He would single her out
for a dance as he would single out almost no other woman.
He would even perhaps call on her at Amanda's if he did
not change his mind. But she must clearly understand the

nature of his interest. Of course she understood it. He had not needed even to hint.

"What I really want to do, Harriet," he said, "is go home and to bed and relive in memory our waltz and that near collision."

He really was shameless.

"I recall your blushes very well indeed," he said when it became obvious that she was not going to reply. "What I do not remember, Harriet, is the slight tightening of the lips that goes along with them. Did you not realize six years ago that I was a rogue but realize it now?"

"Perhaps." She looked up at him. "When do you expect to marry?"

He grimaced and then laughed. "By September," he said. "I have promised my grandmother that it will be no later than that. I have also promised that by Christmas . . . But never mind. The completion of that sentence would draw your blushes, Harriet, but I will spare them this time."

That by Christmas his heir would have been safely begotten. He would have married and done his duty and would be able to return to his mistresses by this time next year.

He laughed softly. "You have completed the sentence for yourself," he said. "For shame, Harriet. Shall I seat you beside Hammond and his partner and fetch you a plate?"

"Yes, please," she said.

Mr. Hammond smiled at her and introduced her to Miss Grainger. She watched the Duke of Tenby as he made his way to the food table, settled two plates in the same hand, and began to select dainties to place on them. She remembered seeing him for the first time in Bath at Clara's wedding and thinking him quite the most gorgeous man she had ever set eyes upon. Clara's Freddie was incredibly handsome too, of course, but in a darker, more sensuous way. And she had disliked Frederick Sullivan quite intensely at that time because she had known that he was a mere smooth-tongued fortune hunter. But Lord Archibald Vinney . . .

She remembered his having Mr. Lesley Sullivan, Freddie's brother, present him to her after the wedding was over and her sense of surprise that he had even noticed her, a mere lady's companion. She remembered the way those remarkable silver eyes had moved over her appreciatively and the pleasure she had felt despite the prim indignation. She had been lost from the start. As she was still lost now. He was in search of a wife, a woman of suitably noble rank.

Harriet turned her eyes and her mind determinedly toward the conversation Mr. Hammond and Miss Grainger had begun.

Even after the Duke of Tenby had had his favorite horse saddled and brought around and was riding on it away from his mansion on St. James's Square, he still did not know quite where he was going. To White's Club? But he had been there in the morning to read the papers and to exchange news and gossip with various acquaintances. It was too fine a day to spend the afternoon cooped up there too. For a ride in the park? It was a little late in the day to do so merely for air and exercise and yet still too early for the fashionable hour when the place would be crowded with gentlemen to converse with and ladies to ogle. To Bridget's? But he did not even give the idea serious consideration. The thought of spending the rest of the afternoon in her stuffy and perfumed boudoir was a trifle nauseating. Besides, he had spent all night with her, or what had remained of it after the Avingleigh ball, and had not particularly enjoyed himself. He had found himself wishing that he had gone home to bed after all to dream of a soft and shapely little body that he had held protectively against his own for a moment during the supper waltz.

Should he go to call at Barthorpe's, then? That had been his declared intention when he had called for his horse. He had danced with Lady Phyllis after supper the evening before and discovered that in addition to being pretty and amiable, she had some conversation too, even if it was not profound. One did not expect profundity from prospective wives, anyway. Her mama and papa had been openly interested too. But that was the trouble, the duke thought with a frown. If he called at Barthorpe's today, the afternoon following the ball, speculation would be rife. Especially since he had had a posy sent around during the morning. He might well find himself backed into a corner before he was quite sure that he wished to be there.

No, he thought, turning a corner abruptly enough to cause his horse to snort in protest, and taking the opposite direction from that which would take him to the Earl of Barthorpe's house, he would leave that call for another day. Tomorrow, probably. He would not leave it too long or he would lose his nerve. But today would make him appear altogether too eager. In fact, he was not eager at all. Only resigned.

He knew where he was going. Of course. He had known deep down all along. Just as he had known the incredible truth the evening before while he had danced with her. He had loved her six years ago, his love for her had prevented him from caring for any other woman in the intervening years, and he loved her now. Quite maddeningly but quite irrevocably. He was bone deep in love with her. He could not think of her in terms of marriage, of course. And not in terms of dalliance either. She was a virtuous woman who claimed to have loved a man more than thirty years her senior who had suffered from a weak heart. And she probably *had* loved him. Harriet would not marry for money, though she had seemed to believe that he would think so.

She was a decent, virtuous woman. It was incredible to know that he could be so deeply in love with a woman like that. The mere description was enough to make him shudder. And he had probably been right about her reason for coming to town. She had come to find a second husband. Another reason why he could not dally with her himself. She deserved love and marriage. She would not be happy without. She would have been desperately unhappy if she had given in to the temptation he knew she had felt six years before to become his paid mistress. He was glad she had said no.

Liar, he told himself with a wry smile as he approached Sir Clive Forbes's house and wondered how he would be received.

* * *

When Harriet returned from a walk in the park with Susan after luncheon, she discovered from the butler that she had missed Mr. Hammond, who had called to pay his respects and left again after a half hour had not brought her home, and that Mr, Kershaw was with Lady Forbes in the drawing room. Harriet took her daughter upstairs to the nursery and hurried to her room to tidy her hair and wash her hands. She had run on the grass, playing ball with Susan, and was looking somewhat disheveled.

He had not come after all, then, she thought, satisfied again with her appearance and going back downstairs. He had either not been serious or he had changed his mind. It was just as well. There was no future whatsoever in pursuing that acquaintance. She smiled at Mr. Kershaw and thanked him for the nosegay he had sent that morning. She accepted a cup of tea from Amanda and sat down. She had had two nosegays that morning and two gentlemen visitors that afternoon. Life as a wealthy widow showed every sign of being a great deal more exciting than life as impoverished Miss Harriet Pope had ever been, she thought ruefully.

And then the drawing-room doors opened again and Sir Clive's butler announced the Duke of Tenby. Yes, a great deal more exciting indeed.

"How d'ye do, ma'am," he said, bowing over Lady Forbes's hand and carrying it to his lips. "Lady Wingham?" He bowed again and let his eyes rest on her face for a moment. "Kershaw?"

When they all sat down, they immediately became two couples, the duke conversing with Lady Forbes, Mr. Kershaw with Harriet. Perhaps, after all, he had not come to see her, Harriet thought after five minutes had passed. Though why he would be calling on Amanda she did not know. Perhaps it was just a courtesy call since he had mentioned calling last evening. He had danced a set with Lady Phyllis Reeder after supper and made Harriet ridiculously jealous, though she had been partnered for every single set herself and had even had to reject the offers of several gentlemen because there simply were not enough sets in the evening.

"It is a beautiful afternoon for spring," Mr. Kershaw said, looking toward the windows. "Far too lovely to be spent indoors, Lady Wingham."

"My feeling exactly, Kershaw," the duke said, raising his voice and entering their conversation for the first time. "I came to ask if you would drive in the park with me, Lady Wingham."

Mr. Kershaw, she noticed, looked distinctly annoyed. He had been going to ask her himself, she realized. And the duke had realized it too and cut him out very deftly. One could do such things when one was a duke and get away with them, she supposed. She felt inclined to refuse his offer, but then of course she would be unable to accept Mr. Kershaw's if he made it. And she wanted to drive in Hyde Park. It was the thing to do in the afternoon during the Season, she knew. And it had been so lovely there earlier when she was with Susan. Besides, she wanted to say yes.

He was looking amused when she glanced into his face. He had felt her hesitation. She wondered why he had come calling and why he was going to take her for a drive when he had made it quite clear the evening before that he had a mission to accomplish before the Season was out or at the latest before September. But of course she knew why. It was silly of her to pretend that she did not.

"That would be very pleasant, your grace," she said.

He got to his feet. "I will return home for my curricle, then," he said, "and be back in half an hour, ma'am." He bowed to Lady Forbes and Mr. Kershaw and left the room. And Mr. Kershaw, who had been there longer than he, of course felt obliged to take his leave too, though he might in all courtesy have stayed longer.

"Perhaps you will drive with me another afternoon, Lady Wingham," he said.

"I would be delighted, sir," she said, smiling at him. He was a pleasant young man, quiet and amiable, good-looking rather than handsome, her own age or perhaps even a year or two younger at a guess. He was the heir to a fortune but not a title, Lady Forbes had told her the evening before.

And he seemed to have made no secret about town of the fact that he was in search of a wife.

"You could scarcely do better, Harriet, dear," Lady Forbes had said. "But of course you must make no hasty decisions. I would predict that you will have at least a dozen serious suitors before the Season is out. You can afford to wait for that very special gentleman to come along. And he will, you know. You have a gift for inspiring devotion and a gift for giving love too."

Lady Forbes had been in Harriet's dressing room after the ball and had dabbed at moist eyes. "How sentimental I become in my old age," she had said, though she was in truth only in her early fifties. "But I cannot help remembering how Godfrey married you after remaining stubbornly single for so long and spent the rest of his life worshipping you. And dear little Susan, of course. She was the great joy of his old age. Though he was not so very old, was he? Poor Godfrey."

When Mr. Kershaw had taken his leave, Harriet turned toward the stairs to get ready for her drive. "You do not mind my going?" she asked Lady Forbes. "We might have walked out together, Amanda. It is indeed a lovely day. One could almost believe it is summer except that the air is fresh."

"Fresh air and walks were never my idea of pleasure," Lady Forbes said. "No, my dear, you must go out whenever you have the opportunity and not mind me. That is why you are here, is it not? To enjoy yourself and to see and be seen. To find yourself that special gentleman. Though I could not help being a little annoyed when Mr. Kershaw was ousted with such naughty skill by Tenby. And I am a little worried by his attentions, Harriet, though they are flattering and will definitely ensure that you are brought into fashion. You could see that last evening, could you not? But what can he mean by them?"

"I met him when I was with Clara Sullivan," Harriet said. "Six years ago. He is a close friend of Mr. Sullivan's. I believe he is being polite to an old acquaintance."

"If you believe that," Lady Forbes said, "you must be naive indeed. You are an extremely pretty young lady, Harriet, and his every glance at you shows that he appreciates the fact. He would not marry more than a notch or two below his rank at the greatest, you know. The Vinneys have always been incredibly high in the instep."

"You mean he would not marry the daughter of a poor country clergyman?" Harriet said with a laugh. "Even after she had elevated herself by marrying a baron? I know that, Amanda. You need not fear for me. I am not a total innocent. He danced with me last evening. He is taking me for a drive this afternoon. Do those few facts have to mean anything? I am not going to be shattered by disappointment when he does not arrive tomorrow with a marriage offer."

Lady Forbes climbed the stairs at her side. "No, I suppose not," she said. "I just hope he does not think you are the typical widow."

"Typical widow?" Harriet raised her eyebrows.

"Well, if there is such a thing," Lady Forbes said. "It seems to be the general belief that widows enjoy far greater freedom than either unmarried girls or married ladies. They have less to lose than the girls, if you understand my meaning, my dear, and yet they do not owe fidelity to any man."

"Widows are expected to have affairs, then?" Harriet said.

"Well, perhaps not *expected*," Lady Forbes said. "Let us just say that it is believed many of them do. And it is not considered to be particularly scandalous if done discreetly."

"As long as people do not know for sure," Harriet said, "they will continue to treat the widow with all due respect?"

"But of course," Lady Forbes said, "you are not that type of widow, Harriet. The very thought! I really cannot imagine you . . . But I just hope Tenby realizes it. If he does not, it is a good thing you are not the type, dear, for I imagine that Tenby is the sort of man who could easily break a woman's heart. He is an extremely attractive young man. Even I, who am old enough to be his mother, can appreciate that. What color would you say his eyes are?"

"Silver," Harriet said.

"Let him bring you into fashion, dear," Lady Forbes said. "But don't let him break your heart. I am foolish to worry, though, am I not?" She reached out to squeeze Harriet's arm before allowing her to escape into her dressing room. "You are a very sensible young lady despite your affectionate heart. You would not allow someone like Tenby to turn your head."

Harriet smiled rather bleakly as she let herself into her room.

4

He had to look across at her occasionally to remind himself that she was not in fact a young girl. She was dainty and slim and looked remarkably pretty in primrose muslin and shawl and flower-trimmed straw bonnet. Wingham must have left her quite comfortably well off, he decided. Both last night and today she had been fashionably and tastefully dressed. He remembered the serviceable, rather prim clothes she had worn as Clara Sullivan's companion, though they had done nothing to dull her charms.

"I have never ridden in a curricle," she said by way of apology for the fact that she had just grasped his sleeve as they turned a corner and relinquished it again almost immediately. "It seems far more dangerous up here than it appears from down there."

"By all means hang on," he said. "Though I would not put you in any danger, Harriet. My reputation as a gentleman on it."

In any other woman the clinging, the explanation of feminine weakness, the wide-eyed look, would have appeared flirtatious and quite incongruous with her age. He would have been feeling nauseated. But then in any other woman both words and actions would have been studied, designed to arouse his gallantry. There was no artifice in Harriet. He felt a wave of unwilling tenderness for her as he turned his curricle into Hyde Park and her face took on a sparkle of excitement. Most young ladies would immediately have assumed an air of ennui.

"It is your first visit to the park, I assume?" he said.

"Oh—no," she said. "In fact, I was here earlier today,

walking. But it is the first time I have been a participant in the fashionable hour. How splendid it all looks."

The Season and the fine weather had brought out the *ton* in force. Horses, carriages of all descriptions, pedestrians— all blocked the thoroughfare so that moving at faster than snail's pace would be quite impossible. But then one did not come to Hyde Park at five o'clock of an afternoon in order to move fast. One came to mingle. For perhaps the first time since being unmannerly enough to cut into Kershaw's invitation to Harriet, the duke wondered how the *ton* was going to interpret his appearance in their midst with Lady Wingham when his dancing with her the evening before had caused such an undoubted sensation. They would assume that he was beginning a liaison with her. Somehow the thought irritated him.

"You must smile and be prepared to discuss the weather ad infinitum, Harriet," he said. "You must be prepared for an hour of crashing boredom."

She laughed. "You forget that I live in Bath," she said. "I am a thorough expert at discussing the weather. And how could it be boring to be a part of all this?" She looked about her with bright, happy eyes and lifted one slim arm encased in its primrose glove.

And he looked about him too, seeing it all as she must be seeing it. She had lived most of her life in a country parsonage and in Bath. For a short while she had lived at Ebury Court with the Sullivans, but in the capacity of a servant. More recently she had been married to an elderly man with a weak heart. She would have been in mourning for his death for a year. She had probably been out of mourning for only a short while. Looking with new eyes at the park and the people thronging there, he could see that the scene did have a certain magic. He had taken the privileges of his life very much for granted.

There was no chance for further private conversation. They became a part of the throng and the duke knew that his entry into Avingleigh's ballroom the night before really had begun something that he might find hard to reverse. Gentlemen friends and acquaintances gazed appreciatively at Harriet and touched their hats to her and grinned at him.

Others who had been presented to her during the ball and had perhaps even danced with her made a point of maneuvering their horses or their curricles or phaetons close enough that they could pay their respects to her. A few lady friends of Lady Forbes's ordered their carriages drawn alongside so that they might greet her. And all and sundry looked at him with varying degrees of shrewd calculation. It was not usual to see the Duke of Tenby tooling a young lady of quality about the park during the fashionable hour.

He wondered if Harriet realized how dazzlingly successful her entrée into society was being. And how dangerous it might be to her reputation if her name became linked too closely with his.

He touched the brim of his hat to Dan Wilkes, the Earl of Beaconswood, whose barouche had drawn alongside his curricle, and would have driven on. But the countess, eager face alight, had other ideas.

"Harriet Pope?" she said. "It *is* Harriet, is it not?"

"Lady Wingham, Julia," her husband said pointedly. "How are you, ma'am? Archie?"

"Oh, good afternoon, your grace," the countess said with a laugh. "And I am sorry, Harriet, to have greeted you by a long-outdated name. And sorry about your husband. Clara told us and about your being here. We have been looking out for you, have we not, Daniel?"

The earl chuckled. "We have left scarce a stone unturned," he said.

"Foolish," the countess said. "You look very smart indeed, Harriet. I am glad we have found you at last."

The duke remembered that the earl was Freddie Sullivan's cousin. He and his countess must have met Harriet when she was working for Freddie's wife.

"But how lovely it is to see you." Harriet was smiling with warm eagerness. "I thought I knew no one at all in town, but I have been pleasantly surprised. You were not at Lady Avingleigh's ball last evening?"

The countess laughed. "I am not—" she said, and broke off what she was saying to turn her head and smile at her husband. "I am not dancing this Season, am I, Daniel? It is very bothersome. Though not entirely so."

The duke watched in some amusement as his companion blushed while her eyes took in what he had noticed immediately. Beneath the loose and carefully arranged folds of her carriage dress, the Countess of Beaconswood was very noticeably with child.

"I shall call on you," the countess said. "May I? Daniel always feels obliged to do the gentlemanly thing when we are in town and spend the morning at White's or about some other male pursuit. I am expected to do the ladylike thing and stay abed until noon. Can you imagine anything more tiresome, Harriet, and more unfair to our sex? I shall come and visit you instead. Where are you staying?"

A minute or two later they were on their way again. But the duke had had enough of sharing her. As soon as he could, he drew his curricle off the main thoroughfare and drove it in the direction of less frequented, more secluded paths.

"You did not lie when you said you were experienced, Harriet," he said. "You discussed the weather with at least eight different people but did not once repeat the same thing. Did you enjoy yourself?"

"Yes, indeed," she said. "I thank you for bringing me here, your grace."

"No thanks are necessary," he said. "You would have come anyway, would you not?" He looked at her sidelong. "With Kershaw."

"That was not very kind of you," she said.

"Tell me," he said, turning his head to look fully at her, "would you have preferred to come here with him, Harriet?"

"That is not the point, surely," she said.

"Why not?" he asked. "What is the use of being a duke if one cannot take advantage of one's rank occasionally?"

"It is not kind," she said.

"But you have not said," he reminded her, "that you would prefer to be driving with Kershaw."

She looked at him and blushed. He grinned at her, wondering if she had any idea at all of the butterflies she set to dancing in his stomach when she did so.

"You danced with Lady Phyllis Reeder last night," she

said. "An earl's daughter. Your grandmother will be pleased."

"Ecstatic," he said. "I did not enjoy the dance nearly as much as our waltz, though, Harriet."

"I would have thought," she said, "that you would be better employed driving her in the park this afternoon, your grace."

"Would you?" he said. "One has to be very careful when there is even the whisper of the possibility of matrimony in a situation, though, Harriet. How would it appear to the *ton* if I danced with the girl last night and drove her in the park this afternoon? They would all be scanning their newspapers tomorrow looking for the announcement of our betrothal."

"And you are not ready for that announcement?" she asked. "Even though it must be made, and the announcement of your marriage too, before September?"

"It will be made," he said. "They both will be. But give me time to catch my breath, Harriet. Marriage is a very irrevocable step to take. Did you not think so?"

"Yes," she said. She looked at the palms of her gloved hands for a few moments before turning them over to rest in her lap.

"But for you it lasted only a short while after all," he said. "How long?"

"A little over four years," she said.

"Do you miss him, Harriet?" he asked. He looked at her curiously.

"All the time," she said quietly. "Sometimes marriage can bring rewards that you did not dream of even if you enter into it in perfect good faith. Perhaps you will find that too, your grace."

With Lady Phyllis? He doubted it. But really, he was beginning to feel, it was damnable bad luck that had brought Harriet to town at this particular time. He had been so determined to grit his teeth and do his duty this spring. He still was determined. In fact, he had even made up his mind to rid himself of Bridget before the Season's end, since it seemed to him rather distasteful to be courting a bride and bedding a mistress all at the same time. But Harriet's arrival had thrown everything into turmoil. He wanted her. And yet somehow the desire he felt was different from the sort of desire with which he was long familiar. It was not just the desire to get a mattress at her back and his body inside hers. Somehow there was more to it than that. But he was on unfamiliar territory. He did not know what that something was.

"And what about your prospects?" he asked. "Did you come to town in search of a husband, Harriet?"

"No." Her eyes widened in shock and her cheeks flamed.

"It would not be at all shameful," he said. "Women more than men, I believe, feel the need for the security of marriage. And London during the Season is the great marriage mart. Your experiences of last evening and this afternoon must both have shown you that you are all the rage, as the saying goes."

"How foolish," she said with a laugh.

"But it is true," he said. "You will not lack for partners and escorts morning, afternoon, or evening for the rest of the Season, Harriet. It is a confident prediction I make. You will not lack for suitors, either. What do you look for? Handsome features and figure? A steady character? Wealth? Youth? Age? You will have your choice."

And may the man who takes her fancy fry in the hottest pit of hell, he thought uncharitably.

"None of those things," she said. He smiled, knowing that she was intensely embarrassed and knowing therefore that she had indeed come in search of Wingham's successor. "I am not looking for a husband."

"For a lover, then?" he asked for the sheer joy of seeing the expected color flood her cheeks again. "Is that what you have come for, Harriet? An *affaire de coeur*? That is nothing to be ashamed of, either. Your husband has been gone for longer than a year."

He knew he was being unpardonably outrageous. He even wondered suddenly if the ailing Lord Wingham had been able to consummate their marriage. Perhaps it was a virgin he was teasing. He thought she was not going to answer. He was surprised and a little alarmed to see her lower lip tremble. He had hit a nerve that he had had no intention of even touching.

"I miss him," she said almost in a whisper.

Well, at least one of his unasked questions had been answered. She and Wingham had had a sexual relationship. One that she missed. He eased his horses to a halt and turned to her.

"I am sorry," he said. "I did not mean to hurt you."

"You did not." She directed her eyes at his neckcloth. "I do not know why you danced with me or brought me driving, your grace, especially when you knew that I would have had another escort even if you had not asked. But I think you should not have done either. I think you should be with Lady Phyllis Reeder or someone else eligible to be your bride."

"You know very well why, Harriet," he said. When her eyes slipped even lower, he set one hand beneath her chin and raised her face. "For the same reason that you granted me that set and accepted this invitation." He kissed her, parting his lips over hers so that he could both feel and taste her. Her own lips tightened and then trembled and then pushed back against his own. He felt instantly as if someone had lit a fire all around them, heating the air and cutting off their supply of oxygen. He lifted his head and released her chin.

"That is why," he said. "You have lost none of your charms in six years, my little blusher. Quite the contrary."

"Take me home," she said. But there was none of the indignation in her voice that he might have expected, only a calm dignity.

Ah, Harriet!

"Yes," he said. "I think I had better. Talk to me. Discuss the weather."

She did not do so. They returned to Sir Clive Forbes's in silence. It was not an angry silence or even a particularly uncomfortable one. Just a silence that acknowledged the fact that that brief kiss had spoken volumes that both of them needed time alone to digest and interpret.

He lifted her to the ground from the high perch of her

seat when they arrived, noting the tininess of her waist and her soft femininity. "Harriet," he said.

But she was smiling and extending a hand to him. "Thank you, your grace," she said. "That was very pleasant indeed. You are very kind."

Ah. She had raised a stone wall between them. He took his cue from her and bowed over her hand before raising it to his lips. "My pleasure, ma'am," he said. "I was, I believe, the envy of every other gentleman in the park this afternoon."

She turned without a smile or a blush and entered the house. He stood with pursed lips, staring ruefully at the door, which a servant had closed behind her. She was right. That must be the end of it. The end of something that had never really begun.

Every day brought its dizzying array of activities. Mornings were spent with Susan. Harriet played with her and read to her indoors and took her out to play in the park or to feed the swans on the Serpentine or to view the Tower of London and other sights suitable for the enjoyment of a young child. Life would be very dreary without the existence of her daughter, she often thought, and she often gazed at her in vain for signs of Godfrey. But Susan was all her mother, even to the golden-blond hair and the green eyes, as Godfrey had always maintained with great pride and delight. But though she could not see him in their child, she cherished the most dear gift of all they had been able to give each other.

Sometimes she went shopping with Amanda or to exchange her books at the library. Occasionally Lady Beaconswood, who insisted on being called Julia, called, and once it was established that they both liked the outdoors, they sometimes went together to the park with their children—with Julia's five-year-old daughter and three-year-old son and with Susan.

"I have done my duty marvelously well," Julia said with a laugh on the first occasion when they took the children out. "A son and a daughter though in the wrong order and now another for insurance if it is a boy, though Daniel was very cross with himself when I broke the news that I was *enceinte* again. He is of the opinion that wives should be forced to perform that particular duty no more than twice in their lives—even if the first two are girls. He affects to believe all the business about getting heirs to be so much nonsense. Was Lord Wingham disappointed not to have a son?"

"Oh, no," Harriet said. "He wanted a daughter so badly that I was terrified of giving birth to a son. And he wanted her to look just like me."

"He certainly had his wish," Julia said. "I do wish Annabel would grow out of the habit of bossing James. Just look at her. It is a good thing Daniel is not here. He would spank her and then tell me how much she resembles me. He disliked me heartily when we were both children, you know. I was what might be described as a hoyden. And Daniel would tell you that I understate the case." She laughed and hurried forward as quickly as she could considering her bulk to scold her daughter and encourage her mild-natured son to stand up for himself.

The afternoons were spent out visiting with Amanda or being visited or in company with one of the surprising number of gentlemen who were showing an interest in her. Mr. Kershaw proposed marriage to her after knowing her for one week and was gently refused. Sir Philip Grafton hinted at the idea that they might come to some mutually satisfying arrangement that did not include marriage and was more firmly rejected. The other gentlemen showed varying degrees of ardor. Some showed no more than a comforting pleasure in her company. But after a couple of weeks Harriet could count six gentlemen, if she included Sir Henry Newman, who was older than Godfrey would have been, whom she could probably lead toward thoughts of matrimony if she so chose. It was all very flattering and very pleasant. Very dizzying, in fact, for a woman who remembered what it had felt like to be Harriet Pope.

Almost every evening brought its outing—to a ball or a party or rout, to a concert or the theater or opera, to a pleasure garden. She almost forgot what it was like to spend a quiet evening at home with a book or her embroidery. Fortunately most evening social functions began late enough that she could get Susan ready for bed herself and play with her for a while and read her a bedtime story.

She saw the Duke of Tenby frequently. He never went out of his way to avoid her. Indeed, sometimes he made a point of strolling up to her at a party or riding up to her in the park to exchange a few pleasantries, often discussing the weather with a mocking gleam in his eyes. It was becoming an accepted fact among members of the *ton* that he was choosing himself a bride at long last and that that bride was very likely to be Lady Phyllis Reeder. He danced with her once at every ball and with almost no one else, drove her in the park occasionally, escorted her once to the theater. It seemed that he was set on doing his duty to his family and rank. His grandmother would be happy.

He clouded Harriet's joy. Whenever he was in her sight—and he frequently was—she could concentrate on no one else. He was an extremely handsome man, of course, but it was not just that. There were other handsome men, a few of them even among what it amused Clive to call her court. He was attractive. He drew eyes wherever he went, not only hers. And it was not just his rank that caused him to be noticed, she felt. But of course she noticed him more than anyone else. She had always loved him and still did.

She cried one night when she made the admission to herself. For if it was true, then she had loved him all during her marriage to Godfrey. But she dried her eyes determinedly. Her love for Lord Archibald Vinney had not diminished her feelings for Godfrey. It had been a different kind of love she had felt for him, a deep and devoted affection, and she had always been true to it, even though she had married him with a sore and despairing heart.

She was glad that the duke had accepted her tacit dismissal after their drive in the park. She had been disturbed by his open admission that he was going to choose a wife of suitable rank within the next few months. An admission he had made while singling her out for attention and not even trying to hide the admiration in his eyes. It had been very obvious what his interest in her was. If she was not wife material, then what was she? It was a rhetorical question, of course. And his actions had answered it even if she had been obtuse enough to need an answer. He had kissed her mouth in a place where they might well have been seen, and caused a scandal.

Of course, she had lied to him. She really had come to town in the hope of finding herself another husband. Not in any cold-blooded way. She would never marry anyone just for the sake of marrying or just because he was a rich man. She did not need riches. She had more than enough of her own. She would marry only for love. Or for deep affection, anyway. She had already proved to herself that affection was enough to make a successful marriage.

She did not know whether he had been serious in suggesting that perhaps she had come in search of a lover, of an *affaire de coeur*. He had always delighted in teasing her and embarrassing her as much as possible. But suddenly, treacherously, his suggestion, combined with what Amanda had said about widows, had its attraction. Although her cheeks could grow hot at the very thought, she knew that she had felt stricken when he had reminded her that Godfrey had been gone for more than a year and she had realized with dreadful force how very much she did miss him. Him, yes. And *that* too. She had not really expected it in her marriage and at first when she knew that it was to happen she had expected to have to endure it. But Godfrey had always worshiped her body, treating her in bed with gentleness and tenderness and respect. She had often wished that it could happen more than its regular once a week. She had liked it. It had made her feel cherished. Now she yearned for just once a week.

The idea that she could even be tempted by the thought of an affair alarmed her. And so she was very thankful that the Duke of Tenby had kept his distance since that afternoon. For she was not sure how she would react if he did not. It was a shocking admission to make. What was even more shocking was the fact that she could not be sure that she was being honest with herself when she told herself that she was glad he did not come close. She was sure finally on the evening of Lady Myder's ball. Sure that she was not being honest with herself, that was.

Mr. Shaw had gone to fetch her a glass of lemonade and had got himself involved in a lengthy conversation with another gentleman over at the drink table. She was not desperate for the drink. Cool air would have felt even better. The Duke of Tenby had just finished his usual dance with Lady Phyllis Reeder and Harriet had been denying to herself as usual that she was depressed and jealous. She did not want him to see her standing alone. One could not very well smile when alone, but she had made sure during the past weeks that he had always seen her smiling and enjoying herself—without him. Although of course she *had* been enjoying herself.

She wandered to the French windows and through them onto the balcony. And because that was crowded with couples, she went down the steep steps onto the small but very dark lawn. She leaned against a pillar of the balcony, closed her eyes, and drew in a breath of the deliciously cool air.

She could not see him clearly when he came down the steps a minute or so after her and stood silently in front of her, looking at her—if he could see her. But she knew it was he. Every nerve ending in her body told her that it was he.

It was a curious encounter. Neither of them spoke. They both stood still for an indeterminate length of time, and then he leaned forward and downward until their mouths met. It was a warm, light embrace for a time until their arms came about each other at the same moment and their bodies fit against each other and their mouths opened. Reality intruded for Harriet only when his tongue, exploring her lips and the soft flesh behind, suddenly became more bold in its demands and pushed, hard and firm and deep into her mouth. She moaned her shock but arched further into him.

And then she was alone again against the pillar and he was standing silently before her again. Her eyes, more accustomed to the dark, could make out the outline of his features.

"This has to be settled, Harriet," he said, his voice low, almost harsh, "this thing that is between us. Tomorrow. You will come driving with me? Not to the park. To Kew. Tomorrow afternoon?" The inflection of his voice suggested a question. But it was more a command than an invitation he was issuing.

"Yes," she whispered.

He stood there a few moments longer and then turned and was gone.

This has to be settled, this thing that is between us. She closed her eyes and rested her head back against the pillar. She knew how it would be settled if it were settled on his terms.

And if it were settled on hers? What were her terms?

She did not know. But she was very frightened. And very excited. And strangely serene. Something that had been started and never ended for her six years ago was to be settled tomorrow. And for him too. Obviously what had happened then—or not happened—had affected him deeply also, though she had not realized it at the time. It was going to be settled tomorrow.

And yet if he offered and she refused again, nothing would have been settled after all, would it? If she refused. Would she? The very thought that perhaps she would not should have terrified her but did not. It excited her. And—yes—terrified her too.

It was a long time before Harriet returned to the ballroom.

5

If his valet had not had to wake him up when his shaving water was brought to his dressing room, the Duke of Tenby would have sworn that he had not slept a wink all night. He had paced for hours, first in the library downstairs and then in his bedchamber. Then he had lain down on his back, his fingers laced behind his head, staring upward at the ornate canopy of his bed.

He had known from earliest infancy that he would be a duke one day. During his boyhood he had known it even more fully. He had been eleven when his father died. Only his grandfather's life had stood between him and the title. He had been groomed by his grandfather, with whom he and his mother had been taken to live, and by his grandmother.

He had never rebelled. Not really, anyway. Not in essentials. He had always known what his duty was and had been ready to assume it whenever the time came. Not that he had craved it. He had been fond of his grandfather. It was true that he had procrastinated about the performance of one of his primary duties. But his grandfather had not married until the age of thirty-four. His father had been thirty-six. So waiting until he was thirty-two had seemed no great dereliction of duty despite the frequently expressed anxieties of his mother and grandmother.

He had not relished the thought of marriage. Not yet. But he had come up for the Season fully prepared to find himself a bride at last and a bride of whom his relatives could be proud. A Duke of Tenby had never married below the rank of earl's daughter. Most of them had done considerably better. His mother was herself a duke's daughter.

He was not particularly fond of Lady Phyllis Reeder. But he felt no great aversion to her, either, and that was what counted. A man in his position could not expect to marry for love. His parents' and his grandparents' marriages had not been love matches. He had taken all the right steps since the beginning of the Season, singling her out regularly for attention while not making his attentions so particular as to lead to a rushed decision. He had by no means reached a point from which he could not return, though he was in no doubt that he had raised expectations in both the girl's family and in the *ton*. It could be expected that in the course of time, probably before the Season ended, he would make his offer and the betrothal would be announced. The wedding would take place during the summer. She would be rounding with his child by Christmas.

If only Harriet had not come, he had thought over and over again as he paced. She complicated everything. She was constantly in his thoughts, almost like a gnawing toothache. And the sight of her almost wherever he went was a constant reminder that though he did not love Lady Phyllis, he did love another woman. He could not and would not avoid the places where she might be. He had tried very hard to be sensible, to treat her just like any other attractive woman of his acquaintance. He deliberately had not avoided either meeting her or talking with her. Familiarity would breed indifference, he had persuaded himself.

But familiarity had bred only frustration and longing. He had settled with Bridget and sent her on her way, not just to be fair to Lady Phyllis, as he had planned, but because he could no longer bear the thought of going to her. Seeing Harriet became a torment to him. It was impossible to know if she felt a like tension when she saw him. She was always surrounded by admiring escorts and was always smiling and laughing. She appeared to be enjoying her Season with a carefree heart.

But then at Lady Myder's ball temptation had presented itself and he had been quite unable to resist. Free of partners himself—he never danced more than one set in one evening with Lady Phyllis and never lingered in her presence—he had watched what happened. Her partner had

gone to fetch her a drink and had been detained by someone wanting to speak with him. She had stood alone, an unusual occurrence with Harriet. He had waited, trying to
resist the urge to stroll across the room to her. He did not
like to be alone with her. And then she had looked at the
French windows with obvious longing and had gone
through them onto the balcony—alone.

He had gone after her to stroll there with her. It was not
quite proper for a lady to go out of doors alone. But she
was not there. He knew she had not returned to the ballroom. She must have gone down the dark steps to the garden below. He went down after her. And there he had had
the answer to one question that had been in his mind. She
had been leaning against a pillar in the darkness, apparently
enjoying the air. If she had felt nothing for him, none of the
tensions he had been feeling for a number of weeks, she
would have said something, started some conversation. Instead she had stood still and quiet, waiting.

God, but he had not planned what followed. He had not
gone out after her with even the hope of a stolen kiss on his
mind. He had realized during that afternoon in Hyde Park
the full danger of kissing her. If only she had said something or if only he had, what had happened would not have
happened. But it had. And what had happened had been far
more than a stolen kiss in a dark garden. Far more.

That something more was what had kept him pacing and
lying awake through most of the night. And the words he
had spoken to her afterward, words that were as unplanned
as the embrace had been. He was to take her to Kew. They
were to settle whatever it was that was between them.

There was only one way to settle it. No, perhaps two. He
could tell her that he was leaving London. He could go
home and inform his grandmother that she must wait until
next spring for him to choose a bride. Or perhaps he could
arrange for a houseful of guests during the summer and invite a suitably eligible young lady and her family. Though
he hated the thought of conducting a courtship under the interested eyes of his mother and grandmother. And of making his intentions so obvious that he would be left with no
choice.

No, there was really only one way to settle what was between him and Harriet. He could not offer her *carte blanche* as he had done six years ago. She was a virtuous and a respectable woman. She would refuse now as she had refused then. Besides, he did not want her as his mistress. There seemed something a little sordid about the idea. He wanted her . . .

There would be all hell to pay with his family, of course. Harriet was a lady, but her birth and background in no way fitted her to be the wife of a Duke of Tenby. She had even been forced to take genteel employment for a few years before making an advantageous marriage. Even the fact that she was a widow would tell against her. Only a virgin would do for his bride.

By the time he had shaved and dressed and exercised his horse with a gallop in the park, the Duke of Tenby had decided that for once in his life he was going to be a rebel. Surely his choice of bride should be his own. Surely he should be allowed to marry whom he would, provided he did not bring into the family someone who would disgrace it. Harriet would hardly do that. And his mother and his grandmother would come to love her once they had met her and given themselves a little time to get to know her.

He was rationalizing, he knew. They would never approve his choice or his decision to marry for love. He picked at his breakfast, his decision made, though he was grim and uneasy with it. Unhappy even. He was going to marry her. For once in his life he was going to put personal inclination before duty. At Kew that afternoon he was going to make his offer. He was glad he had made the appointment for today. If he had made it for tomorrow or the day after, he might lose his nerve. He wanted it done. He wanted the whole thing to be irrevocable. Then he would be able to relax and enjoy loving her.

The clouds of the morning had moved off to give place to yet another lovely day. Harriet had certainly chosen the right spring to be in London, Sir Clive Forbes had said at luncheon. Sometimes it rained all through the Season and plunged everyone into the deepest of low spirits.

"Tenby again?" Lady Forbes said when Harriet excused herself to go to her room to prepare for the drive to Kew. "It is the general belief that he is beginning a serious courtship with Lady Phyllis Reeder."

"I do believe he is," Harriet said, smiling. "We are just old friends, Amanda. It is just an afternoon drive. It is several weeks since I drove with him last."

"Just old friends," Amanda said. "I always distrust those words, dear. But I am sure you are right. You have been out with many young men since the Season began, with several of them more than once. There is no reason for me to be worried just because Tenby shows occasional interest in you, is there? You will enjoy Kew. Be sure to see the botanical gardens. They are not to be missed."

Harriet smiled again and made her escape. She felt dreadfully guilty, although she could see no reason why she should. That kiss—though *kiss* seemed a woefully inadequate word to describe their embrace—had hurt no one. She was a mature adult, not a green girl. They were going for a drive this afternoon to settle things between them. She knew very well what that meant, of course, and she had made up her mind what she was going to do. She felt quite calm about her decision. She was certainly not going to let her narrow upbringing gnaw at her conscience. If she did not say yes this time, she would regret it for the rest of her life, she knew.

She was going to say yes. She was going to become his mistress. Just for a short while. Just long enough to satisfy her curiosity and her craving. During the summer he would be marrying someone else, and she knew that she would not be able to continue the liaison once that had happened. But perhaps by the summer she would have settled for one of her own suitors—Mr. Hardinge, perhaps. His interest in her was leading him toward a declaration, she was sure, and she both liked and respected him. Of course, she might find that she could not in all conscience accept him when the courtship had been taking place during her affair with another man. She did not know yet just how badly her conscience would bother her.

But she was not going to change her mind. She was

going to say yes. She watched the street from the window of her bedchamber after she was ready until she saw his curricle approaching. He was two or three minutes early. Her heart and her stomach performed painful somersaults, and she drew back from the window lest he should see that she was watching for him. She waited with heavily beating heart to be summoned downstairs.

All the way to Kew they conversed on a variety of general topics, including the weather, just as if the night before had never happened and they were just two friendly acquaintances taking a drive together. Since Harriet had mentioned the botanical gardens, they viewed them first on their arrival, admiring and commenting on every plant they saw until almost an hour had passed.

Perhaps, Harriet thought eventually, there had been nothing as significant about the evening before as she had thought. Perhaps he had meant nothing more than that they should take a drive together again. Perhaps in her naiveté she had read into the incident far more than had been there and had given herself a sleepless night for nothing.

"The pagodas," he said when they emerged from the botanical gardens. "It is obligatory to see them, Harriet, when one is at Kew. And to stroll the lawns and view all the trees and flowers. Are you enjoying yourself?"

"Yes, your grace," she said.

"Are you?" He was looking at her, and she knew that his question heralded a change in the afternoon. Gone was the relaxed friendliness. There was a breathless tension in its place.

"You must consider that your courtship of Lady Phyllis is proceeding at a satisfactory pace," she said. She was afraid to bring on the moment. She wanted to hold it at bay. Almost as if there was still time to change her decision. As she supposed there was.

"Must I?" he said.

"It certainly seems to be the general opinion that a betrothal is imminent," she said.

"Sometimes," he said, "one could wish that the *ton* would allow its members to conduct their own courtships."

"Your grandmother must be pleased," she said. "Is she?"

"I believe," he said, "she is already planning the wedding breakfast. And dusting off the christening robes that both my father and I wore for use again within the year. Is it indelicate to mention such a thing to you?"

She smiled. "It is obvious," she said, "that if she is anxious to see you married, her real eagerness is to see an heir born."

"Sometimes," he said, "one wonders if the idea of marriage has been debased so much that it has no other function to serve. There is very little consideration given to the lifelong contentment of the husband or the wife, for example. Do you think perhaps people have gone wrong somewhere, Harriet?"

"Perhaps people of your rank," she said. "The same does not apply to most people. Godfrey and I married for our mutual happiness."

"Did you?" he said. "He was not obsessed with the need to get his heir on you even though he was an older man with a title and I believe a fortune to leave behind him?"

"No," she said. "I think he had made the decision as a young man not to marry or secure his succession. Marrying me was an afterthought, so to speak. He never spoke of an heir. In that sense I suppose I was fortunate. I knew that I was being married for myself."

"Ah, yes," he said. "That would be something. When one is a duke, with title, property, and fortune, one wonders if any woman can see beyond them to the man himself."

"You are afraid Lady Phyllis will not?" she said. "Just as you will see nothing of her beyond her rank and her breeding capabilities? I suppose that will be the challenge of your marriage. Can you get to know each other and like each other and perhaps even love each other despite the calculated way in which you must both choose each other?"

"You make it sound," he said, "as if being a duke is the most undesirable thing in the world."

She smiled.

"I want you," he said abruptly, and her smile faded.

"Yes, I know," she said quietly.

"Do you want me?"

She resisted the impulse to pause, to hesitate. "Yes." She kept her voice firm and her eyes on his. They had stopped walking.

"I have resisted it, you know," he said. "For obvious reasons, if you will pardon me for saying so."

Now that the moment had come, she could not bear to let it develop slowly. She would lose her nerve if it was not over with quickly. They were on a path surrounded by rhododendron bushes. There was no one else in sight.

"When you asked six years ago," she said, "I refused. I had to refuse. For one thing, I was still young enough and naive enough to be shocked. For another, I had a great deal to lose and not sufficient to gain. My virtue and my reputation would have been gone. I would have been putting myself into a world that I would have been trapped in forever. I could not contemplate that, even though I am sure you would have provided well for me and been generous when you tired of me. A great deal has changed since that time."

He looked at her in silence for a while. "What has changed?" he asked.

She could feel herself flushing. "I am older," she said. "I am no longer a v— I have been married. I am a widow."

She was disconcerted by his silence. "I have been assured," she said, "that it is quite acceptable for widows as long as they are discreet." She wished heartily that she had kept her mouth shut and let him approach the subject in his own way. She was not after all speeding things up. She fixed her eyes on his neckcloth.

"That what is acceptable?" he asked. He waited for an answer.

"You are deliberately trying to put me to the blush," she said, obliging him and hating him for teasing her so.

"Taking a lover?" he said. "Having a discreet, clandestine affair?"

His voice sounded strained. Too late she thought that perhaps she had completely misunderstood him, that he had had no intention of offering her *carte blanche*. The thought was deeply mortifying and made her feel as if her cheeks must have burst into flame. She forced herself to look up into his eyes.

"Is that not what you meant?" she asked. "Last evening? When you said that the thing that was between us must be settled? Have I misunderstood?"

"I thought, Harriet," he said, "that you were a woman of unassailable virtue. That you had come here in search of a husband."

He thought that she was throwing herself at his head. He thought that she was trying to trap him into making her a marriage offer. "I may well marry again," she said, "if I find someone with whom I believe I can live with mutual affection. There are already gentlemen . . . Mr. Hardinge is attentive . . . I don't know. But in the meanwhile—"

"In the meanwhile you are prepared to take me as a lover?" he asked.

He did not sound his usual mocking self. But then he had not last night either. There was this thing between them to be settled. She forced herself to keep her eyes on his.

"Yes," she said. "If that is what you wish. If that is what you meant. I—I should have let you speak first. I am nervous. I have never done anything like this before." She smiled and then wished she had not done so. He did not smile back.

"How could it not be what I wish?" he asked. "I have made no secret of my desire for you, Harriet, either six years ago or this year. I did not believe you would accept *carte blanche*."

Was he disappointed that she had said yes? Disappointed in her? But why would he have brought her here to make such an offer if he had expected to be rejected?

"You said yourself," she told him, "that there is something between us. There is. I believe I will always be sorry if I do not seize this opportunity to put that something to rest. It will be put to rest, will it not? Once we have h-had each other, we will gradually begin to t-tire of each other. We will, won't we?" The absurdity of her words struck her so forcibly that she wanted to laugh. She clamped her teeth together so that she would not do anything so embarrassingly inappropriate. The words would doubtless be true of him. As for herself—she wondered if she was letting herself in for a heartache that would be too great to bear. She thought she probably was. But she would not change her mind.

"Yes," he said. "I suppose we will. Did you have in mind an affair for this Season only, Harriet? Not a continuing one? It would be just as well, I suppose. I have never found my interest in a mistress lasting beyond a few months."

It felt a little like a slap on the face. His silver eyes seemed suddenly and inexplicably icy.

"I think I have been mistaken," she said. "I think I have misread this situation, your grace. I believe you fully expected me to refuse as I did before. It was what you wanted, so that you could tease me with my primness for the rest of the Season. That is it, is it not? I'm sorry. I am not too well versed in the ways of polite society. I should like to go home now, if you please."

She made to walk past him, trying very hard to hold on to her dignity. She felt more mortified than she had ever felt in her life. She had thrown herself at a man and been rejected and insulted. *I have never found my interest in a mistress lasting beyond a few months.* And yet it was an idea she had been the first to suggest.

But he caught her arm in a hold that she knew would only tighten if she struggled to get away. She stood still, looking ahead of her along the path.

"I only want you to know, Harriet," he said, "what it is we would be beginning. A purely physical relationship to be conducted in an absolutely clandestine manner. We would have to be quite sure that no breath of scandal could attach itself to either of us—especially to you. Men are excused a certain number of wild oats. We would have to meet during the afternoons for the express purpose of having sexual relations—in broad daylight. There would be no more to it than that. I would continue my courtship with Lady Phyllis Reeder. I will marry her this summer, have my child in her this autumn. You would continue your courtship with Hardinge or with someone else."

"Yes," she said.

"There is no romance in such affairs," he said. "No love."

"No." She swallowed.

"Only sexual gratification," he said.

"Yes."

"Are you sure it is what you want?" he asked. "Are you sure it would be enough for you? Are you sure your conscience will allow you to enjoy it?"

She was not sure of any of the three. She wanted to shake her head and put an end to the madness there and then. She wanted to go home to Susan. Home to Bath. She wanted Godfrey.

"Is it what *you* want?" she asked. "I thought it was. I thought that was what you brought me here to ask. Was I mistaken? Have I made an utter cake of myself? You said at the beginning of this conversation that you wanted me."

He looked at her for a long moment without saying anything. "It is what I want, Harriet," he said. "It is what I have wanted for six years. But I do not want to hurt you. I have had numerous mistresses, my dear, numerous affairs. I know what it is to begin them and I know what it is to end them. It is not always either easy or painless. I would have you understand what it is you are agreeing to."

"We both know when the end is to be," she said. "There need be no awkwardness or pain when the time comes. By then I daresay we will both be glad to move on." She wondered if he believed her words as little as she did.

"Very well, then," he said. "We are agreed."

There was the welling of panic. And terror. And excitement.

"Yes," she said calmly.

He bent his head and kissed her openmouthed but lightly. He made no move to touch any part of her except her mouth.

"It is late today," he said, his tone quite brusque and matter-of-fact. "I don't think either of us would like to be rushed, especially our first time, would we?"

She swallowed.

"Tomorrow," he said. "The same time as today? You must walk from the house. I shall be waiting for you at the corner with a plain carriage."

A carriage.

He must have read her thoughts. "I have a house," he said. "We will go there."

He had a house. Of course he would. She knew that he did not mean his home. That was the very last place he would think of taking her. He had a house where he took his mistresses and his casual amours. An establishment he kept just for that purpose. It must be used often enough to justify the expense of keeping it. But she did not want to think about that. There was humiliation in the thought. A house, after all, was better than a carriage.

"Come," he said, "we have stood here long enough. It is a conveniently deserted and secluded path, is it not? I must remember the fact for future reference."

She smiled, but her lips felt stiff. She took his arm, felt its muscled hardness, and wondered what both arms would feel like tomorrow holding her. She wondered what *he* would feel like and turned her head sharply to try to focus both her eyes and her mind on the bushes at either side of the path.

"Now, Harriet," he said, "we must have a glimpse of these pagodas so that you may give me your opinion of them. Then I shall give you mine at great length and by that time we will have thought of other topics of conversation and be comfortable together again. Agreed?"

"Agreed," she said. "But you speak of the pagodas with the utmost contempt in your voice. Are they so ugly?"

"I shall allow you to judge for yourself," he said. "I would not dream of trying to form your opinions in advance."

Unexpectedly, blessedly, they did find topics with which to fill the silence during the remainder of their time at Kew and during the drive home again. But of course, Harriet thought, he was an expert at dalliance. This situation was nothing very novel for him. It was not a momentous occasion as it was for her. She was being foolish—a woman of eight-and-twenty being so squeamish about beginning an affair that had been mutually agreed upon.

When they arrived back at Sir Clive's, he drew his horses to a halt and paused before jumping down to the pavement. He touched the back of her hand briefly, though he did not take hold of it. It was possible that they were being observed from one of the surrounding houses.

"Harriet," he said, "nothing is written in stone, you know. If you wish to change your mind, I shall not cut up nasty. If you do not appear at the street corner tomorrow afternoon, I shall not come storming into the house demanding an explanation. Until I join my body to yours, nothing is irreversible. Ah, the blush. It always fires my desire. I would think it artful if I did not know you better."

It would be so easy. He was making it easy. She could look at him, or even not look at him, and tell him that after all it was something she just could not do. And she could not do it. The idea had been ingrained in her mind during her growing years and on her heart when she was old enough to make her own decisions—the idea that a woman's body was her exclusive property and the property of whatever man she took in holy matrimony. Her body was hers and had been Godfrey's and was now hers again. She could not give it to the Duke of Tenby in casual lust. It was too precious a possession.

He touched her hand again. "You do not even need to say anything," he told her. "I understand. Shall I find something else to do with myself tomorrow afternoon?"

"No," she said. "I have not changed my mind and will not. I shall be there tomorrow."

He jumped down to the pavement and lifted her down after him. He took her hand and raised it to his lips "Until tomorrow, then, Lady Wingham," he said. "Each hour between now and then will drag by." For the first time there was heat in his eyes.

She smiled and hurried past him into the house.

6

She was only a few minutes late, no more than three or four. Far too punctual for him to have considered giving up and leaving. And yet he had wondered how long he would wait beyond the appointed time. Ten minutes? Fifteen? Half an hour? He watched her walking toward the plain dark carriage in which he waited, not looking at it, gazing about her as if to admire the scenery, not hurrying. And he wondered if he was disappointed that she was so punctual.

Disappointed? He wanted her, did he not? His loins were already aching in anticipation of what was to come within the hour. He had wanted her for a long time. For six years, though he had not consciously thought about her during much of that time. He had always wanted her. He had twice offered to make her his mistress six years ago, once riding all the way from London to Ebury Court in order to do so. Knowing that she would refuse.

Yes, he had known she would refuse. Not the first time, perhaps. When he had lured her into Freddie's carriage after a theater performance knowing that he had several minutes alone with her before Freddie would be able to carry his wife outside—Mrs. Sullivan had been unable to walk in those days—he had fully expected that she would accept *carte blanche*. He had been prepared to offer her a house of her own and servants and a carriage and clothes and jewels, after all, as well as his person. But the second time he had known what his answer was to be even as he rode the distance into Kent.

The question he asked himself now was whether he would have been disappointed if she had said yes. It was a strange question and one he had never thought to ask himself before. Why would he have gone to some pains to offer if he had not wanted her to accept? Because it was her sweetness and her purity that attracted him more than anything else, perhaps? Because he was unconsciously putting her to the test?

And was he disappointed now? He had been about to offer her marriage the day before, but she had forestalled him and offered herself as his mistress instead. Why should he be disappointed? He was to have her today, before another hour had passed, instead of having to wait for banns to be read and other wedding arrangements to be made. And without having to disappoint anyone or give up any of the rules by which he had lived all his life. He did not have to step out into the unknown. Establishing a new mistress, bedding her for the first time, were quite familiar to his experience, after all.

His coachman, dressed plainly and not in the distinctive livery of his household, opened the carriage door, lifted her inside, and closed the door behind her. The duke reached across her without a word and drew the curtain across the window as it was already drawn across the window on his side of the carriage.

"Harriet," he said, looking at her, "you are punctual." And rather drably dressed in a gray cloak that the weather did not really call for and a plain bonnet. Yet in the dimness of the carriage interior her hair gleamed golden. Plain clothes had never succeeded in making Harriet look plain.

"Yes." Her eyes rose to his lips, perhaps to his nose, but not to his own eyes. "I told Amanda that I was going shopping with Julia—with the Countess of Beaconswood. She did not like my leaving the house on foot and without a maid."

"Harriet." He took her hand in his. It was icy cold. He raised it to warm it at his lips. "You are going to have to learn to be devious, my dear."

"Yes." Her fingers were stiff against his lips.

He held her hand in silence for a few minutes. She directed her gaze at the seat opposite him as he examined her profile. She did not look at all like a woman about to begin a love affair. He wondered if it was just the tension of nervousness she was feeling or if it was active unhappiness.

How would she feel, he wondered, if she knew that he had been going to offer the day before to make her his duchess? Would she have accepted? Or was it just an affair she wanted? From what she had said about her marriage, it seemed that she had been fond of the older man she had wed. Perhaps he had been a great lover. Perhaps it was just that she missed it and wanted to satisfy that craving while she looked about her at more leisure for a husband who suited her fancy. He supposed, after all, that women had sexual needs just as men did. He was to service that need for her just as she was for him. He felt his lips tighten with the same anger—was anger the right word?—he had felt the day before.

Why had he not offered her marriage anyway? Why had he not taken her hands in his and laughed at her and assured her that that was not what he wanted at all? That he wanted more than her body, to be taken in clandestine manner at prearranged times. That he wanted all of her for all time. As his love, his wife, his duchess. Why had he kept his mouth shut and fallen in with her plans as if they had been his own?

Had he really felt disappointment? Anger? Surprise that she had offered herself so cheaply? He was not sure. He had not analyzed his feelings at the time, and he had not done so since. He had merely reacted. And his reaction had been that if he could have her without the trouble of marrying her—and marrying her would have caused trouble—then have her he would. He wanted her badly enough, after all. As she had said, they would doubtless tire of each other by the time the Season drew to its end. He would be able to continue with his cautious courtship of Lady Phyllis Reeder. He would be able to marry her in the summer and please his grandmother and his mother. And himself. Lady Phyllis would fit her role as his duchess as to the manner born. His way of life would be changed and upset hardly at all.

"We could merely take a quiet drive for a short while, you know," he said. "I could have you set down at Lady

Beaconswood's house if you wish. You have not yet
reached a point from which you cannot return, Harriet."

He held his breath. Almost, he thought, frowning, as if he
hoped she would take the way out he offered her. Almost as
if he was willing to give up his afternoon's sport.

She looked up into his eyes suddenly, and once more he
was jolted by their wide-eyed candor. "Yes, I have," she
said. "I am here. I'll not turn craven. It is just that I am
nervous and uncertain of myself. I have never—done this
before. What do you expect of me? That I should be—flirtatious? I am not sure that I can be."

Heaven forbid. Harriet flirtatious? Harriet batting her
eyelashes and pouting her lips and entertaining him with
baby talk and trilling little laughs? That was what he was
accustomed to, he realized, what he had always found sexu-
ally stimulating. But not Harriet. His love nest would not
suit Harriet, he thought suddenly. He wished there were
somewhere else to take her.

"I expect only that you be yourself," he said, raising her
hand to his lips again. It was still cold.

He wondered if he should take her into his arms and kiss
away her chill and her nervousness. Normally he did not
wonder what he should do with a woman. He acted from
instinct. Fortunately he did not have to torture himself for
long. The carriage slowed and then stopped and he felt her
stiffen again as they waited in silence for his coachman to
open the door and set down the steps.

She hated the house and the servant who opened the door
and bowed and scraped as he took her cloak and bonnet and
his grace's hat and cane and looked respectable and discreet—as he undoubtedly was. He made her feel like a
scarlet woman. The house was sumptuously decorated and
furnished. At least the hall and the stairway were and the
sitting room through which they passed before the duke led
her through a door leading off it into a bedchamber. The
window- and bed-hangings were wine-colored. Not quite
scarlet but suggestive of luxury and—sin. It was the only
word that would come to mind. The bed was turned neatly
back, ready for use. The sheets and pillowcases, she could

see, were of satin. It was the sort of place where a man of wealth brought women to be bedded. Or housed them if they did not have independent means. It was perhaps where she would have been housed if she had accepted his offer six years ago.

"If you are as nervous as you look or as you said you were when we were in the carriage," he said, closing the door and running his hands up her arms before taking her shoulders in a firm clasp, "you would not wish to be detained in the sitting room for tea or some other refreshments, would you, Harriet?"

Suddenly his height and his muscled physique, his handsome features and very blond hair, his silver eyes, all of which had attracted her powerfully for a long time, seemed quite overwhelming. She was alone with him in a bedchamber. They were there for the express purpose of making love. Though she supposed that was not quite an appropriate term for what was about to happen.

"No," she said, "I would rather—" She swallowed. *Do it without delay,* she had been about to say. Sordid words. She wished on a sudden wave of panic and nausea that she had accepted his suggestion that they merely drive, that he set her down at Julia's so that what she had told Amanda would not after all have been a lie. She wished Godfrey were there. She wanted him desperately, his quiet, almost dull friendship and affection. Dull to anyone who was not emotionally involved with him, that was.

"Yes," he said. "So would I, Harriet."

His kiss was instantly reassuring, for it fired her as it always did. She had been wondering all morning and all during the carriage ride if she desired him after all. She had wondered if she loved him after all. But his mouth, open on hers, his arms that drew her against the length of his body, his tongue, which explored first her lips, and then the flesh behind, and then the cavity of her mouth and the sensitive surfaces there, put her fears to rest, and for the first time all afternoon she felt heat in her body and desire.

It was not sinful, she told herself. It was not. Neither of them was married to anyone else. Neither of them was deceiving the other. Both of them were freely consenting to what was happening. She would not believe it was sinful. Or sordid. There was nothing sordid about two mature adults taking some pleasure from each other if no one else was getting hurt. She closed her eyes so that she would not see the room. She pushed the sudden mental image of Susan from her mind. She would not feel sinful. This was what she had wanted for six years.

"Harriet." He was murmuring into her ear and running one spread palm down her back to her waist, past the curve of her spine and lower and then back up again. "Relax."

She had not realized that she was tense. But of course she was. As taut as a bow. She allowed herself to relax against him. "I am sorry, your grace," she said.

And then his eyes were looking down into hers from a mere few inches away, silver, mocking, heavy with desire. "We had better dispense with that courtesy," he said, "under the circumstances. I have tried to think of a more unfortunate name than Archibald that my parents might have given me, and I have failed miserably, alas. There *is* no more unfortunate name. Most of my intimates call me Archie. If you cannot persuade yourself to do that, it will have to be Tenby. But not 'your grace,' Harriet. Not in this house, anyway."

This house was to be a world apart, of course, and every-thing that happened in it. Outside this house they would maintain the formality of most of their previous dealings. She had known it would be so. It made sense. She would not give in to that feeling of sin that was trying to intrude.

"Archie," she said. It seemed more intimate than a kiss to call him by his given name. She had never ever thought of him by it alone. Always he had figured in her mind with his titles.

"Suddenly," he said, smiling, "I like my name. Do you wish to wear a nightgown? There is a variety hanging in the dressing room through the door behind you. I will wait while you change into one if it will make you feel more comfortable. I would prefer to unclothe you without that lapse of time, of course. Ah, the blush. You make blushes uniquely attractive, Harriet."

It was real suddenly, what was to happen. Godfrey had

never unclothed her or seen her unclothed. He had always made love to her in darkness and beneath the bedclothes, raising her nightgown only as high as was necessary. Even on her wedding night she had felt no great embarrassment.

"It will be as you wish," she said, wanting the decency of a nightgown but not wanting to step inside that dressing room to view the array of nightgowns his former mistresses had worn.

"That," he said, "is quite an invitation, Harriet."

He kissed her again and she knew the moment was coming inexorably closer. She became aware that his hands were opening the buttons that held her dress closed at the back. The buttons extended below her waist. His mouth moved downward, over her chin and along her neck to the pulse at the base of her throat. She tipped back her head and closed her eyes. His hands had drawn her dress off her shoulders and were moving it down her arms. Her chemise, she could feel without either lifting her head or opening her eyes, was coming with it. And then his mouth was at one naked breast and closing, warm and wet and piercingly sweet, over the nipple.

"Ah," she heard herself say. A stabbing ache had taut-ened both nipples and set up a throbbing in her womb. This was what physical desire was, she realized suddenly. She had never really felt it to this extent before.

"Come." His mouth was against hers again, his eyes half closed. "We can pursue this more satisfactorily on the bed."

It was only when he turned her, one arm firmly about her, to lead her to the bed and lay her down on it, that she understood fully that she was naked. In broad daylight. With his eyes on her. He stood beside the bed, his heavy-lidded eyes roaming over her quite unapologetically as he began to unclothe himself.

"I have always wondered," he said, "if the blush covered your whole body down to your toenails. It does. How very charming."

He pulled off his shirt and began on his pantaloons with-out any apparent selfconsciousness. But then why did he need to feel any? He looked even more magnificent without his shirt than he did fully clothed. He must work very hard, she thought, to keep those muscles so splendidly firm. She looked up into his eyes and saw his amusement at the fact that she was appraising his form as frankly as he was appreciating hers.

And then he was on the bed beside her, one powerful and naked arm pushing beneath her head, the other coming behind her waist to draw her against him. She inhaled slowly and smelled warm masculinity. She thought she might swoon.

"What do you like, Harriet?" he asked against her mouth. "What are your preferences? Let me pleasure you."

Her eyes snapped open.

He laughed softly. "You are quite inexperienced, are you not?" he said.

"Yes." She swallowed.

"But not virgin?"

"No." It seemed that he did not know of Susan's existence. She did not know why she had never mentioned her to him. She did not want him to know about her daughter. She wanted her two worlds kept strictly apart. She had never mentioned the Duke of Tenby to Susan.

"Ah," he said. "Well, let me pleasure you even so, Harriet. That is why we are here, is it not?"

Yes, that was why they were there. There would be no romance, he had said the afternoon before in Kew. No love. She had chided herself then for the hurt she had felt. But it was part of what she had decided upon. She had decided to become his mistress. There was no romance, no love in being a man's mistress. Just this. Physical pleasure.

He pleasured her. She forgot embarrassment and her foolish craving for romance in pure physical sensation as his hands and his mouth and his tongue, marvelously skilled, brought her pleasure. No, not pleasure. Pain. Pain that was pleasure. She put all comparisons from her mind. She had decided beforehand that she would under no circumstances make comparisons. But that part of her mind that was beyond her control made them anyway. Although she had been a wife for four years, although she had been used as such regularly once a week during those years, although she was a mother, she came to understand that her

body had been unawakened until now. She came to understand that what had happened in her marriage bed had been
more emotional than physical—for her, anyway. She had
enjoyed physical union with Godfrey because it had
brought her as close to him in every way as she could be
and she had loved him. Her body had never rejoiced in
what he did to it, only her mind and her emotions.

And then the splendidly young and muscular body with
which her own was awakening to the pleasures of the flesh
lifted over her and came down on her. Her legs moved
wide, the sensitive flesh of her inner thighs riding against
powerful masculine ones. She longed, with a sudden re-
newal of her earlier panic, for love, for the older, thinner,
more angular body of the man who had loved her with gentleness and reverence and had never excited her at all.

"Easy, Harriet." The Duke of Tenby set his mouth lightly
to hers and murmured into it. "You are as skittish as a
maiden. Easy."

He kissed her lightly, warmly, while she accustomed herself to the feel of him, hard against the entrance to her. He
did not move immediately inside.

"Archie." Her voice sounded high-pitched. It did not
sound quite like her own. She loved him. She had always
loved him. She wanted it with love. Not like this. She
wanted him to love her. She wondered fleetingly what he
would say if she told him she loved him, and pressed her
lips back against his lest she should do the unthinkable and
say it aloud.

"At last." He had raised himself on his forearms and was
looking down into her eyes, his own liquid silver, heavy
with passion. "At last, after six long years, Harriet."

He pressed into her so slowly that at first she was able to
control her panic. His eyes held hers. But when he came
deep and deeper, she bit her lower lip and cringed away
from his penetration. He stopped.

"All the way, Harriet," he commanded. "Give it all to
me, my dear."

And so she closed her eyes and relaxed beneath him and
allowed him all the way in. It was a moment she recognized
for what it was. Surrender. Surrender of her virtue, of what

had always been one of her most firmly held values. Surrender of herself. To the man whose mistress she had agreed to become until they tired of each other. *Until I join my body to yours, nothing is irreversible,* he had said. Now everything was irreversible.

"Beautiful," he said when she opened her eyes again. "As beautiful inside as out, Harriet. Hot and wet. But you are realizing that you have done something irrevocable, are you not? Your eyes look stricken. I'll make it good for you—this time and all the other times we will meet here. I promise. Close your eyes and let me lo—. Let me make it good for you."

He took her hands, crossed them at the wrist above her head, laced his fingers with hers, and lowered most of his weight onto her, setting his cheek against her hair. And then he began to move in her and to keep his promise so that after a couple of minutes she was mindless with need and with pain that hovered on the brink of pleasure and that suddenly spilled over the brink, bringing her a pleasure so intense that it was unbearable, and then was replaced by a sense of peace so unexpected that she felt all energy, all will to live beyond the moment, drain out of her.

He held deep in her while she settled with a sigh into the peace and then drove to his own climax as she held him, loving him more tenderly than she had ever loved before. Except perhaps for the moment when Susan had burst from her womb. She did not fight the fact that the two loves mingled in the same thought, that her two worlds came suddenly and quite unexpectedly together.

"Well, Harriet," he said several minutes later, having uncoupled them and moved to her side. His arm was about her, holding her against him.

"Well, Archie." She set her face against his chest, heavy with drowsiness. *Don't say anything more,* she begged him silently. *Don't ask how it was. Don't ask if it was pleasurable.* She did not want to be reminded yet that it had been pleasure, not love. She did not want to remember that she was mistress, not wife.

But he tucked her more snugly against him, kissed the top of her head, and said no more. She relaxed gratefully against him and marveled at how she could be thinking only of sleep after such a very carnal experience.

And sleep she did, she realized with surprise only when she was waking up again some time later. She was not waking of her own accord. His hand was on her breast, and her nipple was coming to life between the light squeezing of his finger and thumb. His tongue was moving lazily across the seam of her lips. She opened her eyes and looked into his.

"Again?" she said and wished even as the word was passing her lips that she could have swallowed it. His eyes twinkled into hers with lazy amusement and he chuckled.

"We will make regular appointments for twice a week, I believe," he said. "Once a week would quite frankly not be enough, yet more than twice would court detection and scandal. Twice a week is going to seem woefully inadequate, especially while we are still new to each other. Don't you agree? But we must be sensible. If we are to have each other only twice a week, then, we must make the most of each encounter. We will have to curtail the sleeping as much as possible so that we may enjoy each other two or three times. Agreed?"

Twice. Or *three* times? It did not seem possible. She had never thought of it as a possibility. He was going to have her again? And perhaps again after that?

"Yes," she said.

And she found that it was indeed possible. And equally pleasurable. And a third time too, so closely following the second that they did not even uncouple between times. Life as a mistress, Harriet realized, her face against his damp chest after it was all over, was vastly different from life as a wife. She was too exhausted to explore those differences.

He dressed beside the bed while she dressed at the other side of the room. He had seen her hesitate and then seem to decide that it would be pointless modesty to take her clothes into the dressing room. She stood with her back to him.

He watched her as he dressed. Harriet. Small and neat and beautiful. No longer a mystery to him. Known. His body felt the languor and satisfaction of its knowledge. No longer the pure, unattainable little Harriet of his dreams. She was his mistress. She had become very thoroughly so during the past hour and a half.

He wondered if she would still be his mistress if she had accepted his offer six years ago. He had never kept a mistress for longer than eight months. Six years? He surely would have tired of her long ago. By now she would be forgotten. Not just in his past but forgotten. He could not remember either the names or faces of the women with whom he had taken his pleasure six or even five years ago.

With any luck, if they kept their twice weekly appointments and if he worked her hard enough during those encounters, as he had today, he would have her out of his system by the end of the Season. She was just a woman, when all was said and done, with whose beautiful body his own would become sated through frequent and vigorous use. He was glad he had not proposed marriage to her. She was not close enough to his world for any satisfactory relationship to be a reasonable expectation. She had saved him from making the biggest and most disastrous mistake of his life.

He had had her and he was satisfied. Very satisfied. There were a good number of weeks left during which he could get his fill of her. But he was a little disappointed, nevertheless. He would admit it to himself now. He had just bedded the mistress who had satisfied him more than any other he could remember, perhaps more than anyone even if he could remember all. And he had a great deal more to look forward to. But he felt as if he had lost something too. Someone. Harriet. She was not the person he had thought her. He strode across the room to help her with the top buttons of her dress.

"Thank you," she said, turning after he had finished and looking up at him. Her face was flushed, not with a blush, but with the aftermath of vigorous sex.

God, when she looked at him like that, all wide beautiful eyes, she was Harriet all over again. And the remaining weeks seemed terrifyingly short.

"Twice a week will suit you?" he asked, drawing mentally back from her and hearing in some surprise the cold businesslike tone of his voice.

"Yes, Archie," she said.

"Mondays and Thursdays, then," he said. "The same time?"

"Yes."

"We will have to protect your reputation," he said. "And mine too since I am courting another lady and it would be discourteous to her to have this liaison become public knowledge. I will have my carriage pick you up each time, but not always in the same place. We will arrange each time where it is to meet you the next time. Will that be suitable?"

"Yes, Archie," she said.

"We must meet formally whenever we are attending the same social function," he said. "You must never use my given name except here, Harriet."

She flushed but continued to look at him quietly and steadily. He knew that he was humiliating her, by his businesslike manner as much as by the words he spoke. But curiously he could not seem to stop himself. He felt the quite unreasonable urge to hurt her. Because she had fallen off her pedestal? But he had been very ready to sweep her up when she fell and to lay her down in his bed.

He leaned forward and kissed her firmly on the lips. "Thank you," he said. "You are very good, my dear. You gave me great pleasure." The words were intended to placate her, to redeem himself. But they were spoken as briskly as the words that had preceded them. "Come, I shall escort you most of the way home."

"Thank you," she said.

He rested a hand against the slender and shapely small of her back as he guided her from the room. He wanted to stop and turn her against him and hold her there until she knew that he had not meant the coldness or the brusqueness. But he did not do so. It was almost two hours since he had picked her up. They could not risk being alone together for much longer.

For a man who had just experienced three powerfully satisfying bouts of sexual activity, he thought as they made their way downstairs and outside to his waiting carriage, he was feeling remarkably depressed. It must be just that he was tired. He was more used to resident mistresses with whom he could sleep all night whenever he so wished. Or it was just that he had to wait until Monday before having her again. At the beginning of an affair he liked to indulge himself with daily beddings. In Harriet's case, four days were going to drag by, he knew.

They sat silently side by side in the carriage. She looked prim and virginal again in the drab cloak and bonnet that refused to hide her beauty. He wondered if she had regrets, but he would not ask her. He wondered if she was feeling euphoric—but she did not look euphoric—or as depressed as he was. Perhaps she was feeling neither. Perhaps for her it was as she had indicated, a mere physical affair. Perhaps her body was satisfied and her mind was looking ahead to whatever she had planned for the evening.

He kissed her hand when the carriage came to a stop and watched as his coachman lifted her to the roadway. She did not look into his eyes as she took her leave of him or look back before the carriage door closed again.

7

Mr. Hardinge seemed more than usually attentive. He seated himself beside her at Mrs. Crofton's concert and leaned slightly toward her, making their conversation exclusive to themselves for the ten minutes or so before the first performance, a pianoforte recital, was to begin. He smiled engagingly at her and talked about the violinist who was to play later and whom he had heard play in Vienna. He really was a very charming and interesting man, Harriet thought. He was also young and tolerably handsome. She smiled warmly at him.

"It must be wonderful to have traveled and to have seen the most beautiful places in Europe," she said.

"It is," he agreed. "But I realized at the time and I realize more fully now that seeing it all in company with a like-minded companion, someone one cared for, would make the experience that much more wonderful."

"Yes," she said. "I can believe that."

She wondered how soon he would declare himself. She did not think it was vanity that made her believe he surely would. He would be a wonderful catch. Amanda had said so when she knew that he was to escort Harriet to the concert. And Harriet knew it and felt it herself. With him she could find all the security and potentially all the contentment she had known with Godfrey. But none of the heartache over his weak health. She could marry Mr. Hardinge and be safe again.

Except that the thought sickened her. How could she consider becoming his wife when she was another man's mistress? He could she even consider doing that to him?

She had wondered before taking the irrevocable step how her conscience would react. Now she knew.

"I suspected as much when I first set eyes on you this evening, Lady Wingham," Mr. Hardinge said, touching his fingers to the back of her hand for a moment and looking into her face with a twinkle in his eyes, "but now I know it for certain. You outshine every other lady present tonight. You always do, of course, but tonight you look especially lovely."

"Why, thank you, sir." She laughed lightly. He was not given to paying her lavish compliments. She had fallen in love with the rich green satin the moment she had set eyes on it, and her modiste had assured her that it was an inspired choice with her eyes. But Susan had said it was not the gown.

"You're pretty, Mama," she had said when Harriet had gone into the nursery earlier to hug her and kiss her and tuck her into bed.

"I feel pretty," Harriet had said. "It is a lovely gown, is it not?"

"Not the gown." Susan had held her face in her two small hands and gazed into it. "You, Mama. You're pretty."

Harriet had laughed and rubbed her nose against Susan's.

But she knew what Susan must have meant. And Mr. Hardinge too. She had noticed it herself in her looking glass. A heightened rosiness in her cheeks and brightness in her eyes. She had been alarmed and had held her palms to her cheeks for a while. It had seemed so very obvious to her that it was the face of a woman who had been awakened to the pleasure of the flesh that very day. It amazed her that everyone who looked at her did not immediately point an accusing finger. Yet when she had arrived home late in the afternoon, Amanda had greeted her quite placidly and asked her how she had enjoyed her shopping trip with Lady Beaconswood.

Harriet had sat through the tea telling a pack of lies in a brightly enthusiastic voice. She wondered how many other lies she was going to have to tell in the coming weeks. A whole set of them for every Monday and Thursday afternoon, she supposed.

"Ah," Mr. Hardinge said, "the concert is about to begin."

Mrs. Crofton had stepped into the empty center of her large drawing room and was smiling graciously about her, waiting for the growing hush to become complete silence.

The Earl and Countess of Barthorpe and Lady Phyllis Reeder were sitting across the room from Harriet and Mr. Hardinge, close to the doors. Harriet had noticed them earlier and had looked away from the girl, quelling a twinge of guilt. Why should she feel guilty? If she had not become his mistress, someone else would have. There must be dozens, perhaps hundreds, of women in his past. And he was the kind of man who would have mistresses throughout his life, despite marriage. Harriet certainly did not need that particular guilt on her shoulders.

She looked across the room again as everyone applauded Mrs. Crofton's opening remarks and the pianist settled himself with a flourish of coattails and a theatrical flexing of fingers at the instrument. The Duke of Tenby was just seating himself beside Lady Phyllis and bowing and raising her hand to his lips. He glanced about the room in the moments before the music began, paused at Harriet, lifted his quizzing glass languidly to his eye, and then lowered it again before inclining his head rather stiffly in her direction.

Harriet concentrated her full attention on the pianoforte and harp recitals that followed and on the soprano's aria. It was what she had expected and the way he had warned her it must be. She would become accustomed to the double lives they must lead. There were probably a dozen such couples in this very room, couples who lived separately and respectably in society yet together and intimately in private. She did not find the thought particularly comforting.

He looked extremely handsome and elegant and rather haughty, she thought. And of course she was not the only person who had noticed his late arrival. The Duke of Tenby had a way of attracting general attention wherever he went, though she did not believe he did so deliberately. Everyone was marvelously interested in his apparent courtship of Lady Phyllis. Harriet heard talk about it wherever she went. He would be married to Lady Phyllis before September.

Harriet kept her eyes off the two of them and listened to the music. And yet all the while she was aware of her body as she had never been during her marriage except perhaps the day after her wedding night. She was aware of a new tenderness in her breasts, caused by his hands and fingers, by his mouth and tongue, by the press of his chest against hers. And of a slight stiffness in her legs, which had been held wide by his for long stretches of time. And of a soreness that was not exactly painful and a deep throbbing in the passage he had occupied and worked for several minutes three separate times.

Her body would become accustomed to the new facts, she told herself. But she felt amazed that other people did not look at her and see her for what she was. She felt naked. Her hand strayed to her bosom to check that her low-cut gown covered her decently enough. She felt like a scarlet woman.

Yes, she now knew what her conscience was going to do to her.

After the interval, during which she allowed Mr. Hardinge to fetch her a drink without relinquishing her seat, the chair beside Lady Phyllis remained empty. Obviously the Duke of Tenby was pursuing his courtship with his customary caution. Harriet let out a silent sigh of relief and prepared to enjoy the violinist Mr. Hardinge had heard in Vienna. She also felt unreasonably bereft. He had not even crossed the room to bid her a good evening.

Lord Bruce Ingram paused on the threshold of the Duke of Tenby's breakfast room on Monday morning and grinned.

"You are looking thoroughly out of sorts, Archie," he said. "Might I be permitted to say 'I told you so'? You would not come to Annette's last night even though you dismissed Bridget a few weeks ago. Annette's girls were in fine form—at least Elsie was. Celibacy never did suit you."

"Have a beefsteak," the duke said, waving his friend to a chair at the table. "I had one cooked for you, knowing you were coming. Though *cooked* seems an inappropriate word to describe the way you like it. I believe my chef showed it to the fire and set it on the plate. Behold it swimming in its own juice. It is revolting."

"Ah." Lord Bruce rubbed his hands together in appreciation as his grace's butler placed the beefsteak before him. "My compliments to your chef, Archie. It is just the way I like it. I had better haul you off to Annette's tonight. There is a new girl I want to try. And you are looking green about the gills. A sure sign of sexual deprivation, old chap."

The duke dragged his eyes away from the plate with its almost raw beefsteak and scowled down at the small pile of letters beside his plate. "I am coming under inspection," he said.

"Not a comfortable feeling," Lord Bruce said sympathetically, tucking into his breakfast, "especially when one is a duke and should be a law unto oneself. Your mother is coming to town?"

"Worse," the duke said gloomily. "Ten times worse."

Lord Bruce grimaced. "The duchess?" he said.

"My grandmother, yes," the duke said. "She is not coming to keep an eye on me and press forward my nuptials, of course. She is coming because Aunt Sophie has arrived from Bath and has taken it into her head that she wants to enjoy the pleasures of town one more time before the everlasting silence descends."

Lord Bruce tittered.

"The woman must be a hundred if she is a day," the duke said. "I can remember going to Bath with family greetings on the occasion of her eightieth or ninetieth birthday—I was never sure which. And that was when I discovered Freddie Sullivan about to get married. Six years ago. That makes my greaty aunt eighty-six or ninety-six now. My grandmother is eighty, or will be in August. And they are coming to enjoy the Season, Bruce. Here. They are going to be staying here."

Lord Bruce threw back his head and roared with laughter, a dripping cube of steak pierced by his fork halfway between the plate and his mouth.

"All the ladies will expire from envy when you drive them in the park, Arch," he said. "This is going to be priceless. You must warn me when you are to take them there first. I would not miss it for a hundred of Annette's girls."

"As far as that is concerned," the duke said rather haughtily, "it is no great joke, Bruce, if you would care to stop guffawing and dripping blood over my tablecloth. Ladies do not become figures of fun merely because they have grown old. I am fond of my grandmother and would be of Aunt Sophie if she were not as deaf as a post but quite insistent on being involved in everyone's conversation. No, what concerns me is that I am going to be a dead duck."

"Better than being a live one, old boy," Lord Bruce said with a chuckle. "You would not enjoy quacking your way through the rest of your life. I thought you had steeled your will to wedding and bedding the delectable Lady Phyllis. She is rather delectable, Arch. I have taken a good look at her since you began to lay siege."

"I hate being rushed," the duke said, scowling again. "I hate having my hand forced. I know just how it will be. As soon as my grandmother finds out which way the wind is blowing, there will be teas for the countess and Lady Phyllis and picnics with them and visits to the theater with them and doubtless a visit to Vauxhall with them. And while we are there, Grandmama will doubtless send the two of us down the darkest alley and stand guard at the end of it until the girl has been thoroughly kissed and proposed to. I'll be betrothed before the month is out, Bruce."

Lord Bruce shrugged. "You have my deepest commiserations, Arch," he said. "But it is going to come sooner or later, is it not? It might as well be sooner, I suppose."

"Not until Season's end," the duke said. "I want to be free at least until Season's end."

His friend looked at him with some interest. "Indeed?" he said. "You dark horse, Arch. You did not tell me that you have someone else on the mount already. No wonder you would not come to Annette's. Who is she?"

"No one," the duke said hastily. "You misunderstood me, Bruce."

But his friend was grinning at him. "And you fear the old girls will stop you from enjoying her?" he said. "Poor Archie. But they cannot demand your company twenty-four hours a day, can they? Don't old girls nod off with pleasing regularity? When do you, ah, exert yourself with her, Arch? Morning, afternoon, or night?"

"I told you you had misunderstood, Bruce," the duke said, looking his friend sternly in the eye.

But Lord Bruce Ingram was not easily cowed. "If it is night, she is resident," he said, gazing musingly up to the ceiling, the last piece of steak waving on his fork. "If it is daytime, she is not. Is she resident, Archie?"

"You are in danger of finding that fork embedded between your eyes," the duke said quietly. "Have done, old fellow."

"No, she would not be," Lord Bruce said. "You would be all eagerness to share the news of your latest conquest if she were a courtesan. If she is not resident, of course, then she must be someone respectable. Someone of good *ton*. A married lady. Arch, Arch, you could be getting yourself into deep waters, old boy. Is she good? Who is she?"

"Put that disgusting piece of raw flesh into your mouth," the Duke of Tenby, said, getting resolutely to his feet, "and swallow it, Bruce. We are going to Tattersall's, as planned. And if you say another word"—he held up a staying hand as his friend opened his mouth to speak—"I shall ram it back down your throat with my fist."

Lord Bruce ate the final piece of steak in philosophical silence, washed it down with the inch of ale that was left in his cup, wiped his mouth with his napkin, and got to his feet. "I shall find out for myself, anyway," he said as if to himself as he followed the duke from the room. "All it needs is to remember every lady with whom you have conversed apart from Lady Phyllis since the Season began. There have not been many, have there, Arch? Indeed, I can think of only one below the age of forty. Interesting." He chuckled.

The Duke of Tenby chose to ignore him.

He appeared not to be in a good mood. After his initial greeting when his coachman had lifted her into his carriage, he had sat in silence beside her all the way to his love nest, staring gloomily out of the window. Except that the curtain had been drawn across it. Now, inside the bedchamber, he had drawn her hard against him and was undoing the buttons of her dress without kissing her or saying anything remotely tender. Almost as if she were no more than a body to him.

She was probably not.

She wished she had done what she had promised herself all weekend that she would do. She wished she had neglected to meet his carriage. It would be as easy as that to end the affair, she felt sure. He would not come after her if she did. She had been miserable with guilt for four days and even more miserable over the lies she was going to have to think up to tell Amanda on Monday afternoon. She did not want to continue the affair.

And yet it seemed that her body had become quite separate from either her mind or her emotions. And stronger than either. When Monday luncheon came and was over and Amanda had suggested a stroll in the park before it became too crowded, she had excused herself, claiming that she had promised to accompany Lady Beaconswood on a visit to another lady. She must not use Julia on Thursday too, she thought. She must think of another excuse for leaving home alone.

Her body had ached with the knowledge that it could be loved by him again during the afternoon, though she used the word "love" in her mind only because she did not know any of the coarser words that men knew. What would happen to her body had nothing to do with love. But she had known too that she would not be able to resist the temptation to continue the affair for at least one more afternoon. After all, it must become easier with time. She was not quite sure what she meant by *it*.

And so she was here, to find him silent and rather morose. He drew her dress and her chemise off her shoulders and down her arms, watching what he did, examining her breasts with cold, clinical eyes. There would be no romance, he had said. She had accepted that. But she had not realized that a sexual relationship might be entirely without—tenderness. Without any closeness at all beyond the physical.

"We are going to have to be doubly careful," he said. "My grandmother and my aunt are coming to town tomorrow or Wednesday. I'll not have my grandmother's name sullied by any sort of scandal of mine."

"What do you expect me to do?" she asked. "Climb onto Sir Clive's roof and shout out the glad tidings?" The sarcasm in her voice shocked her. She was never sarcastic.

His silver eyes regarded her coldly. "Shrew," he said quietly, his hands cupping her breasts. He removed his hands and set one at her back to guide her toward the bed.

She lay down and looked up at him as he undressed. His grandmother was coming? "She has been pleased by your news concerning Lady Phyllis?" she asked. "And is coming to see for herself?"

"I suspect that is her real reason," he said, frowning. "She will try to hasten our betrothal. I don't want it hastened. There are two months until the end of the Season. I want to be free to enjoy you during those months. Indeed, I will insist on doing so. But it will not be easy. She has a will of iron."

So his bad mood had not been occasioned by any desire to end their affair almost before it had begun. Quite the contrary. He wanted to enjoy her for two months. Enjoy. There was no tenderness in the word. She did not know why she looked for any.

"But let's not waste time," he said. "These four days have been endless, Harriet. I am ravenous. Are you?"

"Yes." She reached up her arms for him as he came down onto the bed beside her.

"I would kill to have you daily," he said. "I hope you are prepared for an hour and a half of bodily pleasure." His mouth came against hers. "That is what you are going to get."

"Yes, Archie," she said. "That is what I came for."

It was not really, she discovered over the next hour and a half. She had come for sexual activity, of course. She was quite prepared to be honest with herself, since she knew there was no real excuse for her behavior. But even though she had known there would be no more, even though he had said so from the start and she had known he spoke the truth, she knew too that she had come looking for more. Hoping for more. For some affection, some tenderness, if not love. For some awareness of each other's personhood. She wanted to know—she longed to know—that he was aware of her as Harriet.

He had promised an hour and a half of bodily pleasure, and that was precisely what he gave her. She realized today that the last time he had made allowances for her inexperience, her skittishness. Today he made no such allowances but made love with her—or made pleasure with her—with fierce demand for both her own response and his own release. The last time he had been prepared to treat her as a novice, allowing her to remain essentially passive except in her response. Today he began to teach her what he wanted, and demanded that she give it to him. And today he used new, more intimate touches on her and taught her different postures that could heighten sensation until she realized that the boundaries of pleasure could be pushed back to infinity and beyond.

There was not a moment for sleep and very few for relaxation. When he had said he was ravenous, he had spoken the truth. He took her as if he could not possibly have enough of her. And yet as she lay panting and damp against him at the end of the hour and a half, waiting for him to get up from the bed, she felt far, far away from him. There had been a sense of impersonality about everything that had happened between them on the bed. It had been a powerful and exhausting physical performance, something from which their real selves had stood back and hidden.

She closed her eyes. She longed for those selves to touch even if for just one moment. "Archie," she whispered.

He lifted her chin with one hand and kissed her languidly and lingeringly. "Time to be up and on our way," he said. "It was an adequate meal, Harriet? Your appetite has been satisfied?"

"Yes," she said. It was true. Her body was satisfied and contented. "And yours?"

"Utterly," he said. "Unfortunately I do not like having to go three or four days without any meal, at all, but there is nothing we can do about that, is there?" He pulled away from her, swung his legs over the side of the bed, and sat up to begin dressing. Harriet got out at the other side.

He kissed her before they left the room. "You really are very good, you know," he said. "You learn fast and well. You are the best I have had, Harriet."

She did not want to be the best. Being the best meant that she had been compared. She did not want to be compared. She wanted to be unique. How foolish! "I suppose," she said with a smile, "you would not tell me if I were not, would you?"

He kissed her hand and then watched as his coachman lifted her down from the carriage. As on the last occasion, she did not look back. He closed his eyes and set his head back against the cushions as the carriage moved on again. He was exhausted. He was going to have to sleep for an hour or two when he got home.

He swallowed and realized in some surprise that he was on the verge of tears. He could not remember when he had last cried. Certainly not at his grandfather's death. Perhaps it was at his father's. He could remember crying his heart out when his father was carried inside from a morning ride, his neck broken. And sniveling all through the funeral when he should have been comforting his mother and behaving like a man and a future duke—as his grandfather had pointed out to him sternly afterward and even emphasized with a cane swished painfully five times across his backside as he was bent over a desk. He did not believe he had cried since.

He was very much afraid that it had been a dreadful mistake. Not to change his mind about marrying her. He had done the right thing there. Marriage with Harriet would never have worked, not six years ago and not now. His mistake had been in beginning a liaison with her. It had seemed like a good idea and heaven knew he had desired her strongly enough. But it was not working. And yet it was far too late now to go back. What had happened was irreversible.

The trouble was that he could not seem to school himself into thinking of her only as a woman—only as a body to be enjoyed. He had just spent an hour and a half desperately trying to do just that, using her with a power and an energy that must have exhausted her strength almost beyond endurance. Three separate times—although there had been almost no interval between—he had wound up her desire and his own almost to breaking point and then pounded into her quite ruthlessly, denying both of them release until the tension could be borne not one second longer. He had played with her without tenderness or mercy, making pleasure an agony for her as well as for himself.

And yet he had failed in what he had tried to do. For every moment of that hour and a half she had been Harriet, his sweet, prim, grave, charming little blusher. Even though he had used her far more vigorously than he had ever used even the most hardened whore. She had been Harriet. And her body had done what her eyes had always done. It had given openly and candidly, reserving no secrets for itself.

Two months. That was what he had left with her if he could hold his grandmother at bay for that long. Two months during which to have enough of her, during which to begin to tire of her. It was bound to happen, was it not? Especially if he went at her with such vigor twice each week for those two months. It had to be long enough.

He knew it would not be nearly long enough.

He knew it would be far too long.

He loved her, now as always. He would still love her in July. And in July of next year. And ten years from now.

8

"Interesting letters, dear?" Lady Forbes asked at the breakfast table.

Harriet's head snapped up. "Oh, I do beg your pardon, Amanda," she said. "Am I being unpardonably rude? I shall leave the other one until later."

"No, no." Lady Forbes waved a careless hand. "I have told you repeatedly, Harriet, that you must not stand on ceremony here. You must treat our house as if it were your own."

"Thank you." Harriet smiled gratefully. "Clara and Mr. Sullivan are at Ebury Court with the children. They will not come to town this Season, she says, as they consider the baby still too young to be taken from the country. And, of course, they will not leave him behind."

"I still cannot believe the transformation of Freddie Sullivan," Lady Forbes said. "It seems that what they say about reformed rakes must have some truth in it, if you will forgive me for using such an indelicate word, my dear."

"Well, he was one," Harriet said. "I was dreadfully dismayed when Clara decided to marry him even though she knew very well that all he wanted was her fortune. Their marriage has turned out marvelously well." She sighed and returned her attention to her plate.

"You may open your other letter too without regard for me," Lady Forbes said.

"Very well, then." Harriet smiled at her again and picked it up. "Clara wants me to go there, you know. Either for a few days during the Season or for a lengthier stay during the summer. Or both."

"I do hope you will not leave us before the Season is

out," Lady Forbes said in some alarm. "Not when I have such high hopes for you, dear. Mr. Hardinge must be on the very brink of a declaration, surely. And such a very proper and pleasant young man."

"No." Harriet colored. "I don't believe I will be able to drag myself away before the Season is out. But I think I will go to Ebury Court during the summer. I will enjoy seeing Clara again, and it will be lovely for Susan to have the countryside to run and play in and Clara's boys to play with." She looked down at her other letter.

"Perhaps by that time," Lady Forbes said coyly, "you will have a wedding to plan, dear. And Mr. Hardinge has a small country estate, as you must know."

"Oh," Harriet said. "Lady Sophia Davenport is in town. With her sister-in-law. What an amazing lady she is. She never makes a secret of the fact that she is eighty-six years old. And yet she has traveled from home. She is inviting us to call on her this afternoon, Amanda."

Lady Forbes pulled a face. "I am afraid I make a point of avoiding her as much as I can when we are in Bath," she said. "It is very unkind of me, but I hate having to say everything twice, once loudly and the second time in a shout. I believe Clive and I will definitely be attending the Smith garden party this afternoon that I have been dithering over. In fact, we are under some obligation to go. And you too, my dear."

"I think I should go to see Lady Sophia," Harriet said.

Lady Forbes grimaced. "You put me to shame, Harriet," she said. "It was that saintliness and that kindness to the elderly that Godfrey always adored in you and that made Clive and me come to love you when we had been prepared to dislike you intensely. There, I have never told you that, have I?"

"Well," Harriet said, "I *was* a penniless nobody. And I *did* marry Godfrey for the security he could offer me."

"And made his last four years heaven on earth," Lady Forbes said briskly, pushing back her chair and getting to her feet. "Are you coming to Bond Street with me this morning? I feel the urge to purchase a new bonnet, though I need one about as much as I need a headache."

"But there is a garden party this afternoon to wear a new bonnet for," Harriet said with a smile. "No, I plan to spend the morning with Susan. Sometimes I feel guilty about spending so little time with her."

Lady Forbes raised her eyes to the ceiling. "My dear," she said, "many children are fortunate if they see their mothers for two minutes after breakfast and for one at bedtime." She went off about her business while Harriet finished her breakfast.

Harriet looked down at Lady Sophia Davenport's letter and smiled ruefully. It was rather difficult to be in company with her, especially if there were several people in the room and more than one conversation in progress. But then the lady could not help the fact that she had grown old and lost most of her hearing any more than Godfrey had been able to help having a weak heart and being unable to walk fast or dance or do a number of other things that his wife had had energy for. Age and physical infirmity did not make a person less human and did not excuse the impatience and even contempt with which they were so often treated. Harriet—and her husband—had always visited Lady Sophia more often than anyone else in Bath.

The house to which she had been invited was on St. James's Square. Very grand. Lady Sophia was a duke's daughter and a marquess's widow, Harriet remembered. The sister-in-law must be the wife of the present duke or the sister of the marquess if her home was on St. James's Square. It was Wednesday and Harriet's afternoon was free. It was a good thing the letter had not come one day later. She would have had to send an excuse.

Tomorrow. Harriet went into a dream while her finger unconsciously traced a pattern on the letter. She knew she would go—again. There was no point in trying to persuade herself that she would think about it and come to a decision later. She longed for him. Three days seemed an eternity. It did not matter that she hated the lies she had to tell and felt that she was abusing the hospitality of Sir Clive and Lady Forbes. It did not matter that she felt unclean, unworthy of Mr. Hardinge or any of the other gentlemen who still crowded about her wherever she appeared in public. It did not even matter that she sometimes had the feeling she would contaminate Susan.

For the desires of the flesh were more powerful to her than conscience at the moment. And more powerful than pride. She knew what she was to him, and there was humiliation in the knowledge if she allowed herself to dwell on it. But she would not allow any such thing. He had spoken with her and Mr. Selway for a few minutes the evening before at a ball. His manner had been formal and correct, even haughty. His eyes, when they had rested on her for a moment, had been expressionless. But she remembered his saying that the four days before their last meeting had been endless. Tomorrow—oh, tomorrow.

Harriet gave herself a mental shake and got to her feet, folding and picking up her letters as she did so. Susan would be waiting for her and she would not deprive either of them of a single minute of the rest of the morning.

"Five o'clock in the afternoon," the Duchess of Tenby yelled.

"Eh? What about it?" Lady Sophia Davenport asked, looking impatiently toward the windows of the salon in which they sat and the sunlight streaming through them.

The duchess set aside her embroidery with a sigh. It was quite impossible to try to concentrate on her stitches and converse with her sister-in-law at the same time. "It is the correct time to drive in the park, Sophie," she said. "Any earlier and there will be no one there worth seeing. Don't fret. Tenby will return in plenty of time to escort us there."

"Dear Archibald," Lady Sophia said loudly.

"Besides," the duchess reminded her, "you are expecting the ladies from Bath for tea before then."

"Eh?" Lady Sophia asked. But she comprehended the words before the duchess had to yell them once more. "From Bath? Ah, yes. Dear little Lady Wingham. Not one of your sneering, pert misses, Sadie. A very proper-behaved little girl. Too bad Wingham failed to wake up one morning. He was a mere boy."

"You told me he was sixty," the duchess yelled. "You show your age by calling him a boy, Sophie."

Lady Sophia sighed. "A mere boy," she said again, proving to her sister-in-law that she had not heard a word. "I don't like that Forbes woman. She does not appreciate a good conversation. But what could I do? I had to invite her too."

"Of course you did," the duchess said, "since Lady Wingham is staying with her and you have an acquaintance with her and Sir Clive. I do believe they must have arrived. I must admit it will be pleasant to have company."

"Archibald will not forget?" Lady Sophia asked anxiously as the duchess got to her feet.

"Of course he will not forget," the duchess said firmly. "There is no more dutiful grandson—or nephew—than Tenby, Sophie."

The butler entered the room at that moment to announce the arrival of Lady Wingham. She followed close behind him, a dainty, remarkably pretty girl with her pale green muslin dress and a flower-trimmed straw bonnet on her golden-blond hair. The duchess had distrusted her sister-in-law's description of her as a girl. She had expected someone considerably older. Lady Wingham curtsied deeply and blushed. A very charming little girl, the duchess decided.

"Lady Wingham." Lady Sophia's voice boomed across the room. "I cannot get up, gel, unless you have half an hour to spare. Come and hug me."

The duchess raised her eyebrows and looked at her sister-in-law in some surprise. But there she sat, arms outstretched, her face beaming, and the little creature tripped across the room on light feet, smiling as if she was feeling nothing but delight. She bent and allowed the old arms to come about her and even kissed the withered cheek.

"Lady Sophia," she said, lifting her head so that the old lady could see her face, "how lovely to see you. A little piece of home has come and found me here."

She did not speak loudly, the duchess noticed in some surprise, and yet Sophie appeared to hear her every word. She reached up to tap one of the girl's cheeks. She herself had known Sophie from girlhood on and had always had a close friendship with her. Sophie had been a beauty and a high-spirited young woman. But the duchess knew that very few people could now remember what she had been like. Most people avoided her because of her deafness.

"Meet my sister-in-law, the duchess," Lady Sophia boomed. "My dear little Lady Wingham, Sadie."

Lady Wingham turned and curtsied deeply again. "Your grace," she said. "I hope you do not mind that I have come alone. Lady Forbes sends her apologies, but she and Sir Clive had an obligation to attend Mrs. Smith's garden party this afternoon."

"Eh?" Lady Sophia said.

Lady Wingham turned back with a smile and repeated what she had said without any sign of impatience.

"Come here, child," Lady Sophia said gruffly, "and sit on this pouf at my feet. How is that young daughter of yours, eh?"

"Sophie!" the duchess said, rather shocked. "Do take a more comfortable chair, Lady Wingham, I beg you. I shall have tea brought in without further delay."

"If you will forgive me, your grace," Lady Wingham said, "I will be happier sitting here. It is easier to converse with her ladyship when I sit close and she can see my lips."

Bless the child, the duchess thought, and noticed how Sophie took her hand and patted and held it, just as if she really were a child. And the girl turned her face upward, a face bright with affection, and told Sophie about her four-year-old daughter and their various excursions since coming to town. And then when Sophie asked, she told about the balls and parties she had attended and about the newest styles in dresses and gowns and bonnets. It was a treat, the duchess decided, feeling disloyal at the thought, to be able to rest her own vocal cords for a while and allow someone else to entertain Sophie. The girl spoke in a soft voice yet was forced to repeat almost nothing.

"There. You must come and see me again, my pet," Lady Sophia said when half an hour had passed and tea had been drunk and the cakes eaten. "Frequently. You do my heart good."

The duchess's eyebrows rose again as the girl got to her feet and leaned over her sister-in-law to kiss her cheek once more. "It will be my pleasure," she said.

But before she could turn to make her curtsy to the duchess and take her leave, the salon door opened abruptly to admit the duchess's grandson.

"Ah, so this is where my favorite ladies are hiding," he said, and then stopped abruptly when he saw that they had a visitor. His eyes fixed themselves on Lady Wingham for several silent, ill-mannered moments, the duchess noticed. But then she was a very pretty child and Tenby had ever had an eye for beauty. The child's eyes had grown enormous and her cheeks were flooded with color, the duchess saw at a glance. How very ill-bred of her grandson so to embarrass her.

"I do beg your pardon, Grandmama," he said, his voice stiff and haughty—just like his grandpapa's. "I did not realize you and Aunt Sophie were entertaining. I suppose I should have asked Knowles."

"Dear Archibald," Lady Sophia boomed.

"Allow me to present my grandson, the Duke of Tenby, to you," the duchess said, smiling at her visitor. "Lady Wingham, Tenby. Or perhaps you have met before?"

Her grandson bowed stiffly and Lady Wingham sank into a curtsy. "Ma'am?" he said. "I met Lady Wingham in Bath, Grandmama, at Freddie Sullivan's wedding, and have made my bow to her on one or two occasions this spring."

"Eh?" Lady Sophia said.

He repeated loudly and distinctly what he had said.

"Have you come to take us driving, Archibald?" his aunt asked.

"It was my intention, Aunt Sophie," he yelled. "If you and Grandmama feel up to it, that is. The sun is quite warm and there is scarcely any breeze."

"I do not blow away easily in the wind, lad," Lady Sophia said with a rumble that her sister-in-law recognized as a laugh. "You shall come with us too, my pet."

"I?" Lady Wingham flushed to the roots of her hair. "Oh, no, indeed, ma'am. I was about to take my leave. The carriage will be waiting for me. I—"

"We will not take no for an answer, will we, Sadie?" Lady Sophia said. "You shall sit on the seat opposite me, child, and tell me who everyone is. I can hear you far better than I can hear dear Archibald, for all that he shouts very loudly. And you are too young and too pretty not to ride in the park for all the young sparks to see. Can you give me one good reason why you should not come?"

"I must go home to my d—" The girl bit her lip. "I really should go home, ma'am."

Sophie had embarrassed her, poor child. "If you have no pressing reason to return home, you really must favor us with your company, Lady Wingham," the duchess said graciously. "It will please Sophie so. And me too. Do say yes, dear. Tenby shall have your carriage sent home and we shall let you down at Sir Clive Forbes's door when we are on the way home."

The girl did not want to accept, the duchess could tell. Doubtless she felt somewhat beyond her depth. The duchess smiled kindly at her.

"Thank you, your grace," she said quietly.

It would be amusing, the duchess thought, to have a pretty little girl with them when they drove in the park. And Sophie would indeed be pleased. But it was not something that should be encouraged again. The girl was altogether too pretty and charming. Tenby appeared to have been struck dumb by her beauty, though he claimed already to be acquainted with her. And she, of course, was far from indifferent to him. She had not stopped blushing since his entry into the room. It was not uncommon for women to blush in Tenby's presence, of course. He had his looks all from his mother's side of the family, the dear boy, his father and his grandfather not having been renowned for handsome features.

It would not do, the duchess decided. Lady Wingham was a charming girl but hardly an eligible connection for Tenby. Now that he seemed to have fixed his interest on Lady Phyllis Reeder—eminently eligible—he must not be distracted. Not that he was likely to be turned entirely from his purpose. He had been a good and dutiful boy ever since his grandfather had taken him in hand. Her husband had been strict with the boy and had turned him into an obedient grandson. He would not disgrace the Vinney name or his ducal title either.

"We will sit here while you have the barouche brought around, then, Tenby," she said, seating herself and motioning Lady Wingham back to her pouf. He bowed and left the room without another word.

He handed her into the barouche after his grandmother and his aunt—she kept her eyes lowered and did not grip his hand at all—and then climbed in after her. He was forced to sit beside her since his aunt had asked her to sit opposite so that she could hear her. His aunt apparently listened to her lips since Harriet did not speak above her usual soft volume. And his grandmother had settled herself beside Aunt Sophie, facing the horses. His sleeve brushed Harriet's arm as he seated himself, and both of them edged slightly to the outsides of the seat.

To say he was furious was to understate the case quite drastically. If he just had her alone, he was convinced that he would do what he had never done to any woman and had never thought to do. He would bend her over his knee and wallop her until she cried for mercy. Until she could not sit down. Perhaps that was how he would begin proceedings tomorrow afternoon, he thought grimly.

How dared she! How dared she set foot beneath his roof? And wangle an introduction to his grandmother, using what was doubtless a fleeting acquaintance with his aunt in Bath as an excuse. When he had told her that his grandmother and his aunt were coming to town, she must have realized immediately who the aunt was. Obviously she had her spies who had informed her that they had arrived the afternoon before, and had wasted no time at all in coming to pay her respects. And she had used her sweet charm to such effect that she had drawn this invitation.

Good Lord. His hands felt clammy with sweat for a moment. His mistress had arrived at his own home and been presented to his grandmother, the Duchess of Tenby, and his aunt, the Dowager Marchioness of Davenport. And now he was seated beside her and opposite them for a drive in the park. For all the world to see.

Tomorrow she would explain herself. And if she was not quick about it, he would encourage her with the flat of his hand. He just wished he really could. He wished he could bring himself to use violence on her. She had asked for it.

She was leaning forward in her seat, pointing out to his aunt various landmarks on their way to the park, landmarks that Aunt Sophie claimed to have forgotten. His grandmother was looking steadily at him. He smiled at her and launched into a discussion of the weather before he remembered that Harriet beside him would hear and perhaps be amused.

Let her show amusement at her peril. Good Lord! He had fleeting and graphic memories of Monday afternoon and smiled harder and talked more determinedly.

Harriet was wonderful with his aunt. He admitted that grudgingly to himself over the next hour. She talked to her constantly, relieving him and his grandmother of the rather tedious necessity of yelling out everything they said and often having to repeat themselves even then. And she somehow succeeded in both looking and sounding as if it were no trouble at all, as if she actually enjoyed talking with the old girl.

And of course she looked quite remarkably pretty and made his aunt's references to her as a child and a pet seem not as nonsensical as they should have seemed considering the fact that she must be close to thirty years of age.

They certainly did not lack for attention in the park. Several older people recognized his grandmother and drew close to pay their respects and be presented to his aunt. A few people who were familiar with Bath society came to greet her. Some of his acquaintances touched their hats to his relatives and a few drew near to chat. And of course Harriet attracted her usual court. It seemed to be growing with time. He wondered which one of them she would marry when the Season was over. It seemed reasonable to believe that she would not wait longer. He knew from personal experience that she was a passionate woman who must feel the need of a man. She would not have him to serve that need beyond July. He glanced self-consciously at his grandmother just as if she might have read his thoughts, but she was too busy looking about her.

They must present a strange picture, he reflected, inter-

cepting more than a few curious glances from the members
of the *ton* who were riding or walking in the park. His
grandmother, his aunt, and himself—with Lady Wingham.
But he could console himself that the glances could be no
more than curious. He had avoided being alone with Harriet
for even a single minute in public since she had become his
mistress. It was bad enough that Bruce seemed to have
guessed. He certainly did not want any other speculation
along those lines. The tiniest whisper of gossip had a nasty
habit of becoming a great thundering in no time at all—especially in London during the Season.

But today he did not have to worry. Even the most evil
mind would not dream that he could possibly have the au-
dacity to drive his mistress with his grandmother and his
aunt. His fury returned.

"I knew the young bucks would be swarming all over
you, my pet," his aunt said with embarrassing loudness.
"Do you have one of them singled out, eh?"

The duke and duchess exchanged glances.

"I do not," Harriet said with perfect amiability, though a
glance in her direction revealed to him the expected
blush—which unexpectedly had the usual effect on his
stomach. "I loved Godfrey, ma'am, as you know. I am
quite content to enjoy every moment of the Season as it arrives."

"Yes, you were good to him, child," his aunt said. "But
he was too old for you. You need someone more sprightly.
Someone who does not have a weak heart. A man with a
weak heart cannot give a gel what she needs and wants.
Can he, Archibald? You would know, I wager. If I were
only fifty years younger and you were not my nephew . . ."
She rumbled, a sound the duke was beginning to recognize
as a laugh.

"Sophie!" His grandmother was quite outraged. "You
have quite put poor Lady Wingham to the blush. Not to
mention Tenby and myself."

"Eh?" his aunt said, but she appeared to have heard. She
rumbled again. "I was ever outspoken, Sadie. Many is the
young buck I put to the blush in my time, my dear Lady
Wingham."

"If you were fifty years younger, Aunt Sophie," the duke said, desperate to release them all from the embarrassment of the moment, "I should set my glass to my eye, favor you with my most haughty stare, and deliver a blistering set-down. After which I would doubtless flirt quite outrageously with you."

The rumbling occupied all of the next thirty seconds.

"Saucy boy!" his aunt said.

The duke gave his coachman the signal to leave the park and take the direction to Sir Clive Forbes's home.

"This has been very pleasant, Lady Wingham," his grandmother said with all the grandeur she had acquired in her many years as a duchess. "I do thank you for postponing your return home in order to accompany us on our drive."

"It has been my pleasure, your grace," Harriet said.

"Eh?" Lady Sophia demanded.

The duchess repeated what she had said.

"You will come to see me again, my pet," Lady Sophia said to Harriet. "I missed you sorely after you left Bath. You bring sunshine into my life."

Harriet smiled at her.

The duke jumped down from the barouche when it stopped outside Sir Clive's door and handed her down to the pavement. He bowed over her hand and raised it to his lips. His aunt was bellowing something at his grandmother, something about Harriet being a very prettily behaved gel.

"Doubtless," he said very quietly, and was almost distracted when her eyelashes came sweeping up and her green eyes looked directly into his, "you will have an explanation for this tomorrow, ma'am."

Her eyes widened slightly but she said nothing. She turned and hurried through the door that a servant was already holding open for her.

His aunt appeared to fall into a doze. His grandmother regarded him steadily for a while in silence.

"When will I meet Lord Barthorpe and his wife and Lady Phyllis?" she asked. "We will have them to tea, Tenby?"

"Will that not be rather pointed?" he asked. "Perhaps a

dinner would be better, Grandmama, and a larger number of guests."

"You do not wish it to be pointed?" she asked. "You have an objection to the girl?"

"None," he said. "She appears to have all the qualities I could look for in a duchess. She is even pretty."

"Yet you have not declared yourself," she said.

"Give me time, Grandmama." He smiled at her. "I have until September before I am in danger of breaking my promise. I will not break it."

She was quiet for a while, but he could feel her eyes on him. "Tenby," she said at last, "you will not look lower. You will remember who you are and what you owe your position. And the bloodlines you owe your heir."

The damned woman, he thought irreverently. She always saw far more than he was ever aware of revealing. "I have never thought of looking lower, Grandmama," he lied, "and never will dream of doing so. I know too what I owe you and my memories of Grandpapa. And Mother too."

She looked at him a little longer and then nodded, satisfied.

9

"But my dear Harriet, you would so enjoy the afternoon." Lady Forbes sounded quite crestfallen. "An excursion on the river and a picnic afterward and the weather so lovely again that one wonders how we will have to suffer for it later. It was very kind of the Smiths to include you in the invitation, but they did so because I explained how disappointed you were not to be able to come to the garden party yesterday. Can your visit to the National Gallery with the Beaconswoods not be postponed?"

"I have promised," Harriet said, examining the backs of her hands. "And it is a place I really want to see while in London."

Lady Forbes sighed. "But it could be done just as easily on a rainy day," she said. "And you would not be wasting all this precious sunshine. But how dreadful I am being. I have told you to think of this as your home. You must do as you wish, dear. I am glad to see that your friendship with the countess is becoming such a firm one. She seems to be an amiable lady."

"Yes," Harriet said without raising her eyes, "she is. Our children enjoy one another's company. Not that we will be taking the children to the gallery, of course. They are a little young."

Lady Forbes rose from the luncheon table, from which Sir Clive had departed long ago. "Well, I have a river excursion to get ready for," she said. "I will need to wear my largest hat, I believe."

"Amanda," Harriet said as her friend turned away. She closed her eyes tightly for a moment and clasped her hands together. "I cannot do this any longer. I cannot continue to lie."

"To lie, dear?" Lady Forbes sat down again and turned her head to nod a dismissal to the servant who stood at the sideboard.

"I am not going anywhere with the Beaconswoods this afternoon," Harriet said. "I did not go visiting with Julia on Monday or shopping with her last Thursday despite the accounts I gave you of both outings. The only times I have seen Julia have been in the mornings with the children."

Lady Forbes said nothing.

"I will be going out alone this afternoon and every Monday and Thursday afternoon until the end of the Season," Harriet said. "I have appointments."

Lady Forbes was silent for a few moments longer. "You did not need to burden yourself with lies, Harriet," she said. "And you need say no more now if you do not wish. You do not owe me explanations. Your life is your own."

Harriet opened her eyes at last, but she continued to look down at her hands. "I feel," she said, "that perhaps I should not continue to stay here. I will leave if you wish."

"To go where?" Lady Forbes asked. She sighed. "Who is he, Harriet? Do you want to tell me?"

Harriet unclasped her hands and spread her fingers wide.

"Not Tenby," Lady Forbes said. "Oh, Harriet, not Tenby. Is that why you were so agitated yesterday? It was not just that you felt the duchess had been forced into offering you a place in Tenby's carriage for a drive in the park?"

Harriet shuddered. "It was horrible, Amanda," she said. "Sitting beside him all the time with his grandmother opposite. You cannot imagine how like a nightmare it was."

"Tenby." Lady Forbes drew a deep breath and let it out slowly. "He will never marry you, Harriet."

"I know that," Harriet said quickly. "I have never had any illusions about that. Well, not for six years, anyway."

"He will break your heart," Lady Forbes said.

"No." Harriet looked up for the first time. "I know exactly what the situation is. I know it will end. I even know when it will end. He will marry Lady Phyllis Reeder this summer. I will accept it and be satisfied when the time comes."

"Oh, Harriet." Lady Forbes leaned across the table and set a hand over hers. "No, dear, never. You have a wonderful capacity for love—for unconditional, lasting love. You have no gift for flirtation or—dalliance."

"Then perhaps it is time I grew up," Harriet said. "I am twenty-eight years old."

"And growing up means hardening your heart so that you can have an involvement with a rake and then shrug your shoulders and forget him when it is over?" Lady Forbes asked.

"I'll not forget him," Harriet said. "But I'll be able to put it all behind me when summer comes. He offered me *carte blanche* six years ago when I was still with Clara. I never forgot him. Part of me was always a little sorry that I had refused."

"Your heart was bruised merely because an offer had been made and rejected," Lady Forbes said. "How is your heart going to bear up when you have—spent two afternoons a week with him for more than two months? Oh, Harriet, I think I know your heart better than you know it yourself, dear. It will be badly shattered."

"I suppose I will find out which of us is right," Harriet said with a rather crooked smile. "Besides, Amanda, it is too late." She flushed.

"The man should be horsewhipped and shot between the eyes," Lady Forbes said crossly. "He really should, Harriet. He has no business dallying with someone like you. He should keep to his own kind. There must be any number of women of a certain type who would be only too eager to—to *serve* him for a suitable fee."

Harriet twisted her hands together again. "Would you prefer that I move away?" she asked.

"No." Lady Forbes looked at her bowed head for some time. "You have not put yourself beyond the pale, Harriet, provided you are discreet. Doubtless there are any number of people who assume that if you are enjoying the Season as a young widow, you must be having an affair with someone. It would be surprising to many people if you were not.

Life among members of the *ton* is much like a game, my dear. One must know the rules and keep to them quite rigidly. You may dally with as many gentlemen as you wish, provided no one is ever allowed to see you together in anything like compromising circumstances. No one would dream of judging you even if they suspected the truth. I do not judge you. I know you well enough to believe that you are doing that quite nicely for yourself."

"At least," Harriet said, "I'll not have to tell you any more lies. The lies have bothered me as much as anything."

"Your drive in the park yesterday will have worked to your advantage if anything," Lady Forbes said. "If any people suspected—though I am quite, quite sure that no one does—they will now believe that they must have been mistaken. Tenby would not have done anything as brazen as drive out with his—with you in company with his grandmother and his aunt, they will believe."

Harriet smiled rather wanly. "You have a river excursion to get ready for," she said.

"Yes." Lady Forbes got to her feet again as Harriet stood. "And you have an outing to prepare for too, dear. Take care. Oh, do take care." She hugged her young friend before leaving the dining room with her.

Anger was an emotion that Harriet did not often experience. Her mother had used to tell her sometimes that she was too placid for her own good, that she had a tendency to make a doormat of herself. She was very much in danger of becoming a doormat now. She had been lifted, as usual, into his carriage, but beyond one cool look in her direction he had acted as if he were unaware of her existence. By the time they had reached his love nest and he had escorted her upstairs and through the sitting room into the bedchamber, she knew that he was angry.

Well, she was angry too. She could remember his parting words of the day before. She had been in a little too much distress then to be angry at what he had said. But she was angry now.

"Well?" His first word of the afternoon was like a cold

whiplash. He had released her arm and closed the door. "You have your explanation ready, ma'am?"

"I would be foolish not to," she said, "when I have had a day in which to think of it. I suppose I must tell the simple truth, your grace. I wangled the introduction to your grandmother and maneuvered to be invited to the park on the assumption that she would fall instantly in love with my beauty and refinement and insist that you make me your duchess."

His eyes narrowed and he took a step forward until their bodies almost touched. "Have a care, ma'am," he said. "Sarcasm does not become you."

"On the other hand," she said, "arrogance becomes you very well indeed, your grace."

His silver eyes sparked dangerously. "It was unspeakably improper for you, my mistress, to set foot inside my home," he said, "and to impose your company on my unsuspecting grandmother and aunt."

"I have heard," she said, "that it is infectious, like typhoid. Do you fear for their—health, your grace?"

His hands felt like iron bands riveting themselves to her upper arms. They squeezed even more tightly as he shook her until her head flopped back and forth and her breath was gone and she was reaching blindly for the lapels of his coat.

"Harriet, have done," he said harshly, releasing her abruptly before she could find a handhold.

"You forget, *your grace*," she said, emphasizing his title, "that I am not one of your doxies, that I do not take payment for the favors I grant you on that bed. I am a lady by birth and a baroness by marriage and I will not be made to feel like a soiled whore. If I am a whore, then so are you. Why should women be considered to have fallen when they give themselves outside marriage, but not men?"

She did not know where the words were coming from. She had never been so furious in her life. Perhaps it was because his attitude to her echoed her own, but she was too angry to analyze her feelings fully. If he touched her roughly again, she would go at him with her fists, she knew.

He looked at her steadily, his arms at his sides. "You are not a whore, Harriet," he said. "Or my doxy. Even *mistress* is an inaccurate word since it suggests a kept woman. You are my lover."

Something turned over in her stomach. The word caressed her. And mocked her. They were not lovers. Lovers loved. The very word suggested that. They did not love. They merely had sexual relations.

His eyes and his voice had softened. But only for a moment. They were both cold and hard again when he spoke once more. "Why did you see fit to call at St. James's Square and present yourself to her grace?" he asked. "Did your acquaintance with my aunt seem excuse enough?"

She watched her arm lift as if of its own accord and her hand whip with a satisfyingly stinging slap across his face. And she waited in steely-jawed terror for him to retaliate. He did not do so. She watched in fascinated horror as the imprint of her fingers reddened his cheek.

"Did you not think to ask them?" she asked. "Did you not think that perhaps I was invited?"

"Were you?" he said. "Why did you go?"

"Perhaps," she said, "it was out of courtesy. Perhaps it was because I am fond of Lady Sophia, though of course it is hard to believe that anyone could be fond of a lady who is so very old and so very deaf, is it not? And perhaps it was because I did not know that was your home or that the lady to whom I was presented merely as Lady Sophia's sister-in-law, the duchess, was in fact the Duchess of Tenby. Perhaps I did not know it until you walked into the room."

"You did not know where my home was?" he asked, frowning.

"Why should I?" she asked. "Did you imagine that I paced lovelorn outside it each day and night?"

"I told you my grandmother and my aunt were coming to town," he said.

"Why would I have made the connection when I received the invitation from Lady Sophia?" she asked. "People arrive in London every day. It is the Season."

"I have done you an injustice," he said stiffly. "I beg your pardon, Harriet."

"Granted," she said. She was pleased to hear that her voice was as crisp as his own.

"Well," he said, turning his eyes away from her and looking across the room, "we are wasting time. Let's go to bed."

"No," she said.

"No?" He looked back at her, his eyebrows raised.

"No," she said again, and felt terror for a moment. Was she going to end it all here and now? Was there going to be nothing but emptiness for the rest of the Season—for the rest of her life? "I can't, y-your grace."

His eyes searched hers. He clasped his hands behind his back. "You will doubtless explain," he said.

She was not sure she could, even to herself. "We are angry with each other," she said. "You apologized to me but did not really mean it, and I did not really forgive you. And yet you want me to go to bed with you? I don't expect it to be done with love. We have both agreed that there is no love and no romance, only a mutual seeking for pleasure. But there has to be something a little more personal than that alone. It is not just a—an acrobatic performance. Even though you say I am not a whore and I know I am not, I will not be made to feel like one."

He stood motionless before her for many silent moments while she examined the backs of her hands. "Harriet," he said finally, his voice soft again, "I am truly sorry for my anger. It was quite unjustified. And for my arrogance. I can see no possible reason why you are less worthy of being acquainted with my grandmother than I am. And I was touched by your kindness to my aunt. Most people find her tedious. Will you forgive me? Please?"

She nodded imperceptibly without looking up.

"It is not love, what happens here," he said, "or romance. But it is more than an acrobatic performance, Harriet. Good heaven, is that how you have seen our encounters here? You give me more pleasure than any other woman I have known. You are still the sweet, prim little Harriet who so enchanted me six years ago. Sweet little Harriet with a temper. I like it." He placed one long finger beneath her chin and lifted her face. "When you are on that bed with me, I am aware every moment that you are Harriet."

She gazed into his eyes, but it was impossible to know if the smile she saw there mocked her or not. But there was gentleness in his voice. Yes, it was enough. It was enough to know that she was not just any woman to him. That was all she wanted. She knew there could be no love. She had never expected love.

"Harriet." He drew one knuckle along her jaw to the point of her chin. "You are right. I did treat you yesterday as if you were some kind of fallen woman. I am accustomed to a different type of—lover, I suppose. Please forgive me. It will not happen again."

"Archie." She touched her fingertips to his chest and removed them again. "For what it is worth, I was as horrified and as embarrassed as you when I knew that I was in your home and with your relatives."

"Forgive me?" he said.

"Yes." When she looked up at him this time, she found his eyes burning into hers. He surprised her by taking her hand and carrying it to his lips. Then he leaned forward to set his lips against hers.

Ah, but it felt very much like love, she thought as her arms came about his neck. Too similar. Far too sweet. He kissed her with a gentleness he had not used on her before. She relaxed against him, trying not to feel the danger, the terrible danger of believing that she was more to him than just a body that he liked to enjoy. She must never start believing that they came here to make love. The only way to make the end bearable, and the rest of her life bearable, was to keep herself ruthlessly aware of the truth, that there was no love at all. They had both said it again just this afternoon. It was finally agreed between them that there was to be none.

Ah, but his kiss felt very like love.

"Come to bed?" he asked, his mouth against her ear.

She nodded and shivered. She had just refused to go because there was no personal feeling between them at all. Now she was afraid there was too much. Perversely, she willed him to be more impersonal again—as he had been the last time.

"We will take it more slowly today, shall we?" he said, leading her to the bed even though he had not yet unclothed her. "More—tenderly, Harriet? Will you like that better? I will try to be less frantically aware of what little time we have together. And we will rest when our bodies need rest. It is part of the experience of—enjoying each other. You must teach me to be the kind of lover you want."

She looked into his eyes as he undressed her beside the bed, but she could see no trace of mockery there. Surely that idea was a topsy-turvy one. Did not a man usually demand that his woman be the kind of lover he wanted? Could it be true that her feelings, her needs, her preferences, were important to him? Or was he humoring her because she had been angry and had refused him at first?

"Will that please you?" he asked.

"Yes," she said.

"Lie down, then," he said, "while I get ready to give you your gentle lovemaking."

Lovemaking. She felt suddenly, more than she had felt on the previous two occasions, that she was playing with fire. And that there was no escaping being burned. He was going to do it too, she thought, looking into his smiling eyes as he undressed. He was going to make love to her. He was going to give her what he thought she wanted.

And what she had thought she wanted.

"Dinner for twenty-four," the Duchess of Tenby said, presenting her grandson with a written list when they had retired to the drawing room after dinner. The duchess had never allowed her menfolk to linger over their port when they dined *en famille*. "I have included the people you especially asked for this morning, Tenby. The other suggestions are my own. You will notice that in addition to Lady Phyllis Reeder, I have listed the Kingsleys and their daughter, Lady Leila. She has been presented this spring, I gather, though she is barely seventeen. You may wish to consider her. Girls who are fresh from the schoolroom are often more easily bent to a husband's will than those who are in their third Season. And she is a marquess's daughter."

The girl did slightly resemble a horse. Bruce's words had been unkind but true. It was the narrow face and prominent teeth and rather long nose that did it. Now he was being unkind, even though he did not speak his thoughts aloud. The girl was just an infant and often looked frightened. Her mother should have insisted that she remain in the schoolroom for at least another year. The thought of bending her to his will did not appeal.

He looked at the list broodingly.

"So you see, Tenby," his grandmother said, "that I am not tightening the noose about your neck. There will be twenty-three other persons here apart from Lady Phyllis. I will be interested in looking her over."

His grandmother was amazing, the duke thought, his eyes scanning the names on the list. She had been in London for two days and had not been here for two years before that, yet already she knew who else was there and who was eligible to be invited for her public viewing of his prospective bride.

"There are only twenty-three names on the list," he said, counting.

"Eh?" His aunt had finished pouring the tea and had become interested in the conversation. He repeated what he had said in a yell.

"We need one more lady," his grandmother said. "I did not know if you would prefer Lady Trevor, Lady Howden, or Lady Pryde, Tenby. I waited to consult you."

"Eh?" Lady Sophia demanded.

The duchess repeated her words.

"Is my dear Lady Wingham on that list, Archibald?" the old lady roared. "I told Sadie to put her there, but I do not know if she heard me. Sometimes I think Sadie must be going deaf." She rumbled.

The duke forced his fingers not to tighten on the paper.

"Her name is not here, Aunt," he said.

"Put it down, then, dear Archibald," she said. "And seat her next to me at dinner. She is the only person willing to speak loudly enough for me to hear. I would swear every-

one else talks nothing but secrets all day long that they
must whisper so."

"I believe, Sophie," the duchess yelled, "that Lady Wingham might feel out of place in such company. Perhaps you
could invite her to tea again one day next week."

"You know I do not like to be difficult, Sadie," Lady
Sophia said. "I am the most agreeable of persons, am I not,
Archibald? You need not answer, dear boy. But I will not
sit through that dinner unless I have my little pet beside me.
I have never forgiven Wingham for marrying the gel. I was
going to take her for my companion after her mother died.
But there, he was good to her, so I must forgive him after
all. Put her name on the list, Archibald."

"Well, Tenby?" The duchess looked at him steadily.
"You have no objection to Lady Wingham as a guest?"

"None at all, Grandmama," he said. "She seems gen-
uinely fond of Aunt Sophie."

"Eh?" his aunt asked.

He left his grandmother to repeat his words while he
crossed the room to the desk and dipped a quill pen in the
inkwell in order to add the name that would give even num-
bers to his guest list. For Monday evening.

He stayed at the desk rather longer than was necessary,
his eyes reading the list, pausing at Lady Phyllis's name,
Lady Leila's, Harriet's. He was feeling utterly wretched.
Under normal circumstances he would have dined privately
in his own apartments tonight or, more probably, at one of
his clubs. He would have sat and brooded afterward or, if at
the club, he would have found a noisy group of friends with
whom to carouse. He would have sought out a lively game
of cards. Perhaps he would even have persuaded Bruce or
some other friend to go to Annette's with him. No. No, he
would not have done that. But something like that. Instead
of which, he was going to have to cross the room again
soon and entertain his grandmother and his aunt for at least
another hour before they retired to bed.

He wanted only to brood on what he had done.

He had made love to her. He had understood her need for
tenderness as reassurance against the humiliation of his
treatment of her—unpardonably, he had made her feel like

a whore. And because he loved her, or perhaps because he had a conscience, he had decided to give her tenderness. Except that he had been unable to divorce tenderness from love and had given her love, though he had not called it that and she had doubtless not recognized it as that.

God! All his defenses had come crashing down and he had made love to her. Something he had never done before with anyone and something that had frankly terrified him. It was not that he had lost control of himself. He had had more control than perhaps ever before. Every move, every touch during what had remained of their hour and a half after they had finished quarreling, had been devoted to making her enjoy the bedding on her terms, not as a physical performance, but as an encounter between two persons with somewhat tender feelings for each other. He had kept an iron control over his body and yet had lost it completely over his emotions. Every move, every touch, had been given with love.

He did not know if he would ever again be capable of coupling with a woman without the extra dimension that made all the difference. He had understood in a flash why the act was called making love. He did not know how he would be able to give her up at the end of July. Would it be possible, he wondered, to persuade her to remain as his mistress even after his marriage during the summer? He doubted it. He very much doubted it. He had been surprised, even a little disappointed at first, to discover that she was willing to give him her virtue. He was quite sure, though, that she would be unwilling to be involved in an adulterous relationship.

And so the future yawned frightening and empty.

"You are satisfied with the guest list, Tenby?" He had not heard his grandmother come up behind him. She rested a hand on his shoulder.

"Yes, Grandmama," he said. "I need not ask if you have the invitations ready to go out tomorrow, I suppose? Of course you have them ready."

"Of course," she said. "You did not mind giving in to Sophie's whim?"

"About Lady Wingham?" he said. "No, of course not. Why should I?"

"I just hope you are not too pleased," she said. "She is an unusually lovely woman. And she has a freshness and a charm that are beyond the ordinary."

"Yes," he said.

"I could not fail to notice yesterday," she said, "that you were taken with her, Tenby."

"I?" He chuckled. "I am always taken with a lovely face, Grandmama. And half of London is taken with this particular one. You must have noticed in the park how large her court is."

"Yes, dear," she said. "But sometimes a man's pride is challenged by such a fact. We shall consider her to be Sophie's companion on Monday evening, shall we?"

"I doubt if Aunt Sophie would leave us any choice even if we decided otherwise," he said.

His grandmother patted his shoulder. "Come back to the fire," she said, "or she will be thinking we are whispering secrets again. I expect great things of you before the summer is out, Tenby, and an heir on his way into this world by Christmas. You will not let me down, I know. You never do. Your grandfather trained you well."

He took her hand from his shoulder as he got to his feet and kissed it before laying it on his arm. "I just hope, Grandmama," he said, smiling down at her, "that my wife has the good sense to present me with a son the first time and does not make him follow along behind two or three daughters."

She held herself very straight. "The duchesses of our line have always known their duty, Tenby," she said. "There is not a one of us for almost a century who has not produced a son first, and within a year of marriage. It is all in the breeding. Choose a bride of the right breeding and this time next year it will be the christening of the heir to Tenby we will be planning instead of a dinner."

"Eh?" Lady Sophia asked as they drew close.

10

It was with great trepidation that Harriet stepped down from Sir Clive's carriage outside the mansion on St. James's Square the following Monday evening. She had looked hopefully at Lady Forbes's pile of letters on Friday when her own invitation had come, but there was no matching one there. She alone was being invited to dinner and to spend the evening.

Her first instinct had been to refuse. If he had been angry with her for going there to tea, he would be furious if she turned up for dinner, doubtless with other guests. But he must know about the dinner and he must know the guest list. The invitation was in his name and the duchess's. Besides, her unexpected burst of anger when he had accused her of impropriety had reminded her that she was not unrespectable by *ton* standards. There was no reason at all to refuse the invitation.

She did not want to go. She would rather do anything else than go. And yet she would not allow him to make her feel inferior. Besides, she knew why she had been invited. An event like a formal dinner and party was a sore trial to Lady Sophia Davenport, who so much enjoyed company but whose deafness cut off her pleasure in it. Harriet had been invited as her companion. She was not offended. Indeed, she was pleased. She would not have to join the company feeling conspicuously alone.

And yet she felt trepidation as she stepped down from the carriage. She had been awed by the size and magnificence of the mansion the first time she had been there. She had thought then that it was more like a palace than a private home. This time, knowing that it was his, she had to fight against that sense of inferiority she was determined not to feel. But it did seem indeed that he came from a different world from hers.

They had met during the afternoon and said not a word about the evening. She had not asked him why she had been invited. He had not asked her why she had accepted. She did not want to think about the afternoon. Not now. Not until she was home again and alone. It had been too disturbing.

The grand hall was lined at intervals with footmen splendidly liveried in pale blue and white, all wearing snowy white wigs. One servant—the butler, perhaps, or a steward—bowed low to her, clicked his fingers to a footman, who took her wrap, and escorted her upstairs past large and ancient portraits, doubtless of Vinney ancestors, to the drawing room, where he announced her in a voice whose rich tones must have reached to the farthest corners of the room. Harriet wished fervently for Amanda and Clive's presence. Or Godfrey's.

The Duchess of Tenby, regal in purple and nodding plumes, swept toward her. "My dear Lady Wingham," she said, one hand graciously extended, "how gratifying that you were able to attend at such short notice. What a delightful shade of pink." She glanced down at the silk gown of deep rose-pink that Harriet was wearing for the first time.

Harriet curtsied. "Your grace," she murmured.

The room behind the duchess seemed filled with people. But Harriet saw only one of them. He was walking toward her, looking quite magnificently handsome in burgundy and silver and white.

"Lady Wingham," he said, taking her hand, bowing over it, and raising her fingertips to his lips. "I am happy to see you again, ma'am. I hope I see you well?"

"Thank you, your grace." She curtsied again.

He had held her hand in the carriage during the afternoon, and talked to her the whole way on a variety of topics. It was the first time they had not traveled in near silence. They had been silent on the return journey, but it had been a comfortable silence, and he had held her hand again. He looked at her now with a polite expression and blank eyes.

"You will see to it that Lady Wingham has a drink, Tenby," the duchess said. "I do believe Sophie is eagerly awaiting her arrival."

Harriet smiled. She had not mistaken, then. She took the duke's arm and was borne off to where Lady Sophia was sitting talking with the Earl and Countess of Barthorpe. They smiled rather gratefully at the interruption and moved off.

"Ah, my dear Lady Wingham," Lady Sophia said, indicating by the movement of her hands that she expected to be kissed. "Looking as fresh as a rosebud in June. And twice as lovely. Wouldn't you agree, Archibald?"

"I could hardly have put it better, Aunt," he said. "I shall fetch you a glass of sherry, Lady Wingham."

Harriet bent over the old lady and kissed her heavily rouged cheek before sitting down close to her. "Thank you, ma'am," she said quietly, making sure that she enunciated her words clearly and that Lady Sophia could see her lips. "It is the color Godfrey always liked me to wear."

"Everyone else here tonight is whispering," Lady Sophia said irritably. "I told Sadie and Archibald in no uncertain terms that I would not attend if I could not have my little pet here to bear me company. You shall tell me all the gossip that you hear at the table, and you will tell me all that you have been doing in the past week and how many slain bucks you have left in your wake. Ah, it does my heart good to see your pretty, smiling face, child."

"Fourteen," Harriet said with a laugh. "Fourteen slain bucks, ma'am, if one discounts the Prince of Wales."

The old lady barked with laughter, drawing to herself not inconsiderable attention. The Duke of Tenby handed a glass to Harriet.

"That must have been too rich a joke not to be shared," he said.

"My little pet here has stolen the hearts of fifteen young bucks in the past week, including Prinny's!" Lady Sophia roared. "Ah, if I were only fifty or sixty years younger, child. We would make a team such as the *ton* has never seen before."

Harriet's cheeks flamed scarlet. She did not look up to note the duke's expression—or anyone else's.

"One must be careful, then," he said softly, "to stay away from Lady Wingham unless one wishes to leave one's heart behind."

"Eh?" Lady Sophia asked. "What did he say, my pet?"

Harriet, still feeling uncomfortably hot, repeated his words just as softly, and the old lady chuckled.

It quickly became clear to Harriet what the purpose of the occasion was. The duke bowed over the hand of the Countess of Barthorpe, Lady Phyllis's mother, when dinner was announced, and led her into the dining room. He seated her to his right at the head of the table. The arrival of the duchess in town was obviously moving the courtship into another phase, making it almost official. Or perhaps entirely official. Perhaps an announcement was to be made after dinner. Harriet's stomach lurched at the very thought. But no. He would have led in Lady Phyllis herself if matters were that far advanced.

Harriet exchanged a few words with Viscount Travers to her right, though most of her attention during dinner was taken by Lady Sophia to her left. She was glad of the necessity of talking almost without ceasing. It took her mind off the strangeness of the occasion. She was dining with the Duke and Duchess of Tenby. There were twenty-four at table. She held the lowest rank of all of them, being a mere baroness.

She tried to keep her eyes and her mind off the Duke of Tenby at the head of the table. It was hard on such an occasion to think of him by any other name. And hard to realize that the same man was her lover.

Lover. Harriet's stomach lurched again. Somehow she was beginning to think of him as her lover, although of course he was not that. But he appeared to have taken her accusations during last week's quarrel seriously. Even today. After talking with her throughout the carriage ride, he had been silent in the bedchamber. He had kissed her long and lingeringly—and tenderly—as soon as they had arrived there and then he had made long and slow love to her. It was treacherously easy to start using that term to describe what was happening between them. It had seemed that he was making love to her. Her head knew differently, of course, but her heart . . .

She had closed her eyes and given in to fantasy. When she had once opened her eyes on the bed, after he had raised himself onto his elbows as he moved rhythmically in her so that she would not be oppressed by his weight, she had found that his too were closed. Almost as if he did not want to see reality any more than she did. Afterward he had held her close and covered her with the bedclothes and allowed her to sleep. And when she had woken up later, although his hand gently massaging her head had told her that he was awake too, he had not taken her again but had lain quietly with her until it was time to get up. Strangely, it had felt like love. More so than if he had had her again.

Oh, so very, very like love. She had been disturbed by it after she had arrived home. She was losing touch with reality. She was allowing her dreams to become too real. Dreams and reality should never be allowed to mix. The reality was that they were having a physical relationship and that there was a certain fondness between them. That was all. Next time she must keep her eyes open.

But she knew that she had made the biggest mistake of her life when she had agreed to become his mistress. Better to have him briefly than never at all, she had told herself. She had even persuaded herself that once she had had him a few times she would be satisfied and would be quite able to go back home and forget about him. How very foolishly naive she had been. She dared not contemplate the extent of the heartache she was facing when it was all over. Amanda was quite right, of course. But it was too late now to benefit from either good advice or her own newly acquired experience.

The Duchess of Tenby motioned the ladies to rise and follow her back to the drawing room. The Marquess of Kingsley on one side and Harriet on the other helped Lady Sophia to her feet.

* * *

He had had an argument with his grandmother on his return from his assignation with Harriet earlier in the afternoon. Not that one ever really argued with the duchess, of course. One could only hope to negotiate with her. She had wanted him to lead Lady Phyllis in to dinner. And she had decided that there was to be dancing in the drawing room after dinner. She had even taken it upon herself during the day to hire a pianist and a violinist and cellist to come and play. He was to lead Lady Phyllis into the first dance—an old-fashioned minuet.

He knew very well what his grandmother was about, although she had not yet even met Lady Phyllis. She was trying to force his hand, make it impossible for him to back out of his vow to marry during the summer. She was even trying to precipitate matters, forcing him into such marked attentions to the girl that he would feel constrained to offer for her long before the Season's end.

He would dance first with the girl, he had reluctantly agreed. He would not lead her in to dinner. It was too marked a favor to offer a young unmarried girl whom he was not even officially courting yet. He remained adamant against his grandmother's hard look and stubborn jaw.

"You have not even set eyes on her yet, Grandmama," he had said in exasperation. "How do you know that you will want to promote this courtship so ruthlessly?"

"It really does not matter what my eyes see, Tenby, does it?" she had said. "Or what yours see, for that matter. She is Barthorpe's girl and will be a suitable hostess for you in the coming years. And, more important, a worthy mother for your heir."

He had sighed. "I will lead the countess in to dinner," he had suggested eventually. "Will that satisfy you?"

"It will be most proper, Tenby," she had said after a moment's consideration, "since the girl is being presented to me for the first time. Better than my suggestion. Very well."

It had been quite a minor victory. Everyone, from his servants upward, could be in no doubt of the purpose of the dinner and informal dance afterward. It seemed that one did not have to announce a courtship. One merely made one's bow to an eligible party and speculation quickly gave place to certainty. Once he had led Lady Barthorpe in to dinner and opened the dancing with Lady Phyllis, any boats he had left to him would be quite effectively burned. He tried to imagine spending the rest of his life with the girl. He tried to picture himself in bed with her. But such thoughts could only bring a feeling of gloom, even nausea. He wished sometimes that he had been born a commoner. What a luxury it would be to be free to choose his own bride or no bride at all.

What he should have been adamant about, he realized after all his guests had arrived and they were all seated at dinner, was that Harriet not be on the guest list. He could not have done so easily, of course, out of courtesy to his aunt, but he should have hardened his heart. His grandmother, at least, would have been relieved. He found that he could concentrate on nothing and no one except Harriet, sitting and smiling cheerfully beside his aunt, eating very little because the demand of talking to her was taking almost all her time. She looked quite breathtakingly beautiful. He wished she had not worn that particular gown. How could one be expected to keep one's eyes off her? But then Harriet would look beautiful in a faded sack.

He relaxed somewhat when the ladies left the dining room, but he knew he must not do so for too long. There was the necessity of returning to the drawing room before the ladies could start to feel neglected. And so he rose from the table less than half an hour after the ladies' departure.

He danced with Lady Phyllis, Lady Leila, and the Duchess of Crail. Lady Phyllis was quiet, Lady Leila giggly, the duchess talkative. His grandmother, he knew, would count the evening a success. Harriet had danced once, with Sotheby, Barthorpe's brother, who had an eye to her and was one of her regular court. Travers had sat beside her for a while until he moved away, doubtless as a result of having to repeat everything he said for Aunt Sophie's benefit. The duke smiled inwardly. Good old Aunt Sophie! He struggled with himself not to laugh aloud and startle the Duchess of Crail as he remembered Harriet's little joke before dinner and the embarrassment she had suffered when it had suddenly become very public. Ah, his sweet little blusher.

He wandered to his aunt's side between dances. He knew that his grandmother was well aware of his attraction to Harriet and that she would be watching him like a hawk. But Harriet was, after all, his guest. And it was only polite to spend a little time in his aunt's company. Most of the other guests were assiduously avoiding her. Not that she appeared to notice. She was doting on Harriet like a grandmother.

"Ah, there you are, dear Archibald," she said, raising to her eye the jeweled lorgnette she had affected for the occasion. "You dance prettily, my boy."

"Prettily." He played with the ribbon of his quizzing glass. "Do I thank you, Aunt Sophie, or stare at you haughtily through my quizzing glass?"

She rumbled. "It would not work on me, boy," she said. "I had perfected the art with this little jeweled toy long before you were even thought of." She tapped her lorgnette on his sleeve.

Harriet was playing with a fan, opening it on her lap to reveal a spreading bouquet of pink rosebuds, and sliding it shut again. He did not realize he was watching her until his aunt spoke.

"You must dance with her Archibald," she said. "She is without a doubt the prettiest little girl here tonight and has been drawing more than her share of glances. Yours included, dear boy. Dance, my pet. You should not be stuck here with an old woman when there is dancing to be done and more bucks to be slain."

Harriet's fingers whitened against the sides of the fan after she closed it. But she looked up with a smile. "I can think of no one I would rather be with, ma'am," she said, reaching out a hand and resting it on the back of his aunt's gnarled one. "You remind me of home and of—of Godfrey."

His grandmother would have his head on a platter. The duke bowed and reached out one hand. "Ma'am?" he said. "It is to be a waltz, I believe. Will you do me the honor?" It had been agreed between his grandmother and himself that he would dance the first waltz with Lady Phyllis—though he had thought it might be bad form to dance with her twice.

Harriet's eyes traveled up his waistcoat and his neckcloth to his chin, paused there, and lifted finally to his own. Those beautiful candid green eyes that he had purposefully avoided looking into as he had made love to her during the afternoon. She blushed as deep a pink as her gown. "Thank you, your grace," she said, and placed her hand in his. The same soft little hand he had held on the way to and from their assignation earlier.

His aunt nodded in triumph. His grandmother was smiling and yet looking tight-lipped all at the same time. He would suffer a tongue-lashing for this before he went to bed that night, he would wager. Bruce grinned at him and winked. Travers and Sotheby were looking envious—as was the Marquess of Yarborough, interestingly enough. The man was old enough to be her father and was one of London's most persistent rakes. Lady Phyllis was being led onto the floor by the Duke of Crail. And he himself was to waltz with the prettiest, daintiest lady in the room—even considering his bias, his aunt had been in the right of it there. Harriet's eyes were fixed on the diamond pin in his neckcloth as she set her other hand on his shoulder.

"I wonder," he said softly, "if there will be any clumsy oxen to protect you from this evening." She looked up at him fleetingly and smiled. It seemed a long time ago, that waltz with her at Lady Avingleigh's ball. And yet none of the wonder of finding her again had worn off. Alarmingly none of it had, although she had been his mistress for two weeks now and he had uncovered all her mysteries. Except the mystery of what it was that drew him to her, that made him want more of her the more he had. The mystery of what it was that made him love her when she used none of the lures that other women used and when he had never loved before—or since.

He smiled and looked about him, remembering that he was a host at his own party. There were six couples on the floor. Bruce was dancing with Lady Leila and enduring her giggles with a polite smile. Bruce was going to have to be careful or he would be snared himself. Crail, his father, was not likely to remain indulgent about his single state for much longer.

"You are making the evening a pleasant one for my aunt," he said. "She does not bear her deafness with patience."

"It must be a distressing affliction," Harriet said. "Partly because it makes other people impatient. I always remind myself that I may be old and somewhat infirm myself one day. I would hope that someone will show me a kindness if that time comes."

How could anyone not be kind to Harriet? "Somehow," he said, "one cannot think of Aunt Sophie as being infirm. She is the very devil."

She looked up at him, startled, and smiled. "I am sorry," she said. "You did not want to dance with me. Or to invite me here. Lady Sophia has a gift for having her own way."

"On the contrary," he said for the sheer pleasure of drawing the blush he knew would flood her cheeks. "I wanted too much to dance with you, Harriet. And to invite you here. Sometimes—most of the time—I feel a great fondness for the old devil."

She blushed and he smiled. And totally forgot his surroundings and his audience of twenty-two. And the particular audience of his grandmother, who knew of his attraction to Harriet. He danced and his eyes and his senses feasted on his partner and he felt himself perfectly happy. She had made love that afternoon in silence with closed eyes. And with a compliant, passionate body. He had discovered the best way to give her pleasure. She liked slow, almost languorous lovemaking more than an energetic "performance," as she had described their earlier encounters. She liked to sleep and to cuddle afterward. And she had taught him to enjoy those times too—the tenderness of shared physical passion and its aftermath rather than the frenzy of it.

Inexperienced as she was, she had taught him that one extra dimension of love that was both entrancing him and breaking his heart. The meeting and joining of bodies in the act of union could also be the fullest, most complete expression of love, the most total giving of self. He wondered sometimes—he wondered now—if she loved him. Sometimes he thought she must. Surely Harriet would not have given herself just for the sake of physical pleasure. And yet it was of no moment. He could not reveal his own love. He had nothing more to offer her than he was already giving—his body for her delight.

He dreaded the coming of summer more than he had dreaded anything else in his life.

"Harriet." He did not realize he had spoken her name until she raised her eyes to him. But he had nothing more to say unless he poured out a confession of his love for her. He gazed into her eyes and she gazed back for what might have been an eternity but was probably no longer than a few seconds or a minute at the longest before she looked down to his diamond pin again.

He wanted to take her somewhere where he could kiss her, but there was nowhere. The realization brought him back to an awareness of his surroundings. He felt rather as if he had been gone for a long time. And perhaps he had been. The music was drawing to an end. He set Harriet's hand on his sleeve and returned her to the empty chair beside his aunt. He bowed over her hand and thanked her. What was it about Harriet, he wondered, that made her seem sweet and pure even now after she had shared his love nest with him on several occasions?

"You were the handsomest couple I have seen tread a measure together for many a long day," his aunt said with embarrassing loudness. "You dance as prettily as Archibald, my pet. But then I remember that from Bath, when Wingham used to bring you to the assemblies and all the gentlemen would crowd about to lead you out. None of them as handsome as Archibald, though, eh?"

Harriet was saying something quietly as the duke bowed and walked away, noting with an inward wince of discomfort that his grandmother—and several other of his guests—had been well within earshot of his aunt's remarks. The next dance, he quickly discovered, was also to be a waltz—his grandmother's doing, doubtless. He crossed the room to solicit the hand of Lady Phyllis.

After waltzing with the Marquess of Yarborough, Harriet retreated to the ladies' withdrawing room. She still felt flustered about the forced dance with the Duke of Tenby. She had been so achingly aware of him as they waltzed and there had been such an intensity about his silence that she had had the uncomfortable—and doubtless mistaken—impression that they had been the center of attention just as they had been at Lady Avingleigh's ball.

She was about to leave the room five minutes later when the door opened and Lady Phyllis Reeder came inside. Harriet smiled at her as she passed. But the younger girl stopped her.

"There is no maid here?" she said. "Oh, dear. My hem is down at the back. Would you be so good as to pin it for me, Lady Wingham? Thank heaven there is a dish of pins on the washstand."

Harriet went down on her knees, the dish of pins beside her, and began the repair job after assuring Lady Phyllis that the damage was not great.

"Oh," the girl said with a sigh after a few moments of silence, "I do so envy you, Lady Wingham. How wonderful it must be to be a widow and to be free to enjoy the Season. Unless you were fond of your husband, of course," she added hastily.

"I was," Harriet said. But she smiled to show that she had not taken offense. "Are you not enjoying the Season?"

The girl pulled a face. "Is it done? Oh, thank you. I thought it was quite ruined and I must sit in a corner for the rest of the evening. I enjoyed the last two Seasons enormously. But this year Papa made it quite clear that I was to be serious. And as luck would have it, Tenby chose just this year to select a bride."

Harriet wished she could have escaped in time. "You do not like the Duke of Tenby?" she asked unwillingly.

The girl shrugged. "He is handsome enough," she said, "except for those cold, pale eyes. They make me want to shiver, I must confess. It is just that I hate being seen as someone to be bred, no more. Does my outspokenness outrage you? It is the truth, what I say. Do you think he cares a fig for me?"

"I am not privy to his grace's feelings," Harriet said. "Can you not just discourage him?"

"Pooh!" the girl said. "Papa would disown me and Mama would scold from now until Christmas. I dreamed of marrying for love, that is all—for two full years. Foolish when one is the daughter of an earl, is it not?"

"No," Harriet said quietly. "Not foolish."

"Did you marry for love?" Lady Phyllis sighed. "But I have heard that Lord Wingham was ancient. No matter. I wish you were an earl's daughter, Lady Wingham. I wish you could marry Tenby."

"I?" Harriet looked at her, startled.

"He greatly admires you," Lady Phyllis said. "All the world knows that. It is hardly surprising. All the gentlemen admire you. You are so despicably lovely. I would be jealous if I did not have admirers of my own. But they are all falling away now they know I am to be Tenby's bride. One does not trifle with Tenby. I will not even be able to take lovers after my marriage. Have I shocked you again? I would wager a year's pin money that Tenby would not countenance it, though doubtless he will have three or four mistresses in his keeping at any one time."

"You are repaired," Harriet said cheerfully, "and will not have to sit in a corner. I must return to Lady Sophia."

The girl pulled a face again. "Imagine having that for an aunt for the rest of my life," she said.

Harriet smiled stiffly and left the room.

11

The Duchess of Tenby did not expect it to be a good day. She was out of sorts when she joined her grandson at the breakfast table and she was feeling thoroughly disagreeable by the time he left her there, his tossed napkin on the floor instead of the table. He told her coldly that he would do himself the honor of joining her and Sophie for dinner and stalked off she knew not where for the rest of the day to do she knew not what.

The duchess was not accustomed to arguments. Most people crumbled before the power of her will. She had ruled her husband despite his sternness with his subordinates, and she had ruled her quiet, good-natured son. Her grandson was a different matter. He had been trained well and strictly, at least from the age of eleven, and had always been a dutiful boy, to give him his due. But he was stubborn. He liked to do his duty in his own time and in his own way. He was also a charmer and played mercilessly on her love for him—she loved him many times more than she had loved any of the other men in her life. He had always been able to avoid unpleasant confrontations with her. Until this morning, that was. She had not said a word the night before after all the guests had finally left.

"I do not consider it seemly or courteous of you, Tenby," she began this morning when she entered the breakfast room and he sprang to his feet to greet her, "to appear indoors with muddy boots."

"Muddy—?" He frowned down at his riding boots, on one of which was a small splash of mud or dust. "I do beg your pardon, Grandmama. I have been out riding. You are not usually up this early. Would you like me to go and change?"

She was further irritated by the fact that she had complained about a triviality. "Sit down," she said regally, but of course she waited for him to come around the table first to seat her. She tilted her head for his kiss on the cheek.

"It is a fine morning," he said. "Misty and a little chilly, but invigorating. I trust you slept well."

"As well as could be expected," she said. "Dismiss the servants if you please, Tenby."

He did so and then smiled winningly at her. Just as he had always done when he was a boy and was trying to avoid a scolding. It had sometimes worked with her, though never with his grandfather. He was a handsome boy. There was no denying the fact.

"Were you satisfied with the evening?" he asked. "I thought it went rather well."

"She is a pretty girl," the duchess said, "and nicely behaved. Not that the prettiness has anything to say to the matter, but I daresay you would sooner have a pretty bride than an ugly one, Tenby. And she will give you pretty children."

"She is rather lovely," he conceded, sipping his coffee.

"I was extremely disappointed when you chose to break your promise to me and lead another lady into the first waltz," she said.

His smile could almost be called a grin. The duchess stiffened her already straight back. She did not like the levity of his expression. "You must know, Grandmama," he said, "that Aunt Sophie left me with no choice."

"You might have explained," she said, "that the dance was already promised to your intended."

"But it was not," he said. "And I don't believe Lady Phyllis need yet be described in that way, Grandmama."

"You intend breaking your promise to me, then?" she said. "And disgracing the girl when the whole *ton* is in daily expectation of an announcement?"

"If the *ton* is expecting any such thing," he said, "then it has a powerful imagination, Grandmama. We have merely met with strict formality on a few occasions."

"When you are the Duke of Tenby," she said, "and she is Lady Phyllis Reeder, daughter of Barthorpe, a few formal meetings amount to a great deal."

He sipped his coffee. She could see a pulse beating in his temple. He was wisely choosing not to argue with her.

"And I must protest that vulgar display to which I and your other guests were subjected during the first waltz," she said.

"Ah." He set his cup down none too gently on its saucer. "I wondered how soon we would get to the point. She was my guest, Grandmama. I was forced into dancing with her unless I choose to be extremely rude to both her and Aunt Sophie. I danced with her once. I danced once with almost every other lady guest. I danced with Lady Phyllis twice."

"It was not the fact of the dance," the duchess said, her irritability at its peak, "but the manner of it, Tenby."

"Meaning?" He looked as angry as she felt. She did not like the impertinent abruptness of his tone. His grandfather would have known how to deal with that tone of voice.

"It was vulgar in the extreme, Tenby," she said. "I can only describe the way you looked at her throughout the dance as *devouring* her with your eyes."

There was a dull flush on his cheeks. "She is a beautiful woman, ma'am," he said. "Perhaps you did not notice the way Travers and Sotheby were looking at her. And Yarborough too. Men appreciate beauty. There is surely no vulgarity in doing so."

"There is when you do so openly in the presence of your own relatives and that of your intended bride and her parents," she said. "Lady Wingham was entitled only to your condescension last evening, Tenby. She was invited specifically as a companion for Sophie."

"She was a guest in my home," he said harshly. "And she does not have employment as a companion, Grandmama. She is the widow of a baron. And a lady in her own right."

"The offspring of a country parson, I believe," she said, "and for several years as a paid companion."

"Ah," he said. "you have been making inquiries."

"Of Sophie," she said. "Sophie knows her well. She was going to employ the girl herself, but she managed to snare herself a wealthy husband in time to escape that fate. I do not blame the girl. She had every right to look after her own interests. But she cannot expect to look as high as a duke. At least not as high as Tenby."

She watched his jaw tighten.

"I do not believe she aspires to my hand," he said. "I do not believe she is in any way conniving, Grandmama. I believe she loved Wingham and was good to him."

"I will grant you," she said, "that the sweetness of her disposition seems genuine enough. And I believe she is a virtuous woman. If you cannot think of yourself, Tenby, and of what you owe your mother and me and your position, then perhaps you should think of her reputation. How do you think the *ton* will interpret the sort of glances with which you were favoring her last evening?"

"I don't know, Grandmama," he said. "Perhaps you will be good enough to enlighten me."

She looked at him severely. "I do not expect impertinence from you, Tenby," she said. "The *ton* will be well aware of the fact that you cannot offer Lady Wingham marriage. But she is no young girl. She is a widow. It will be thought, then, that your dealings with her are of another sort."

"I will meet any man who dares say any such thing aloud," he said.

"In order to defend the lady's honor?" she said. "Would it not be better to defend it by never putting it in jeopardy, Tenby? For her sake, if not your own? I will not have you distracted during the very time when you are engaged in making one of the most important decisions your position will ever call upon you to make."

"And Lady Wingham is a distraction," he said, getting to his feet. "She is of no more significance than that." That was when he tossed his napkin with vicious impatience so that it landed on the floor and when he stalked from the room after the iciest of bows and the assurance that he would do himself the honor of joining his grandmother and his aunt for dinner.

The Duchess of Tenby was far more discomposed than she had been when she came into the breakfast room. Then she had been merely angry. Now she was a little frightened. For perhaps the first time she realized that her grandson was a grown man and a determined and a strong-willed one too. She realized that he was a person quite separate from herself and quite capable of defying her and—more important—of defying his duty. She had held duty most dear since the day she had shut her mind to the man she had loved and married the Duke of Tenby in obedience to her father's command. The situation was far worse than she had thought. Her grandson was not infatuated with Lady Wingham. He was in love with her.

The Duke of Tenby was in no better humor when he arrived home late in the afternoon with only enough time to get dressed for dinner. He had been at White's and at Tattersall's and at the races during the afternoon with Lord Bruce. But he carried with him his anger, which was only worsened by his knowledge that perhaps his grandmother had had a point. If he really had shown his admiration for Harriet the evening before, then he had put her in danger of becoming the subject of gossip.

"Bruce, my good fellow," he had asked languidly at the races, eyeing through his quizzing glass a couple of ladies of doubtful virtue who had been momentarily abandoned by their escorts in favor of the horses, "would you say I was in any way, ah, indiscreet last evening?"

"As pretty a piece of horseflesh as I ever saw," Lord Bruce had said, his eyes moving appreciatively over the favorite for the coming race. "Last evening? Oh, you mean dancing with the chit twice? Most indiscreet, Arch, my lad. I would say you are a goner. The sound of wedding bells is already deafening me. It's a good thing you did not choose the horsy girl. She giggles so incessantly that one wonders how she catches her breath."

"Ah," the duke said. "Pretty, I grant you, Bruce. But lame in all four legs I would wager. And will wager. My bet goes elsewhere with better and surer odds. You observed no other indiscretion?"

"Did you steal a kiss behind a potted palm?" Lord Bruce asked. "No, it was not apparent, old chap."

Ah. His grandmother had seen only what she was looking for, then. It had not been obvious to anyone else.

"If I were you, Arch," Lord Bruce said, "I would reserve certain looks you were giving the little Wingham for the bedchamber. Is she good there, by the way?"

"What looks?" The duke raised his glass to his eye again the better to observe the parading horses. Inside he froze.

Lord Bruce chuckled. "Eyes that devoured her and undressed her and set her back to a mattress and mounted her," he said. "You had me reaching for my cravat to loosen it, Arch. Is she good in bed? If not, there is yet another new girl at Annette's. Very accomplished." He made a circle of his thumb and forefinger and extended the other fingers wide.

Eyes that devoured her. Exactly what his grandmother had said. Obviously he had been very indiscreet. "Bruce," he said softly, continuing his languid survey with his quizzing glass, "when you refer to Lady Wingham, old chap, you will keep a respectful tongue in your head. Unless you are prepared to name your seconds, that is."

Lord Bruce threw back his head and guffawed. "Name my seconds!" he said gleefully. "Arch, Arch, you are head over ears for the woman. I never would have thought it of you. She must be very good indeed." But he held up his hands quickly, palms out. "My apologies. I have to say I admire your taste, old fellow. Yarborough was almost panting over her last evening. Did you notice?"

The race was about to begin at last. The duke lowered his glass. "Yes," he said. "I might have to have a word with him if his interest develops in its usual manner. Lady Wingham is not for the likes of Yarborough."

Lord Bruce chuckled and then whistled. "If he has four lame legs, Archie, my boy," he said, "I will eat my hat."

"Bon appétit," the duke said dryly as the race began.

By the time he arrived home much later, he was still feeling angry, but more at himself than at his grandmother. It was unpardonable of him to have exposed Harriet to possible gossip and speculation by the unguarded way he seemed to have looked at her while waltzing with her the evening before. Looks apparently that he should have con-

fined to their bedchamber. He would not for worlds publicly compromise her virtue. And yet he seemed to have
been in danger of doing just that.

His grandmother at least had put her mood behind her, he
saw when he entered the drawing room later and found
both her and his aunt there, ready for dinner. The duchess
smiled graciously at him. "Ah, you are punctual, Tenby,"
she said. "You know how I hate tardiness for meals."

He knew it well. He bowed over her extended hand and
then over his aunt's.

"You are a handsome lad, dear Archibald," Lady Sophia
said loudly. "You look quite ravishing in pale blue. Like an
ice prince."

He grinned at her and winked.

His grandmother's restored good mood was explained as
soon as they had sat down at table and begun to eat.
"Barthorpe and his countess called this afternoon," she
said. "It was very civil of them, Tenby."

"Yes, indeed," he said, sipping his soup and wondering
what his grandmother had said to them in his absence.

"They brought an invitation with them," she said, smiling almost benevolently at him.

"Oh?" he said politely and waited for her to repeat what
she had said to his aunt. His grandmother had always liked
to milk a particularly good story. It must be a ball, he
thought. It must be something more than a dinner to have
brought that expression to the duchess's face. Damnation.
And he was going to be expected to lead Lady Phyllis into
the first set in full view of the gathered *ton*. Well, he supposed the inevitable could not be postponed much longer.
Not when his grandmother was at work on his behalf, anyway.

"We have been invited to spend a few days at Barthorpe
Hall in the country," the duchess said, "with a few other select guests. From Friday to Tuesday, in fact. It will be a
splendid opportunity for you to fix your interest with Lady
Phyllis, Tenby, and even perhaps to make your offer. There
is no point in postponing the matter longer, is there?
Barthorpe has certainly made his interest clear."

The duke set his spoon down quietly. "You accepted the

invitation on my behalf, I suppose, Grandmama?" he said. His first thought had been that he would be away on Monday. He would have to go a whole week, from this coming Thursday to next, without Harriet. And if a formal betrothal was effected during his visit to the country, perhaps she would not be willing to continue their liaison even until the end of July. Somehow he feared that Harriet would be strict about such matters.

"Eh?" Lady Sophia asked. "What was that, Archibald? You are mumbling, dear."

He repeated his question.

"Of course I accepted," the duchess said, a trace of impatience in her voice. "It is rather short notice, but I am sure you do not have any engagement that you cannot politely withdraw from, Tenby. Everyone will understand. Everything is proceeding wonderfully well."

"Yes," he said. "It seems I will have to have a talk with the earl sometime during our visit."

"At last," his grandmother said in some triumph. "I was beginning to fear that you were never going to commit yourself, Tenby."

"That gel is going to be a handful, if you ask me," Lady Sophia said. "No one can tell me that she has been on the town for two years because no one will have her. She is a stubborn little piece, I would not doubt."

"I am sure she knows where her duty lies, Sophie," the duchess said stiffly.

"I'll have my little pet with me," Lady Sophia said. "She will enjoy a few days in the country."

The duchess looked at her blankly. "I beg your pardon, Sophie?" she said.

"Eh?" Sometimes, the duke thought, looking at his aunt shrewdly, he believed she pretended to be harder of hearing than she actually was. "Oh, it was all arranged while you were in the garden showing the countess the rosebushes, Sadie. Barthorpe would insist on talking in a whisper and turned somewhat purple in the face when he had to repeat everything he said. Sometimes twice." She rumbled. "I told him that I can only ever hear my dear little Lady Wingham clearly."

The duke would perhaps have been amused if he had not felt aghast at what he knew was coming. His grandmother knew it too, he could see from a glance at her taut expression.

"What are you saying, Sophie?" she asked. "What did you force Barthorpe into?"

"Force, Sadie?" A look of wide-eyed innocence did not at all suit his aunt, the duke thought, amused despite himself. "Barthorpe is a gentleman, I'll give him that, even if he does whisper. He was most civil. He promised to invite the child into the country for my greater comfort."

"She will feel remarkably out of place," the duchess said coldly.

Lady Sophia chose to be deaf, and addressed herself to her roast beef. His grandmother had misplaced her good mood, the duke saw in one hasty glance at her. She looked decidedly grim, in fact. And he? Part of him rejoiced. He would not be entirely without her, after all. Another part of him cringed. It seemed that both his grandmother and Barthorpe would expect some sort of declaration during those few days, and he could not see how it was to be avoided. Or whether it was desirable to avoid it. But Harriet would be there. Perhaps she would be present for the announcement of his betrothal.

He remembered that only a few short weeks before he had been prepared to throw caution to the winds and offer Harriet marriage. He seemed a long way now from such a gesture of freedom and defiance. He had backed himself into that corner he had so dreaded.

"Perhaps," his grandmother said distinctly, "Lady Wingham will have the good sense to refuse her invitation."

"Oh, I think not, Sadie," his aunt said. "Not when she reads my letter. She is such a tender-hearted child."

The Duke of Tenby was at Mrs. Robertson's rout that evening. Harriet, in conversation with Mr. Hammond and Lady Forbes, was relieved when she saw him arrive. Though it was not really relief she felt. Her heart beat painfully and she knew that color was flooding her cheeks.

She fanned herself and smiled at what Mr. Hammond was saying.

The Duke of Tenby usually wore dark colors, which always looked striking with his very blond hair. Yet he looked equally distinguished in this evening's ice-blue coat and silver knee breeches with sparkling white linen and lace. Harriet turned away from him so that she would not stare.

And then the Marquess of Yarborough was bowing over her hand and kissing it—on the palm—and gazing into her eyes and complimenting her lavishly on her gown and on her eyes. And yet all the time his own eyes were insolently seeing, not her gown, but her body beneath it. It was strange, she thought, how quickly one could lose one's naiveté—and one's innocence—when one ventured out into society.

The duke kept his distance, as she had expected he would. He would not have danced with her the previous evening, she knew, if Lady Sophia had not trapped both of them into it. He kept his distance because he wished to guard both of their reputations, especially hers, she liked to believe. Or perhaps it was because he no longer felt the need for social intercourse when he had what he wanted from her in private twice a week. She chastised herself with such thoughts as punishment for dreaming of love in his arms when it was merely sex.

Although there were several opportunities to put herself in his way, she left it so late that she began to fear that perhaps he would leave early, as he often did. She finally contrived to be alone approaching a doorway as he came through it in the opposite direction. He saw her, bowed stiffly, and would have passed on. But she caught at his sleeve.

"I need to speak with you," she said, feeling the color flood her cheeks, wishing that the floor would open up to swallow her.

He looked displeased and withdrew his arm under the guise of reaching for the ribbon of his quizzing glass. He bowed again and smiled. "I think it unwise, ma'am," he said softly.

"I cannot keep my appointment on Thursday," she said hastily, wishing that for once she could be a blasé woman of the world.

"Ah," he said. "Another more important engagement?"

"N-no," she said. "I cannot come, that is all."

"Smile," he said. "It is wise when one is undoubtedly being observed. You are having your courses, Harriet?"

Not having a looking glass handy, she was not sure if there was a deeper color than crimson for her face to turn.

"My dear," he said, "I have had dealings with women for many years and know that such an affliction has to be endured monthly. Smile. Ah, yes, and wave your fan too, my little blusher."

"I will be well again by Monday," she said.

"Alas." His hands played with the handle of his quizzing glass. "It seems you cannot have had either your invitation or your letter yet. You and I will be at Barthorpe's in the country on Monday, Harriet, you to save the earl from the tedium of having to repeat his every word—twice—to my esteemed aunt, me to move on to the next stage of my courtship of Lady Phyllis."

"I shall not be there," she said quickly. No, not again. She would not allow herself to be drawn into such an embarrassing and painful situation again.

"You have not yet read my aunt's letter," he said. "I do not doubt it will reduce your tender heart to spasms of pity. I do not doubt that it would do the same if your heart was as hard as rock."

"I do not like it." She raised her chin.

"But you like my aunt," he said, the suggestion of a smile in his eyes. "We have conversed for altogether long enough. Your servant, ma'am." He made her a courtly bow and strolled on to some other destination.

No, she thought. No, she would not be so manipulated. She was beginning to feel quite out of control of her life. She supposed that that was what she might have expected when she gave up one of the most firmly held values of her life in order to become his mistress. But that did not explain why she had become almost inextricably involved with his family and his courtship. It was not right, she told herself. It was most definitely not right. She remembered in some distress the confidences to which Lady Phyllis had made her an unwilling listener the evening before.

The situation was becoming quite bizarre. She longed suddenly, as she seemed so often to do these days, for the safety of Godfrey's presence. She longed to be able to close her eyes and find her head comfortably nestled on his shoulder and his arms about her and her whole world secure.

Someone took her arm and patted her hand. "Gracious, Harriet dear, smile," Lady Forbes said. "Whatever did he say to you to make you look so forlorn? Someone has replaced you in his affections? It was bound to happen, you know. You can do very much better, dear. You can find yourself a husband. What has happened to Mr. Hardinge?"

"I put him off," Harriet said. "It did not seem fair to encourage him. I am being invited out to Lord Barthorpe's country home, Amanda. Probably at Lady Sophie's request. How can I go under the circumstances? It is like a nightmare. But it is so hard to dissapoint Lady Sophia."

"She is a veritable dragon," Lady Forbes said. "Here comes Lord Sotheby."

Harriet smiled brightly. If there had been one spot of brightness in her day, she thought, it was her discovery during the afternoon that she was not with child. She had worried about it, having no idea how conception was to be prevented. At least she would not have that particular concern for another month.

12

She simply would not go, Harriet decided, the expected invitation open before her on the breakfast table. She did not want to go. It would be in very poor taste to do so. How would the Earl and Countess of Barthorpe feel if they knew that they were inviting the mistress of the man they intended for their daughter's husband? For the moment Harriet ignored the other letter beside her plate, the one she knew was from Lady Sophia Davenport.

"I'll not go," she told Lady Forbes. "I shall send a refusal immediately after breakfast, Amanda. I cannot leave Susan alone for so long."

"I would, of course, be delighted to have her to myself for a few days," Lady Forbes said. "But I think your decision is wise, dear. Clive and I are delighted with the way in which your circle of admirers seems to grow larger every day. Even Yarborough has an eye to you. You must at all costs avoid being alone with him, of course, Harriet, but his admiration can do nothing to harm your consequence. Sotheby is very attentive too, and he is a viscount, dear, with a very respectable fortune. He cannot have passed his fortieth birthday yet."

Harriet smiled. "Everyone is very kind," she said. She looked back at her invitation. "I shall certainly not go, Amanda."

"And you will give Tenby up too?" her friend asked hopefully.

Harriet reached for her other letter and opened it. "When the time comes," she said quietly. Perhaps the time had already come. He would be moving on to another phase of his courtship, he had said. The gathering at Barthorpe Hall must surely be for the establishment of a serious courtship, perhaps even for the betrothal. Harriet felt rather sick at the thought. She did not think she would be able to continue as his mistress after he was betrothed. Even now her conscience was being stretched to the limits of its endurance.

Lady Forbes clucked her tongue and drank her coffee.

"Oh, dear," Harriet said, reading. "Oh, dear."

"She is a selfish old woman, Harriet," Lady Forbes said firmly. "She would not think twice about taking you away from your friends and even your daughter merely for her own comfort. She would use you as her servant."

"I think that is a little unjust," Harriet said. "I do believe she loves me, Amanda. I believe she sees me as a kind of granddaughter. I am sure she thinks I will enjoy a few days in the country. And she needs me so badly."

Lady Forbes made a sound that was almost a snort.

"It will be difficult to disappoint her," Harriet said. "It must be so frustrating to live in a world of near silence when one has always reveled in sound and conversation."

"And gossip," Lady Forbes added caustically. "But you will disappoint her?"

"I must," Harriet said. "If you will excuse me, Amanda, I shall go now to write to her and to refuse the earl's invitation."

"You are excused," her friend said, waving a dismissive hand.

Harriet decided to write to Lady Sophia first. It was not an easy letter to write. She realized to her surprise, when she tried to choose words that would disappoint least, that she loved the old lady. Almost like a grandmother. It was not just that Lady Sophia was a reminder of Bath and more secure times. It was more than that. It was hard to deprive her of company that would make those few days in the country more enjoyable for her.

And of course, Harriet thought, drawing the feather of the quill pen absently through her fingers, part of her wanted to go too. It would be both embarrassing and painful to go, but for four days she could be in frequent company with him. The end was so near. She could grasp for herself just a little more. Perhaps by the time Tuesday arrived the end would have come. Perhaps she would never be able to be with him again. Perhaps she had already made love with him for the last time.

Even if the country visit did not result in a betrothal, she should end the affair, Harriet thought. Perhaps next month she would not be as fortunate as she had been this month. It was true that in four years of marriage she had conceived only once, but perhaps it was not her own fertility that was the ruling factor. And even once now would be disastrous. She felt the clawing of a cold fear. What would she do if she was got with child?

"My dear Lady Sophia," she had written when Sir Clive's butler interrupted both her letter writing and her thoughts with the announcement of the arrival of the Earl and Countess of Beaconswood. The countess was laughing when they came into the morning room.

"Industrious Harriet," she said brightly. "Do I look like a ship in full sail? Daniel unkindly insists that I do. He also warns that I must face front when entering a room or I will not be able to pass through the doorway. We have come to disturb you and bear you and Susan off to the park. I will not allow you to make excuses like a pile of letters that need writing. They can wait for this afternoon. The children are outside in the carriage with their nurse. I told Daniel he did not have to deprive himself of a morning at White's, but he has the notion that I am too close to my time to be allowed out of his sight. Don't you, my love? I think he must be right—"

"Julia," he said quietly, "would you pause for a moment so that I may make my bow to Lady Wingham and so that she may say good morning, as I am sure she is burning to do?"

His countess laughed again. "It is a good thing ladies do not have to bow," she said. "I have absolutely no waist to bend from, Harriet. And it is a good thing you are a friend and do not have to be curtsied to. Daniel would have to haul me upright again. I have so much energy. I could not possibly have stayed home this morning. Will you be ready soon? I always have energy when my time is near, don't I, Daniel?"

"Most of it," he said, "is worked off via the tongue, Lady Wingham. If you and your daughter would care to join us to take the air in the park, ma'am, you may leave us to get ready. If you wait for Julia to stop talking, we may still all be here at luncheon time."

"And the children would be as cross as bears," the countess said, "and their nurse threatening again to give in her notice. Do you think . . ."

Harriet left the earl to answer the question, whatever it was to be, and hurried upstairs to fetch Susan and to get ready to go out. There was some urgency about writing both the letter and the note of refusal, of course, but they must wait. Perhaps by the time she had had some exercise and some luncheon she would have found the words with which to explain to Lady Sophia why she could not accompany her into the country.

The Duke of Tenby had been given his orders to return home after luncheon in order to escort his grandmother to the Earl of Barthorpe's. She and the countess were to pay a few afternoon calls together. He would have proceeded about his afternoon's business once his task was complete, but he felt obliged to return home once more to see if his aunt had woken from an afternoon nap and if she needed anything.

"Dear Archibald," she said, "you should not have returned home on my account. I know you young bucks have plenty of occupations for your days, like ogling the ladies in the park. At least that is what young bucks did in my day."

"We have as much red blood pumping through us now as men did then, Aunt Sophie," he assured her with a grin.

"Who is my pet staying with?" she asked. "I have forgotten, Archibald. Someone who frequents Bath."

"Lady Wingham?" he said. "She is at Sir Clive and Lady Forbes's."

"Eh? Forbes? Yes, that's the one," she said. "Take me there, Archibald, if you please."

"Now?" He looked at her in some surprise.

"I daren't wait a year or two," she said. The duke smiled

at the familiar rumbling laugh. "Or even a week or two or a day or two. At my age, Archibald, you act on the spur of the moment. It might be the only part of the moment left. I want to see my little girl."

"She may well be from home, Aunt Sophie," he said. "Ladies usually have plenty with which to occupy their afternoons too, you know."

"In my day, it was going to the park to be ogled by the young bucks and to stick our noses in the air and act haughty while we flirted," she said.

"Times have not changed a great deal," he said with a chuckle.

"Eh?" she said. "What are you waiting for, Archibald? Call out the carriage again and send my woman to fetch my bonnet and shawl, will you?"

The duke bowed and left the room. And admitted to himself as he sent a runner to call back the carriage, which had only just been returned to the carriage house, that he could cheerfully kiss his aunt on both cheeks. He could think of nothing he would prefer to do this afternoon than go where he could look at Harriet and perhaps talk with her. It was a strange admission and one that surprised him. He had never—ever—craved a meeting with a mistress except for one purpose. This meeting was to be at Forbes's house in company with his aunt. Anyway, Harriet was in the middle of her courses and he would be unable to bed her even if he could get her alone. It did not seem to matter, he realized. The mere prospect of seeing her—if she was not out, as she probably would be—frankly excited him just as if he were still a schoolboy.

Getting his aunt into the carriage occupied several minutes of the time of both the duke and a hefty footman, but finally she was comfortably seated with a blanket over her knees.

"She has not answered my letter yet," she said as the carriage started on its way. "Depend upon it, Archibald, the delay means she doesn't know how to refuse. I shall have to persuade her in person."

He had not really thought of her refusing, though she had said the night before that she would. His aunt's letter would persuade her, he had thought. She was fond of the old girl. He could not bear the idea of her refusing, though the realization alarmed him. He should not want her there, surely? His mistress—his lover—in residence while he courted his future duchess. He wished fervently that matters had not proceeded so far, that his courtship had not developed a life of its own quite beyond his control. He wished he had insisted at Kew that he wanted marriage with Harriet instead of falling in with her seemingly more convenient idea that they become lovers for what remained of the Season. Could he really have believed that possessing her body regularly for two months or so would leave him satisfied and content to give her up?

"Do you think you will be able to persuade her?" he asked his aunt.

"Eh?" she said. "Persuade that sweet little child? I persuaded Barthorpe, did I not, Archibald? The very prospect of having me without her was giving the poor man an apoplexy." She barked with laughter.

"Aunt Sophie," he said, chuckling fondly, "you are a manipulator."

"And aren't you thankful for it, dear Archibald," she said. "Fancy my little pet yourself, don't you?"

He sobered instantly. "What do you mean?" he said. "I am practically an engaged man, Aunt."

She clucked her tongue. "Sadie gave up love for duty more than sixty years ago," she said. "For more than sixty years she has been obsessed with duty. She might have been a viscountess instead of marrying my brother, and have taught her grandchildren to love. I never had either children or grandchildren, Archibald, but I loved. Oh, how I loved. One does not forget, you know. Your uncle was the world's greatest lover. Not that I could compare, of course." She rumbled for a moment. "I was virtuous even if I was a brazen flirt as a gel. Do you think there are feather beds and privacy in heaven, eh, boy? I don't have so long before I'll find out, though, I suppose. Maybe your uncle will have everything ready for me."

It was strange, he thought, how one tended to forget that elderly people had a whole life behind them, that at one time they had been young. He could not imagine his grandmother in love—and with someone other than his grandfather. Poor Grandmama. But he frowned out of the window. How many other people had guessed his feelings for Harriet? He had obviously been very indiscreet indeed.

She was at home. She joined them in the salon to which they had been directed only a couple of minutes after them, hurrying into the room and bending over his aunt's chair to kiss her cheek before curtsying to him.

"I was writing letters," she said breathlessly. She was holding one in her hand. "I am sorry that Amanda—Lady Forbes—is not here. Sir Clive has taken her for a drive."

"It is you we came to see, child," Lady Sophia said, reaching for Harriet's free hand and drawing her down to sit beside her on a sofa. "It does my heart good to see your pretty face. Is she not the prettiest child you have ever seen, dear Archibald?"

The duke bowed without replying, looked appreciatively at Harriet's blush, and seated himself.

"Is that letter mine, my pet?" Lady Sophia asked.

"Oh, yes." Harriet held it out. "It is not finished, ma'am, but I believe the meaning is clear. I am sorry."

"Have you replied to Barthorpe's invitation yet?" Lady Sophia asked.

"No, ma'am," Harriet said. "It was to be my next task." She was still holding out the incomplete letter.

She had decided not to go, the duke thought. Her brief apology and the look of regret on her face told him that.

"I cannot read it without my eyeglasses, child," his aunt said. "Read it to me."

Harriet bit her lip. " 'My dear Lady Sophia,' " she read, " 'I deeply regret—' "

His aunt's hand had reached out to tap Harriet's. "There, there," she said, "that is enough, pet. Tear it up."

"Ma'am?" Harriet said.

"Archibald," Lady Sophia said, "ring for tea, dear boy."

Harriet sprang to her feet, dismayed, and flew to the bell pull. "I do beg your pardon, ma'am," she said. "And yours, your grace. My manners have gone begging." She gave instructions to the servant who appeared at the door.

"Now, child," Lady Sophia said when Harriet had resumed her seat, "tell an old woman why you must disappoint her."

The wicked old fiend, the duke thought over the next few minutes as he sat silently watching Harriet being effectively wound about one gnarled finger. Her eyes were big with tears by the time she promised faithfully that nothing could keep her from spending four days at Barthorpe Hall. And then she was suitably rewarded.

"There. Kiss me, my pet," his aunt said, offering one withered cheek. The old devil. He would wager that she had led his uncle a merry dance during the forty-five years of their marriage. He almost smiled suddenly as he caught himself hoping that his uncle would be waiting with a feather bed for her in heaven.

Why was she so insistent that Harriet accompany her to Barthorpe Hall? he wondered. Was it just that Harriet seemed to be the one person who was able to cope with her deafness? Was she as deaf as she sometimes seemed to be? Why had she insisted that Harriet be invited to his dinner? Was she trying to matchmake? Was she hoping to see her favorite become a duchess? It would be as well for her if she realized it was far too late for that, he thought. Her little Harriet had a heart that might be broken.

He wondered what his aunt would have to say if she knew that Harriet was his mistress.

But he had sat silently contemplating Harriet for long enough. He drew her into conversation as she poured the tea and as they drank it and ate the tarts and currant cakes that had come on the tray with it. He had learned something of her trick of sitting facing his aunt and enunciating her words clearly rather than bellowing them. He had to repeat himself no more than twice before his aunt appeared to nod off and he could talk more naturally.

"Well," he said finally, getting regretfully to his feet, "we have taken enough of your time, ma'am. I shall awaken my aunt and see her settled in the carriage."

She awoke so easily that he wondered if she had been asleep at all. "Is it time to leave already, dear Archibald?" she asked. "How time does fly. Run upstairs for your bonnet, child, and we will drive once or twice about the park. I doubt it is the fashionable hour and we have only the closed carriage anyway, but a drive will be pleasant. It is a chilly day. Or perhaps it is just these ancient bones that feel chilled."

Harriet was blushing and looking distressed again. Had she not learned that there was no point whatsoever in trying to argue with his Aunt Sophie?

"It is chilly," he confirmed. "Lady Wingham, will you do us the honor of driving with us?"

"I'll fetch my bonnet, your grace," she said, her eyes unhappy, and went from the room.

Of course there was almost no one in the park and not a great deal to be seen from the windows of a closed carriage. And his aunt had very little to say. He and Harriet talked about the weather and the beauty of the trees in Hyde Park and the need of a good rain to refresh the grass. He smiled at her in some amusement at one point until he remembered that he was sitting opposite his aunt and there was nothing wrong with his aunt's eyes even if she did need eyeglasses to read with. He did not want to feed her suspicions.

But evidently they did not need feeding. She sighed when they were still in the park and complained of stiffness and some chill about the legs, despite the blanket that covered them. And then for good measure she discovered a headache.

"I think you had better convey me home, Archibald, dear," she said. "I sometimes forget that I am too old for a visit and a drive all on the same afternoon. Forgive me, pet." She patted Harriet's hand. "I know Sir Clive's is closer, but it would be too far for me. Never fear, though. Archibald will escort you home afterward."

"Of course, Lady Wingham," he said, inclining his head. The inspired old fiend.

Harriet helped him get his aunt out of the carriage and into the house on St. James's Square. There the old lady assured them that the same stout footman who had assisted her earlier would give her his arm to her room. After an hour's rest she would be as right as rain once more. She dismissed them with a careless wave of the hand.

The duke handed Harriet back inside his carriage, gave instructions to his coachman, and vaulted in after her.

It was not the plain carriage in which they rode on Mondays and Thursdays. This one was far more opulent with its dark blue velvet upholstery. His ducal arms were painted on the outside. Harriet waited while he gave instructions to his coachman and wondered if it was as obvious to him as it was to her that Lady Sophia had deliberately thrown them together. But why? Surely she must realize that the daughter of an impoverished country parson could not aspire to the hand of a duke. And even if she did not, then she must know that he was all but betrothed to someone else.

He drew the blue curtains across the windows as he always did in the plain carriage. Then he settled beside her, his shoulder touching hers. She looked down at her hands in her lap until he covered one with his own and curled his fingers beneath it.

"I wonder," he said, "that you even tried to defy my aunt, Harriet. Did you not know that she is undefyable?"

"It was not a matter of defiance," she said, "but of propriety. She does not know, does she?"

"She knows that I admire you," he said. "That is why she took me to visit you this afternoon and why she developed a stiffness all over and a chill in her legs. Ah, yes, and a headache too, I believe."

"She does not understand," Harriet said, distressed to know that it really had been obvious to him. "But I could not say no to her. I am sorry."

"You need not be." He lifted her hand to his lips. "Harriet, I could not go for even a week without a sight of you."

She turned her head sharply away, but of course there was no longer a window through which to look.

"You are well?" he asked her.

"Well?" She looked at him in some surprise. "Yes, of course, I—"

"Some women have bad cramps, I believe," he said.

"Oh." Yes, she had suffered badly from them until she had had Susan. The experience of childbirth seemed to have cured her. "No. I am well, thank you."

"Harriet." His silver eyes laughed at her. "Will you still be blushing when you are ninety, I wonder? No, don't lower your head." One long finger caught her beneath the chin and held up her face for his scrutiny. "You have many charms, but your blush is the one I find most endearing."

She found his kiss deeply disturbing. Not because there was passion in it, but because there was not. Passion she understood and could feel comfortable with. It was what one expected of a lover. It was a thing more of the body than of either the mind or the emotions. This was more like the way he had made love to her—for want of more accurate words—during their last two assignations. But it was even more disturbing because he knew he could not take the embrace to its physical conclusion. And yet he kissed her.

His mouth moved over hers, caressed hers, played with hers. His tongue touched, stroked, teased. One of his hands caressed a breast, though he made no attempt to slip her dress from her shoulder and avoided touching her nipple and thus arousing her. And then he slipped an arm beneath her knees and lifted her onto his lap and cuddled her there after untying the strings of her bonnet and tossing it to the seat opposite.

"We ought not," she said.

"Ought not what?" he asked, finding her mouth with his again. "Crush my legs, O mighty feather?"

"Be doing this," she said. "Why have we not arrived at Sir Clive's yet?"

"Because my coachman has instructions to take the long route to it," he said. "Don't worry, Harriet. I am not abducting you. You will get there eventually. I want to hold you for a while. It is going to be an eternity before I can have you again."

She rested her head on his shoulder. "I ought not to be here with you," she said. "It is not right."

He chuckled. "What quaint prudery you suffer from, Harriet," he said. "You have given me all on several occasions and yet now you mutter about impropriety because you ride about the streets of London on my lap. Kiss me."

"And because I am going into the country with you and

the duchess and your bride and her family," she said, sitting up, "and no one but you or me knows that I am your mistress. I could not say no, Archie, but I ought to have. Sometimes I am frightened by the changes in myself."

"Hush." There was a harshness in his voice. He drew her head back down to his shoulder and held it there with a hand that was none too gentle. "You were invited to amuse Aunt Sophie, Harriet. It is not very flattering, but under the circumstances you may find it consoling. Amuse Aunt Sophie. Make her happy. Just the sight of you makes her happy."

Yes. She closed her eyes. She would console herself thus. There was truth in it. She would not be simply rationalizing.

"Archie," she said after a short silence, her eyes still closed, "your betrothal is going to be announced, is it not?"

"Not to my knowledge," he said. "But this thing is beyond me, Harriet. It seems to be in the hands of Barthorpe and my grandmother. It does not matter. Kiss me again."

She had not planned to say what she was about to say. She did not want to say it. She felt physically sick. "Archie," she said, "I don't think we should—"

But his mouth, pressed hard to hers, stopped her. "Hush," he said harshly. "Hush."

"It is not—" she began again, but his mouth stopped her again.

"No," he said, looking fiercely into her eyes when he finally lifted his head away. "I'll not let you end it, Harriet. Not yet. I cannot do without you. Not yet. I have not had enough of you. Not nearly enough. Nor you of me. Tell me you are tired of me."

"I—"

"Tell me you are tired of me," he commanded again.

She blinked when her vision became suddenly blurred.

"You cannot," he said. "And you will not end it just because you are having a crisis of conscience again. To hell with conscience. Oh, Harriet." He drew her head down once more and rested a cheek against the top of it. "To hell with conscience. I need you for a while longer yet. Tell me you need me."

She was frightened. There was more in his voice than physical need. What did she mean to him? It seemed to her that a very thin wall was between them and that she could with one hand reach up and send it crashing down. But the thought terrified her. To what end? The future, which already was painful in prospect, would be unbearable.

"Tell me," he whispered urgently.

"I need you," she said. "We need each other for a little while longer i-in bed, Archie."

She did not understand the word he muttered. She thought it was probably a swear word. She closed her eyes and cuddled against him.

13

It was quite as bad as the Duke of Tenby had feared. But no worse than he had expected. Apart from his grandmother, his aunt, and himself—and Harriet, of course—everyone who gathered at Barthorpe Hall on Friday was a relative of the earl's. It really was a family gathering and obviously had only one purpose. The earl, he decided, was a determined man. He was forcing the issue of his daughter's marriage.

Viscount Sotheby, the earl's brother and heir, was a guest, as were Lord and Lady Mingay, the countess's brother and his wife, with their son, Mr. Peter Horn, and three children not yet out of the nursery.

"It is all very satisfactory, Tenby," his grandmother said when he appeared in her dressing room before dinner on the first evening to escort her downstairs. "The way has been made easy for you. I do not need to tell you how to proceed during the coming few days, of course."

No, she did not need to tell him. He had not expected there to be any going back after this particular weekend, and indeed there was not. Strangely, it was almost a relief to know himself so thoroughly trapped. It would be even more of a relief when he was finally betrothed. Except that . . .

"Tenby?" His grandmother spoke rather sharply.

"I shall have a few words with Barthorpe this evening, Grandmama," he said, "and arrange a more formal meeting with him for tomorrow."

She smiled. "Your grandfather would be proud of you if he were here now," she said. "Next week we will make a public announcement and summon your mother to town.

She hates to leave the country, but for such an important occasion she will come. We will plan a splendid ball for the following week. Even the Prince Regent will come, I daresay. And then there will be the wedding plans. I do think it would be a good idea for it to take place before the end of the Season, Tenby, so that everyone of any importance will be there."

"Grandmama," he said, extending his arm for hers, "I am not even betrothed yet."

"But there is a perfect understanding between both families," she said. "One cannot begin plans too early. However, they need not concern you. Lady Barthorpe and I will set our heads together over the coming few days."

Yes, none of the plans need concern him. None of them. His only duties were to make the offer, to make the vows, and to get his child on the girl as soon after their wedding night as was humanly possible. Marriage was really not such a difficult business. Only a damned dreary one.

"One thing, Tenby," his grandmother said, stopping him as his hand was on the handle of the door to open it. "Nothing is to mar the business of these next days. Nothing. Sophie has her companion. They may be safely left to amuse themselves."

He inclined his head.

"If you feel the need for greater beauty than you will be getting in a wife," she said, "or for greater—pleasure, then you may seek them out after your marriage, as all men do. Your intended wife is a woman of good breeding and will turn a blind eye. But these days are to be strictly for business."

Poor Grandmama. He had seen her with new eyes since his brief talk with his aunt. She had once given up love and had made an armor and a shield of duty ever since. She had shielded herself from the humiliation of knowing that his grandfather kept mistresses.

The duke removed his hand from the doorknob and set it over hers. "Grandmama," he said with unaccustomed gentleness, "soon I will present you with a granddaughter-in-law of whom you may be proud. By this time next year, if it is within my power, you will be able to hold my heir or my daughter in your arms. I'll not let you down."

"Certainly not a daughter, Tenby," she said firmly. "You know my views on that."

He bent his head and kissed her cheek before opening the door and escorting her from the room.

Harriet felt awkward. It had been made very obvious by the condescension with which she had been greeted on her arrival the day before and by the smallness of her bedchamber and its position overlooking the kitchen gardens at the back of the house that she had been invited solely for Lady Sophia's sake. It was true that Viscount Sotheby had been attentive to her, seating himself beside her at dinner, but almost all her attention had been taken by Lady Sophia on her other side. And the very young and shy Mr. Horn had tried to engage her in conversation in the drawing room afterward but had been driven away by Lady Sophia's insistence that he repeat everything he said. The poor boy had been almost stammering by the time he had wandered away to stand behind Lady Phyllis, who had been playing the pianoforte.

Harriet had not minded the evening before. But this morning Lady Sophia was still in bed and everyone else had plans for the morning. The duke and the Earl of Barthorpe disappeared from the breakfast room early, and it was obvious from the dignified look of triumph on the duchess's face and the arch comments of the countess's why they had disappeared together. Lady Phyllis, Harriet saw, was picking at the food on her plate with downcast eyes. The duchess, the countess, Lady Mingay, and Lady Phyllis were to pay some morning calls on neighbors.

"What a pity," the countess said with a smile, "that there will be no room in the carriage for you, Lady Wingham. But I daresay you would prefer to be here when Lady Sophia wakes up anyway."

"Yes, indeed, ma'am." Harriet smiled back.

"Perhaps, Lady Wingham," Viscount Sotheby suggested, "you would honor young Peter and me by joining us for a ride."

"I am quite sure, Marvin," the countess said, "that Lady Wingham did not come prepared to ride. She may make free with the morning room. There are a few books in there and paper and ink and pens for the writing of letters. Lady Sophia will expect her to be on hand when she rises from her bed."

The viscount smiled ruefully at Harriet and shrugged. She was being very effectively put in her place, she realized. The countess was coming as close as good manners would allow to treating her as a servant. Harriet wondered if the woman had been offended at the fact that the duke had danced with her at his dinner the week before. Perhaps she even remembered that at Lady Avingleigh's ball, when the duke had made his first appearance in a ballroom for a long time, it was with Harriet he had danced first.

The countess, Harriet guessed, must have been very annoyed with her husband for inviting her into the country to what was otherwise a gathering for the two families about to be linked by marriage. She escaped from the breakfast room to her bedchamber, intending to stay there for a while. She was missing Susan dreadfully. She should never have agreed to leave her for almost five days just because Lady Sophia had sounded pathetically in need of her company. Susan would love the open spaces of this park, she thought with an ache of the heart as she gazed out across the kitchen gardens to the tree-dotted lawns beyond.

She felt foolishly like crying. She really ought not to have come. Especially not at this particular time. Archie was downstairs with the earl. She felt little doubt that they were discussing a marriage contract. It was madness for her to have come.

And then she remembered the children. Three of them. She had caught only a glimpse of them the day before, but she had asked Lady Mingay about them. There were two girls and a boy. The youngest girl was five years old—only a little older than Susan. She wondered if the children's nurse would consider her appearance in the nursery an intrusion, but decided that she would risk it anyway. She need not stay long. But just seeing some children might cheer her up.

The children's nurse did not appear at all sorry to see her. She was shrieking at them when Harriet tapped on the door and was blowing a painfully reddened nose when Harriet opened it. She looked ill and exasperated. The youngest child was wailing, the older girl was loudly scolding, and the boy was wagging his tongue and also his fingers from his ears into which he had stuck his thumbs.

"Oh, my lady," the nurse said.

"Goodness," Harriet said, but the commotion ended as the children looked at her with curiosity and interest. "You have a cold?"

"Oh, my lady," the nurse said, "and I ache all over. You would think they would have pity, but they are naughty children. Just wait until I tell Lady Mingay."

The little boy started dancing and wagging his fingers again. The older girl informed him that his father would give him the cane when he knew.

"Goodness," Harriet said again. "Such energy. But you are all using it so well that I daresay you do not wish to go outdoors. It is a shame. It is such a lovely day out there and I am going out."

There was an immediate hush, broken by the loud blowing of the nurse's nose. "They are not allowed outside in the morning, my lady," she said.

"Their nurse is ill this morning," Harriet said briskly, "and must return to bed with a hot drink. It is not a morning for rules. Of course, the children do not have enough energy left to go outside. I shall send up one of the footmen to watch after them. The one with thick black eyebrows that meet over his nose, I believe. The one who frowns all the time. The one with arms like tree trunks." She turned toward the door, but was stopped by a chorus of voices.

Five minutes later three wild and whooping children were racing across the back lawn while Harriet walked briskly after them. The nurse, amidst halfhearted protests, had retreated to her bed. They were not easy charges, Harriet discovered during the next hour. Neither eight-year-old George nor ten-year-old Sarah wanted to play with little Laura, with the result that the child frequently opened her mouth wide and wailed in angry misery. Neither were they particularly eager to play with each other, the trouble being that everything George suggested was forbidden and drew scolds and threats from Sarah. It seemed the children were not allowed to climb trees or sit down on the grass or get their hands dirty or even run. The two of them finally settled to throwing a ball back and forth to each other, though George was contemptuous and called Sarah a stupid girl because she could not throw a ball properly.

Harriet missed Susan more than ever. But the little one at least became thoroughly happy when she discovered a playmate in Harriet herself. Harriet allowed the child to run toward her, despite Sarah's protests, and then swung her up and around in circles. The little girl was soon flushed and giggling. She wrapped her arms about Harriet's neck after the dozenth repetition of the game had made them both dizzy and breathless.

"I wish you would play with us all the time," she said.

Harriet laughed and hugged her.

"Charming," an aristocratic and familiar voice said, and Harriet turned to find herself being surveyed through the quizzing glass of the Duke of Tenby. "And considerably disheveled."

She set Laura down and smoothed her hands over her dress. She could see errant wisps of hair from the corners of both eyes. She was not even wearing a bonnet.

"Children?" he said. "Mingay's, are they? And you have the charge of them, Harriet?"

"Their nurse was quite ill, poor woman," she said. "She looked quite done in when I peeped in at the nursery. I sent her off to bed."

"You peeped in?" he said. "Are you fond of children?"

She flushed. "Yes," she said. "I miss— Yes, I am fond of them."

"You're a stupid, stupid girl!" George cried suddenly. "And I don't care if you tell, Papa, so there." He went into his characteristic taunting dance, tongue and fingers waving.

"Oh, dear," Harriet said, turning and preparing to wade into the fray.

"Is this, ah, a gentleman I see before me?" The duke's voice was at its haughtiest and iciest. Harriet was not surprised to find when she turned her head that he had his quizzing glass to his eye again. He strolled toward the two older children. "Or is it a particularly nasty overgrown insect? It appears not to have enough legs."

Sarah tittered.

"I believe," the duke said, "it is a young gentleman who has temporarily misplaced his manners. Doubtless when he recalls in a moment that he has been discourteous to a lady, he will beg her pardon."

George gaped. "She's my sister," he said.

"Indeed," the duke said. "Are you a gentleman, sir?"

" 'Course I'm a gentleman," the boy said crossly.

The duke raised haughty eyebrows. "Is not a gentleman's sister a lady?" he asked.

"Papa will cane you for sure, Georgie," Sarah said spitefully.

"Ah, quite." His grace silenced her with his quizzing glass. "You have something to say, sir?"

"You aren't my papa," the boy said sulkily.

"For which fact I shall be eternally grateful," the duke said. "Your papa apparently has a cane, sir. I merely have two hands."

George looked at them shiftily. "I'm sorry, Sare," he muttered, a note of defiance in his voice. He glared at the duke. "There. Are you satisfied?"

"I am accustomed to being addressed as 'your grace,' " the duke said, lowering his glass. "But you are merely a gentleman in embryo. Doubtless you will remember to include it the next time you speak to me." He looked at Sarah. "Are you satisfied, young lady?"

"It was just because he says I can't throw the stupid ball right," she said.

"Yes, I did notice that myself," the duke said. He stared down the crow of delight that came from George. "But one does not expect ladies to be as accomplished at sports as gentlemen. Ladies almost invariably have more useful accomplishments. If you wish, young lady, I shall give you instruction."

"Oh," Sarah said, preening herself on being so addressed. "Will you, your grace?"

His grace proceeded to do so while Laura, with renewed energy, resumed the running and swinging game with Harriet.

"You handle children quite beautifully," Harriet said later when the children had finally been persuaded to start back for the house. It was the duke's hand on the handle of his quizzing glass that had persuaded them, Harriet's suggestion having been met with a chorus of rebellious protests.

"Nasty little specimens, are they not?" he said. "Are all children the same, Harriet? I have had almost nothing to do with them until today."

"My own d—" She bit her lip and took his offered arm. "Not all children are as unruly," she said. "I suppose it is inevitable that three children will sometimes quarrel. I believe these children are hedged about with too many rules and not enough opportunity to work off their energy. They are a great deal calmer now than when I first brought them outside."

"Gracious," he said. "You must have felt the need of a leash, Harriet. You made the little one feel important. You would make a good mother. Blushes? Ah, good. I have accomplished something worthwhile this morning."

"Only one thing?" she asked. "I thought you were to spend the morning with the earl."

"We were closeted together for upward of an hour," he said. Silence fell between them for a few moments. "It was all quite satisfactory."

"Ah," she said. "You must be glad of that." The breeze felt cold suddenly. She wished she had brought a shawl and a bonnet.

"Harriet," he said quietly. "She means nothing to me. You must know that."

And I do? She stopped herself in time from asking the question aloud. She did not want to know the answer. It did not matter if he cared for her or not. It would make no difference to anything. Only perhaps it would cause more pain to know that he cared.

"You must not say that," she said. "You are going to marry her. There must be more commitment than merely a desire for an alliance and an heir of appropriately blue blood. She is a person. She needs love and care as much as anyone else."

"Harriet," he said, "don't try to arouse my conscience. I begin to suspect that I have none."

A footman approached and bowed to them as soon as they had entered the house through a back door, and informed Harriet that Lady Sophia was in the breakfast room and asking for her.

"Bellowing for you more like," the duke said. "Take the children up to the nursery and summon their nurse," he directed the footman and then offered his arm to Harriet again. "I shall escort you into the old dragon's presence."

"We ought not to be seen together," she said.

But he made an impatient sound and his hand strayed to the handle of his quizzing glass. She linked her arm through his.

Lady Sophia, seated at the head of the table, was munching on toast. The Duchess of Tenby was seated beside her, a cup of tea in front of her. The Countess of Barthorpe stood with a cup of tea in hand. It felt rather like walking out into a January morning without coat or muff, Harriet thought as the duke relinquished her arm in order to greet his aunt and the others. She was suddenly aware that she had not gone upstairs to comb her hair.

Lady Sophia opened her arms to Harriet. "You were out walking, my pet? I am glad you have not been wasting this lovely weather," she said. "It has brought roses to your cheeks. Has it not, dear Archibald? Come and kiss me good morning, child."

A marriage contract had been discussed at some length and agreed upon by both parties. The Earl of Barthorpe had shaken his future son-in-law heartily by the hand and that was the end of the matter. Apart from the formality of a marriage proposal to Lady Phyllis herself, of course. That would be accomplished sometime in the course of the day so that they could appear together at church tomorrow morning and the first announcement be made at dinner on

Monday evening. Some of the earl's more prominent neighbors had been invited in anticipation of the occasion.

The duke had wandered out into the garden afterward in order to collect his thoughts. He had gone to the back of the house so that he would not meet anyone. At first he had been annoyed by the sound of children's voices, and then drawn by the sounds of girlish laughter and childish giggles, and then enchanted at the sight of a rather untidy Harriet playing with infants. And looking thoroughly at home with them too, despite the fact that the older ones proved themselves to be little monsters on closer acquaintance.

It struck him forcibly that at her age she should be a mother already but had been deprived of what she would undoubtedly have counted a joy by an elderly husband. It also struck him that she should be in serious search of a husband who could rectify the lack without further delay instead of wasting her time with him. But of course he could not resist the temptation to spend half an hour with her even though doing so took him into unfamiliar waters. He had never had dealings with infants since reaching adulthood himself. It was time, he supposed, that he got some practice.

His grandmother, of course, was so tight-lipped after they had walked into the breakfast room together that one would have needed a crowbar to open her mouth. And if she had held her back any straighter she would have been leaning backward. She made no comment, though he escorted her upstairs as soon as she had finished her tea, and he offered no explanation. Instead he told her that everything was settled satisfactorily with Barthorpe and that he would be making his offer that afternoon. It was to be arranged that Lady Phyllis walk out alone with him. His grandmother unbent enough to tell him rather chillily that she was pleased.

He wished he were pleased, the duke thought as he set off for the walk with Lady Phyllis after luncheon. Everyone else, it seemed, had been warned off joining them, though he politely asked. The girl at his side was pretty and elegant and refined. But he wanted Harriet. More than ever he wished he could go back to Kew and change the way the afternoon there had developed. But thinking of Harriet reminded him of the scolding she had given him that morning. Lady Phyllis was a person who desired to be cared for and loved just like anyone else, she had said. He sighed inwardly. Perhaps he did have some glimmering of a conscience after all.

"The park is very lovely," he said. "I had heard it was one of the most picturesque in England."

"My father's gardeners are dedicated to their job," she said. "But I have heard that your park is quite splendid, your grace."

"It is not so formally arranged," he said. "But it is indeed splendid for riding. And the deer park is well stocked."

They conversed politely for several minutes.

"Perhaps," he said at last, "you will permit me to turn the conversation to more personal matters?"

"Yes, of course," she said.

They both knew why they had come walking without chaperonage of any kind. It seemed very cold and calculated, the duke thought, glancing uneasily at Lady Phyllis. She was lovely. She should be courted with warmth and desire. He wondered if she ever dreamed of love. Did not all women dream of love? And he should be feeling eagerness and anxiety as he offered his hand and his heart to the lady of his choice. There should be more than this arranged, entirely businesslike meeting. The whole weekend was business. That was the word his grandmother had used of it. An alliance—Harriet's word. A treaty. The linking of two houses, not the marriage of two hearts.

"I spoke with your father this morning," he said. "He gave me permission to pay my addresses to you."

"Yes," she said.

"Will you do me the honor of marrying me?" he asked.

"Yes," she said.

He found his mouth opening to say that she had made him the happiest of men, but he could not do so. This was business. Why add the meaningless lies that convention seemed to demand?

He stopped walking and took her hand in his. "Is it what you want?" he asked her.

She looked up at him in some surprise. "Is that relevant?" she asked, surprising him equally. It seemed that she was as reluctant as he to mouth platitudes.

"Have you been forced into this against your will?" he asked, frowning.

"Have you?" she said. "The question seems hardly relevant, your grace. You must marry someone of my rank, and it is an excellent match for me to marry someone of yours."

Somehow it had not struck him that perhaps the girl was actively reluctant to marry him, though when he thought about it he realized that only vanity could have led him to the assumption that any girl must be delighted at the chance to become his duchess.

"Is there someone else?" he asked gently.

"I believe the question is impertinent, your grace," she said. "I have accepted your offer. You will find that I know my duty and will perform it."

Like his grandmother? Would duty become the guiding principle of Phyllis's life, all love snuffed out because she had had the misfortune to be born too nobly?

He raised her hand to his lips. "I shall do my best," he said, "to ease you in the performance of your duty, to ensure that you will not regret your answer to me today."

There was some warmth in her eyes for a moment. "How could I regret it," she said, "when I will be the envy of the *ton*? You have been the biggest prize on the matrimonial mart for many years, your grace."

The girl had spirit and a direct manner of speaking that he liked. Perhaps it would not be a total disaster, this marriage, he thought. Though it would never be that, of course. They would both know how to be civil for the rest of their lives, despite personal feelings.

Yet he could feel no gladness in knowing that his bride was apparently a sensible woman. His heart was aching. He had now reached and passed the final stage. He had just engaged this girl to marry him. He had just made her a pledge. And yet already he was breaking it. Already he was longing to be free. Already he was living for next Thursday afternoon. Already he was scheming of ways to convince Harriet to prolong their affair beyond the end of the Season.

Already he knew that he could not willingly face living without her.

And yet already too he knew that conscience was not dead in him. That being unfaithful to a wife was going to be no light or easy matter.

Harriet!

He smiled at Lady Phyllis and resumed his walk with her. "There," he said. "The moment we have both known was coming has come and is safely in the past. The rest, I suppose, can be left in the hands of your mother and my grandmother. Let us talk, shall we? Become a little less than strangers to each other? Tell me about yourself."

"Oh," she said. "Let me see. I was born in May twenty years ago. Have I started far enough back?"

They looked at each other and both laughed.

14

No announcement was made. But it was perfectly obvious that one was imminent. The duke led Lady Phyllis in to dinner on Saturday evening and turned the pages of her music in the drawing room afterward. They traveled in the same barouche to church on Sunday morning and sat next to each other in the earl's padded pew. They walked out together, unchaperoned and unaccompanied, in the afternoon and partnered each other at cards during the evening. They rode together on Monday morning.

Oh, yes, it was perfectly obvious. There was to be a dinner for guests and neighbors on Monday evening and dancing afterward. The countess, the duchess, numerous maids and footmen, hurried to and fro all day long, busy with preparations. During the afternoon armfuls of flowers were carried into both the dining room and the small ballroom. Obviously it was no ordinary occasion that was being prepared for.

Harriet devoted all her time to Lady Sophia, who seemed unusually pensive during those days and often sat merely patting Harriet's hand. She was doing so on Monday afternoon as they sat out in the formal gardens. She was wrapped about warmly with a shawl and had a blanket over her knees.

"I did not think it would come to this quite so fast, child," she said after gazing and nodding silently at the flowers for several minutes. "I forget how relentless Sadie can be when she has her mind set on something."

Harriet did not pretend to misunderstand. "It is a good match for both of them, ma'am," she said.

"Fiddle!" The old lady rapped her hand almost sharply.

"If they like each other, that is quite as far as their feelings go. They are foolishly sacrificing themselves on the altar of family expectations."

Harriet said nothing.

"And he loves *you*, my pet," Lady Sophia said sadly.

"Oh, no." Harriet pulled her hand away, abruptly. "You must not say so, ma'am. It is not true."

"Never say he has not told you?" the old lady said. "Ah, young bucks are not what they used to be in my time. Or perhaps you have never developed the wiles to draw the truth from him. You are too sweet for your own good, child."

"What would be the point of making him say it?" Harriet said, bowing her head.

The old lady's gnarled hand touched the bright hair at the back of her head. "I did not hear you, my pet," she said. "But I have upset you. There, there, I should have left you at home with your little one, where you wanted to be. I am a selfish old woman and foolishly thought I could work miracles just because I am aged and have acquired some small measure of wisdom during my life."

Harriet looked up and smiled determinedly. "I am not sorry I came," she lied. "Have I made your days a little happier than they would otherwise have been? Everyone seems too busy to sit and talk."

"My days always have a little more sunshine when you are in them, child," Lady Sophia said. "You will help me inside now. I feel chilly."

The announcement was made by the Earl of Barthorpe at the end of dinner before the ladies retired. There were twenty neighboring guests in addition to those staying at the house. No one was surprised, of course, but the announcement was followed by loud exclamations of astonishment and pleasure. The dining room was loud with the noise of congratulations to the newly betrothed couople. Toasts followed.

Harriet sat with a bright smile on her face while Lady Sophia patted her hand.

The duke opened the dancing with Lady Phyllis and then

danced with her mother. Harriet, seated beside Lady
Sophia, kept her eyes away from him as she had done quite
diligently for four days. She conversed with an elderly couple who had come to pay their respects to Lady Sophia. But
then Viscount Sotheby was bowing over her hand and asking for the third set, a country dance.

"Lady Wingham," he said when he had led her onto the
floor, "I hesitated to accept my brother's invitation into the
country until I knew you were on his guest list. And yet I
find your time has been almost totally monopolized, and
my sister-in-law has been determined to keep it that way. I
believe she is jealous of the fact that you are many times
lovelier than Phyllis, who was to be the focus of attention
during these days."

It was difficult to answer such words. Harriet chose to ignore the compliment. "It is only right that she should be,"
she said. "Every woman deserves to be paid attention on
the occasion of her betrothal. It happens only once in life."

"Except, perhaps," he said, "when a woman is widowed
young."

Harriet was alerted by his tone. But the music began and
the steps were intricate. There was no chance of further
conversation. He was a distinguished-looking gentleman,
she thought, and had been attentive in London during the
past few weeks. He was perhaps ten years her senior. A viscount in his own right, he was the heir to an earldom. *Be
sensible*, she told herself suddenly. *Be sensible*. He smiled
at her as they came together after dancing a measure with
other partners according to the pattern of the dance. She
smiled back. But then they were separated again and she
found herself being twirled by the Duke of Tenby, his silver eyes watching her and jolting her into an awareness of
what she had determinedly ignored for the past four days.
She had not realized that he and his partner were part of her
set.

Be sensible, she told herself even more firmly when she
and the viscount came together again. When he suggested a
stroll on the terrace after the set had finished, she smiled
and agreed.

"Ah," he said when they had stepped out through the

open French windows, "fresh air. And a terrace to ourselves. I hope you do not feel the need for a chaperone?"

"No, of course not, my lord," she said. "Do I need one?"

He chuckled. "There is nothing like a betrothal to turn the mind in the direction of romance, is there?" he said. "Though I would have to say that I have not always felt that way."

"I hope they will be happy together," she said.

"Oh, Phyllis will be happy," he said. "She has made the catch of the decade. He is a handsome devil too, is he not?"

"The Duke of Tenby?" she said. "Yes, indeed."

He stopped walking when they had strolled along the terrace in one direction, and covered the hand she had rested on his sleeve. "May I kiss you?" he asked.

She looked up at him in some surprise. *Be sensible*, an inner voice told her quite distinctly. "Yes," she whispered.

He kept his lips closed when he kissed, as Godfrey had always done. He pressed them warmly to her own and set his hands lightly at her waist. It was an entirely unthreatening embrace. It was pleasant. She had that feeling of safety she had always had with Godfrey even though she was alone with the viscount out-of-doors.

"Mm," he said, lifting his head but keeping his hands at her waist. "As sweet as I expected. The rest of your sizable court of admirers in London would be green with envy if they knew I had you alone in the moonlight."

"But I am sure you are a gentleman, my lord," she said.

"If anyone could make a man forget his manners," he said with a smile, "it is surely you, Lady Wingham. But I assure you I mean honorably. Would you do me the great honor of marrying me?"

She had suspected that it was coming. Even so, she was surprised when the words had actually been spoken. It had been equally likely that he would have offered her *carte blanche. Be sensible*, that inner voice warned. But although she opened her mouth and drew breath, no words would come.

"I have taken you by surprise?" he asked, releasing her waist in order to take one of her hands in both of his.

"Yes," she said.

"Perhaps," he said, "I speak too soon after your bereavement? Is this scene in poor taste? If so, I humbly beg your pardon, ma'am."

"No." She shook her head. "I loved my husband dearly, my lord, but I have done my grieving and life must continue. I have a daughter."

"Ah, yes," he said, "I remember hearing as much. I would still be honored to make you my wife."

Say yes. Say yes. She could hardly do better. He was a man of rank and fortune and honor. He was willing to take on her child. She had come to London in the hope of finding such a man. No, he went beyond her hopes.

"I have found myself quite enchanted with you," he said. "With your beauty and your, your—" His free hand described a circle in the air. "What is it about you? Your innocence? Is that the right word? Whatever it is, you enchant me and make me eager to give up a bachelorhood that I have jealously guarded for thirty-nine years. Give me hope. Tell me you will think about my offer even if you cannot say yes now."

Her innocence. Oh, God, her innocence. An image of the bedchamber in the duke's love nest and of herself naked with him on the bed there flashed unwillingly before her eyes.

"My lord," she said, "I c-cannot. I am—I am unworthy of you."

He possessed himself of her free hand and squeezed both of them. "Rumor has it," he said, "that you were once companion to Freddie Sullivan's wife. And I suppose you are aware that I will be Barthorpe one day if I survive my brother and that any son of mine almost certainly will. The fact troubles you? It troubles me not at all, ma'am. Is that your only scruple?"

She closed her eyes and dropped her chin. He was so very—kind. As kind as Godfrey. Surely she could grow to love him as she had Godfrey. He was younger, more personable. "I could not bring you a whole heart, my lord," she heard herself whisper. The words were quite unplanned.

There was a short silence. "Ah," he said, "That is an impediment, ma'am. I would want your heart or at least the hope of making it mine. Is there any chance that in time it will be free?"

She decided that he deserved honesty. She looked up at him, aware that the moonlight was on her face. "It has not been for six years," she said.

"And yet," he said, "you claimed to have done your grieving."

"I do not refer to my husband," she said.

"I see." He squeezed her hands once more, almost painfully, and released them. "I shall remain one of your admirers, ma'am. If at some future time you will permit it, perhaps I shall renew the topic of this conversation. You will wish to return to the ballroom."

Fool, the inner voice told her. *Fool*. "My lord," she said, walking by his side, not touching him, "if my heart were free, I cannot think of anyone on whom I would more wish to bestow it."

He chuckled. "Unfortunately," he said, "hearts are not always in the control of their owners, are they? It is almost invariably the other way around. Or so poets through the ages have assured us. I don't like to see those eyes full of distress. I appreciate your honesty, ma'am, and honor you for it."

"Thank you," she said, distressed nonetheless. She wanted to catch at his arm before they reentered the ballroom and ask him if she might try, if they might attempt a closer relationship, if he would give her a little time. But though she wanted desperately to do just that, decency held her back. He deserved better than anything she could give him. He had misunderstood when she had told him she was unworthy of him. She was unworthy. And she realized in a flash that that sense of unworthiness would very probably keep her from any future marriage.

It was a bleak future she looked into as she stepped back through the French windows.

Lady Sophia was thirsty. Harriet got to her feet and offered to fetch her a glass of lemonade from the dining room. But the old lady was also stiff in the legs. With Harriet's assistance she would go too. The dining room seemed a little too far to walk, though, she decided when they were outside the ballroom. The small, darkened anteroom to their left was unoccupied. She would sit quietly in there until Harriet returned.

Harriet did not return quite as soon as she could have wished. Mr. Horn was in the dining room with another young man from the neighborhood, and he stopped Harriet to make introductions, to stammer out his admiration for her appearance, and to compliment her on her dancing skills.

"I can never remember the steps unless I concentrate on them," he said. "But my partners always want to talk."

"I can never keep my feet from beneath my partner's," the other young man said while Harriet laughed.

"Better that," she said, "than *on* your partner's, sir."

"Oh, the devil, yes," he said, laughing jovially. "You are very witty, Lady Wingham. As well as devilish pretty."

Despite her mood of general depression, Harriet could not help but smile as she made her way back to the anteroom, a glass of lemonade held in one hand. The youth must be all of eighteen years old, swaggering and pretending to be at least a decade older. And probably shaking in his shoes with nervousness, poor boy.

Harriet smiled when she entered the anteroom and opened her mouth to speak. But Lady Sophia frowned and held a finger to her lips. Harriet stood very still and glanced to the door that stood slightly ajar in the wall to her right. There must be another anteroom through there. It was occupied, too.

"No, David. It is no use. It is wrong." The voice was high-pitched and sounded on the verge of tears.

"This whole thing is wrong," a man's exasperated voice said. "That is what is wrong, Phyll."

Harriet closed her eyes briefly and wondered it it were possible to close the door without the couple in the other room realizing that they had an audience.

"There was nothing I could do about it." Lady Phyllis's voice sounded utterly miserable. "I know I made you a promise."

There was a lengthy silence, ending with a kissing sound.

Lady Sophia shook her head and held up one hand as Harriet took two cautious steps in the direction of the door.

"You said you would keep yourself free until you were of age," the man said. "And that then you would marry me even if your papa still objected. You promised, Phyll. I believed you. I trusted you. There was only one more year to go."

"You have no idea," she said. "Oh, don't, Dave. Someone might come. And it is wrong. Don't. Please don't."

There was a repetition of the silence and the sound that ended it.

"You have no idea," she said again. "They were disappointed after my first Season and angry after the second. I thought I could hold out for one more. But then *he* decided this year of all years to choose a wife and of all the misfortunes he looked my way. There was no way I could avoid it. Everything developed a life of its own once he had looked. And Mama and Papa were so determined. What could I do?"

"You could have said no."

"It sounds easy, doesn't it?" She seemed very close to tears again. "Perhaps I am just weak. But I could not say no. Everyone expected me to say yes—Mama and Papa, the duchess, him, the whole *ton*. I could not say no, David."

"So this is good-bye," he said, his voice dull with a misery to match her own.

There was a strangled sob from Lady Phyllis and then a long silence again. Harriet took the remaining steps to the door and shut it as soundlessly as she was able. She turned and set down the glass on a small table and knelt down in front of Lady Sophia.

"How much did you hear?" she asked.

"Not as much as I would have liked, child," Lady Sophia said. "It was Lady Phyllis?"

Harriet nodded. "Please," she said, "we must say nothing to get the poor girl into trouble. She was saying good-bye to him."

"To her young buck," Lady Sophia said. "He was not Archibald, was he?"

Harriet shook her head. "David," she said. "I think Mr.

Lockhart, son of Baron Raven, is David. They were both presented to us before dinner. Please promise that we will say nothing."

Lady Sophia patted Harriet's cheek. "They were kissing," she said. "Even I could hear the silences, child. And they were unhappy. Sometimes I am glad I was unable to have children. Something happens to make parents very foolish creatures. I suppose Barthorpe's ambition has kept the gel from her David?"

Harriet nodded and Lady Sophia tutted. "There," she said, patting Harriet's cheek once more. "Perhaps all is not lost after all. No, child, I am not about to go back into the ballroom to shout out an announcement. Their secret is safe with me, just as yours is. Hand me the drink. And then you shall help me upstairs and call my woman to put me to bed. These old bones have had enough of festivities for one evening. Tomorrow we have to return to town. But I have something else to accomplish before I leave." She sighed. "How we take our energy for granted when we are younger."

Harriet returned to the ballroom after taking Lady Sophia to her room and immediately had her hand solicited for a dance by Mr. Horn. But the necessity of smiling and appearing as if she were enjoying herself was just too great a strain on her nerves. She was rapidly coming to believe that this must be one of the worst days of her life. She could not remember feeling more depressed. She thought back to that day at Ebury Court when Lord Archibald Vinney had come to try for the second time to persuade her to become his mistress and she had sent him on his way with her second refusal. Oh, yes, perhaps that day had been equally bad. And yet she had survived it. She had even gone on to find deep and unexpected contentment after it. She supposed she would survive this too.

Except that that time her honor had been intact.

She could not stay in the ballroom after the set was over. She could tell by the look on his face that the other young man of the dining room was trying to get up the courage to ask her to dance. She could not smile for half an hour longer. She slipped out through the French windows again

and crossed the terrace into the deeper darkness of the grav-
eled walks that made geometric patterns through the formal
gardens. The cool, almost chilly air felt good.

He had felt almost relieved after his offer had been made
to the earl and to Lady Phyllis and both had accepted. All
the doubts and the indecisions were behind him. Once there
was really no way out he was able to begin to accept the
new facts of his life. He expected to feel even more relieved once the betrothal was publicly announced and the
last nail had been pounded into his coffin, so to speak.

But it had not happened that way. In the dining room
when the earl had stood to make the announcement, he had
felt a deep dread, and then, when the announcement had
been made and he had been forced to smile and get to his
feet, bow over Lady Phyllis's hand, and raise it to his lips,
he had had to fight blind panic. He had fought and won, of
course, but black despair had replaced it. And his awareness of Harriet, always acute, almost like a sixth sense, was
further intensified. Although he did not consciously look at
her through much of the evening, he was aware of her
every move, every gesture, every expression. It was sweet
agony to touch her briefly during the one country dance and
twirl her about before returning her to her own partner. He
could have killed when she left the ballroom with Sotheby
in order to step out onto the terrace. He knew almost to the
second how long she was out there. Too damned long.

When she was absent for a long time with his Aunt Sophie, he guessed that both of them had retired for the night.
He fought the urge to go after Harriet, to try to talk with her
in the privacy of her own room. To make love to her there.
His need for her was a raw ache. It was a week—a week
and so many hours—since he had last had her. But he was
betrothed, he reminded himself, and looked about to see
Lady Phyllis coming into the ballroom, brightly smiling, on
the arm of young—Lockhart? It was difficult to recall the
name of everyone to whom he had been presented this
evening. This was the evening on which his betrothal had
been announced. He could hardly go upstairs to make love
to another woman.

And then Harriet came back alone and danced once and disappeared out of doors just when he was fighting the urge to ask her to dance himself and estimating the reaction of his grandmother and the countess if he did so. He also fought the urge to go out after her—and lost. After all, it was unlikely that anyone had seen her go. He would not be gone long enough himself for his absence to be particularly noted. He slipped out through the French windows, looked along the terrace in both directions, and crossed it to look down over the gardens. She was strolling to one side of them, close to some overhanging willow trees. He would not have seen her if he had not been looking for her. He hurried after her.

"It's me," he said when she jerked around suddenly in some alarm as his feet crunched gravel behind her. He stopped walking when he was close to her.

She stood looking at him for a few moments and then gave a low moan and swayed forward. He caught her to him, his arms going about her like iron bands, trying to fold her into himself. Her face was buried against his neckcloth. And in that wretched moment he knew the truth that he supposed he had known all along. Her feelings matched his own.

Too late. By his own foolish, foolish stupidity too late.

"No," she said as his mouth sought and found hers. But he took it anyway and ravished it while she sagged against him and moaned once more. "No. Archie, no."

He lifted his head. "Harriet," he said, "you know it means nothing, what has happened this evening. It is a mere formality."

"A formality sanctioned by church and state," she said. "Go back. You must go back. I shall enter the house by another door and go to my room. Go. Please."

"Harriet," he said, "how can I go? I want you. I need you."

"No," she said. "No longer. You are affianced. You belong to her."

"What are you saying?" he asked harshly. "You are not ending things now, Harriet. I won't let you end it yet. I won't let you." His arms tightened about her again.

"It ended," she said, "when your betrothal was announced. I have been your mistress, Archie, when only we two were concerned. I cannot commit adultery with you. I cannot, no matter what you say."

He looked down at her with wild eyes. "Not yet," he said. "We cannot say good-bye now. Not like this. Once more. We have to meet one more time. On Thursday. We have to have time to say good-bye properly. You cannot deny me that, Harriet. One more time." Panic was on him again. "Please. One more time. Please."

She bent her head forward until her forehead was against his neckcloth. She said nothing for a long time. He fought the humiliation of tears. What sort of damned-fool trap had he allowed others to lead him into? What sort of damned-fool weakling was he? But such questions came too late. It was too late.

"Once more," she whispered. "To say good-bye."

"On Thursday?"

"Yes." He felt her swallow awkwardly.

He lifted her face with hands cupped on either side of it and kissed her lips gently. "Thank you," he said. "Thank you." And he turned to hurry back the way he had come a mere few minutes before.

15

It felt so very good to be back in London. Harriet traveled back alone on Tuesday morning, having declined the offer of a place in the duchess's carriage. The duchess and Lady Sophia were not leaving until the afternoon. Lady Sophia was spending an hour of the morning walking very slowly on the terrace with Lady Phyllis. She was getting to know her future niece-in-law, she explained. Harriet was glad to be alone, to have the whole ghastly weekend behind her.

She flew up to the nursery when she arrived back in London after doing little more than poke her head about the door of the salon to announce her return to Lady Forbes. She picked Susan up and twirled her about and hugged her almost hard enough to bruise her ribs. Never, never again would she leave her for longer than a few hours, she vowed.

Susan launched into an excited account of all the places Sir Clive and Lady Forbes had taken her and of the ices and cakes they had bought her. And the doll. She dashed across the nursery to produce a wonder of porcelain and silk and lace.

"Annabel and James have a new brother," she announced.

Harriet sat down and drew her daughter onto her lap. Julia had been right, then. Her time had been near. And now she had three children. Harriet had hoped after Susan that she would conceive again. But it had not happened. And now she was eight-and-twenty and had refused two marriage offers within the past few weeks. She did not know if she would ever be able to contemplate another marriage. Perhaps she would never have more children than

Susan. But she must count her blessings. At the time she had thought of her daughter as her little miracle. She hugged her again now.

"And I was afraid that you would be missing me as much as I was missing you," she said, smiling.

"I did miss you, Mama," Susan said, regarding her gravely. "I cried one night when I could not show you my doll, but only a little bit. Aunt Amanda read me a story."

Harriet kissed her cheek. "Would you like one now?"

"Yes, please," her daughter said, getting down to fetch her favorite book. "Aunt Amanda does not read the wolf right, Mama."

It was good to be back in London. Perhaps it would be better to be back in Bath. To be home. Harriet longed for it suddenly, for the familiar safe surroundings of her own home. If only she could go back and find Godfrey there. She missed him with a welling of sadness. He had been invariably kind and dependable. There were no ups and downs of emotion with Godfrey, only the even keel of daily living—and the certainty of a deep affection.

No, she did not want to return to Bath yet. She would feel her loneliness more acutely there. Yet she knew she could not stay in London. Not when staying there would mean seeing him wherever she went—as she had done all Season so far. But now he would be more often in company with Lady Phyllis. With his betrothed. Harriet had not expected the actual betrothal to be quite so upsetting. She had known it was coming and had thought herself prepared for it. But there was a raw pain in knowing that he had chosen her as his mistress and another woman as his wife. Even though she understood the reason, she felt soiled, slighted, inferior. Unloved.

Though even that was untrue, she knew, and tried not to know it. She did not want to know if it was true. In the garden on the night the betrothal was announced she had believed it true. He had not said it, but she felt with a deep certainty that he loved her as she loved him. But if it was so, she did not want to know it beyond any doubt. The knowledge could only bring the worse pain of hopelessness.

She would go to Ebury Court, she thought suddenly. Clara had invited her, and it was ages since she had seen the woman who had been her dearest friend as well as her employer. It would be good to spend a few days, perhaps a week, in the country. It would be soothing. It would be good for Susan too.

"Would you like to go into the country for a few days to play with Paul and Kevin?" she asked Susan when the story had been read. "And see Aunt Clara and Uncle Freddie?"

"With you, Mama?" Susan asked.

"Yes, with me," Harriet said. "You and I together. Shall we go?"

Her daughter nodded. "I'll show Aunt Clara my doll."

They should go tomorrow, Harriet decided, eager to be gone now that she had thought of it. She should go and avoid Thursday's painful good-bye. The very idea of that brought on a pain so intense that she wanted to run in panic. And that was what she would be doing if she left for the country without seeing him. Somehow the good-bye was necessary. She knew that if she avoided it she would be forever haunted by something that had never been finished.

Besides, if she was strictly honest with herself, then she must admit that she could not resist the temptation to see him one more time, to be alone with him once more. Except that there could be nothing between them except the good-bye. He was a betrothed man.

"We'll go on Friday," she said. "In the morning bright and early. I'll send word so that they will be expecting us."

"I can't wait," Susan said.

"Neither can I." Harriet hugged her.

He had returned to town with his grandmother and his aunt on Tuesday afternoon. In the evening he had escorted Lady Phyllis to the opera as a member of a party that included her parents. On Wednesday he drove her in the park. In the evening he danced two sets with her at the Sefton ball. If the *ton* had not drawn the obvious conclusion with certainty, then all their doubts were put to rest on Thursday morning when the announcement appeared in the *Morning Post*.

Phyllis was unhappy, he knew. Although they seemed to have set the foundations for a cautious amity while he was at Barthorpe Hall, she had become icy, quite uncommunicative since their return to London. He wondered if he was succeeding in playing a better part. Since for years he had retreated behind a public facade of aloofness and a certain haughtiness, he guessed that he probably was. And he was making every effort to set the girl at her ease, to make himself agreeable to her. He had no intention of deliberately punishing her for the mess he had made of his own life.

He lived for Thursday afternoon and dreaded it. He feared the inflexibility of Harriet's moral principles. She had bent them recently in order to become his mistress, but he knew that doing so had put a severe strain upon her conscience. He suspected that she would go no further. He had encountered her inflexibility, like a brick wall, six years ago. He dreaded that the afternoon would have no more to offer than good-bye. He dreaded that it would be the end, that after Thursday he would not see her again except by chance and at some distance at a social function they both attended.

One of his fears, at least, was eased when he saw her hurrying toward his carriage only three minutes after the appointed time, and his coachman lifted her inside. She glanced at him and sat in the farthest corner, her hands clasped in her lap. Had she not been wearing gloves, he was sure he would have been able to see the white of her knuckles. Perhaps this would be the last time, he thought. He was going to have to fight the battle of his life to get her to continue their liaison for a while longer. He had begged for one more meeting and she had granted it—to say good-bye. He sat in his own corner of the carriage, looking at her, saying nothing.

For the first time since they had begun their affair, she hesitated when they were in the sitting room of his house. But his hand at the small of her back guided her firmly on into the bedchamber. He was not going to lose her. He could not lose her. It was the one thought that pounded through his head. He turned her as he shut the door, drew her to him with both arms, and set his mouth to hers. He felt her mouth and body leap into instant response.

"Harriet." He trailed kisses along her jaw to her ear. "I have missed you. It has been an agony being without you. Tell me you have missed me too. Tell me."

Her body sagged into relaxation. "Don't, Archie." Her voice was flat, devoid of emotion. "Let me go."

He dropped his arms and took a step back from her. "You came," he said. "You promised today. Harriet, we need today." He reached out both hands to her.

"Today is forbidden," she said. "Until today we have harmed no one but ourselves. It has always been wrong, but it is only our own moral values and our own sense of right and wrong that have suffered. Today we harm someone else. Today your fidelity is pledged to someone else. You do wrong to meet me, and I do wrong, knowing that you belong to someone else."

Her face was pale and set. The speech sounded stilted and rehearsed. He guessed that she had been able to persuade herself to come only on the understanding that it was strictly to say good-bye.

"I am not married yet," he said, possessing himself of her hands and tightening his grip when she would have pulled them away. "It is not forbidden yet, Harriet."

"A promise to marry is as binding as the marriage vows," she said. "I came to say good-bye, Archie." There was momentary pain in her eyes, but she blanked them immediately. She had herself under iron control.

"You could have said good-bye at Barthorpe Hall," he said harshly. "Or at Lady Sefton's ball last evening. You could have found a moment to say the single word. You came here to be alone with me. At least let there be some honesty between us."

She raised her chin a little. "Yes," she said, and reached for something else to say. Obviously she had not prepared an answer for just that charge. Her eyes wavered for a moment. "Yes, you are right. I needed to say it—when we were alone."

"A single word?" he said. You needed this clandestine meeting, this place, this whole afternoon, just to say a single word to me?"

"Yes." Her eyes filled with sudden tears and she bit her upper lip and dropped her head. "It is not easy, Archie. I am unaccustomed to *affaires de coeur*. I cannot take them lightly."

"Harriet." He cupped one palm about her cheek. What had he done to her? God, what had he done in his selfishness? He should have known when she offered herself to him at Kew that it would tear her conscience apart if he took her. And now it was too late to correct the error.

She moved forward, as she had done in the garden at Barthorpe Hall, and set her face against his neckcloth. "It is not easy," she repeated, her voice high-pitched with emotion. "Please, let us have done, Archie. Take me home. Please take me home."

It was the only decent thing he could do—take himself out of her life as speedily as he could and give her the only thing that might bring healing to her conscience and her emotions—time. Time without him. He belonged to Phyllis. He should turn and open the door and escort her back downstairs and into his carriage. He would do it—in just a moment.

"Harriet." He set a hand beneath her chin, lifted her wet face, and set his mouth, open, over hers. My love. My love. My love.

"Archie." Her arms were up about his neck, her body pressed to his. "Archie. It is not easy. Oh, please, it is not easy."

Yes. It was the only way to say good-bye. With their bodies. With their whole selves. Just once more. And perhaps then he could persuade her to prolong their affair for a little longer. Until the end of the Season. Until his marriage. She would not have the guilt of adultery on her conscience until his marriage. He was not married yet. Yes, this was the only way.

He heard a button thud onto the carpet as he pulled ungently at the opening at the back of her dress. She was sobbing against his mouth. Her arms had a stranglehold about his neck. He stooped down and scooped her up into his arms. He undressed her when she was lying on the bed, dragging her clothes down over her body, flinging them over the foot of the bed. He tore off his own clothing and came down on top of her, into her reaching arms. He found her mouth with his again, pressed his knees between her thighs and pushed them wide, slid his hands beneath her, and thrust deeply into the welcoming soft heat of her.

Harriet. My love. He could not lose her. He would not lose her. He needed her as he needed the air he breathed. He lay still in her, his mouth covering hers. She was his. They belonged together. This was not good-bye. She must feel it too. He lifted himself onto his elbows and smiled down at her, resisting the urge to begin moving in her, bringing them both to the climax that was not far off. Her face was wet and reddened with tears.

"It need not end yet," he said. "There can be many more times before we need say good-bye. Does that feel good?" He stroked her once and paused again. "Tell me it feels good." He lowered his head to touch his lips softly to hers.

Her eyes filled with tears again. "You are not even an honorable man," she said. "I thought at least you were an honorable man."

A stinging slap across the face or a pail of cold water thrown over him could not have been more effective. He looked down at her for one frozen moment and then withdrew from her body and rolled off the bed. He dressed quickly, his back to her. She did not move.

"Get dressed," he told her. He could hear the coldness in his voice. "Get dressed before I turn around. I might be tempted to continue my rape of you."

He did not turn until he was sure she had clothed herself. Her face was set and pale again when he did so, with traces of redness from the tears.

"It was not rape, Archie," she said. "I consented."

He hated her suddenly and quite unreasonably. And hated himself. No, only himself. He loved her. And yet when he spoke he lashed out at her. "Yes," he said. "It seemed to me that you did, Harriet. You came here to be raped, did you not? So that you could have your final forbidden piece of pleasure without the guilt. No, you say, and then yes, and no when your body is mounted and it seems too late. Were you glad that I am without honor? Were you disappointed when I did not give you what you were asking for? You spoke too soon, Harriet. You could have had your thrill and your little moment of righteousness too if you had waited until after I had spilled into you."

"You are no gentleman," she said.

He laughed. "Men without honor rarely are," he said. "But you have known that fact about me for six years, Harriet. Gentlemen do not take ladies to bed without first making them marriage vows, do they? Or not in your prudish little world, anyway. Did you hope until the last possible moment that I would make you those vows after all? You are naive, my dear. Men do not marry for what is voluntarily and eagerly given free of charge."

He could not believe what he was saying. He watched her eyes widen in shock and bewilderment and wanted to hurt her more. Because he was hurting. He knew what was happening, knew himself for the blackguard he was, and could seem to do nothing to stop himself. He was angry and upset and hurting—and full of self-loathing.

"Good-bye, your grace," she said, moving suddenly in the direction of the door. "I shall walk home."

"The devil." He caught none too gently at her arm. "Men without honor still like to pretend in public that they are gentlemen, ma'am. I shall escort you home. You will be quite safe with me, I assure you. I usually attempt rape only once in an afternoon."

"You are despicable." She was almost whispering. Her large, candid green eyes looked directly into his. "I am glad I have seen you as you are at last. I should have known it, of course. You knew I was an innocent, and an impoverished innocent at that, six years ago, and yet still you pursued me and would have ruined me. And this year you pursued me again, although you knew very well that you must select a bride before the Season was over. I pity Lady Phyllis, your grace. I am glad my eyes have been opened. Suddenly it is not difficult at all to say good-bye. Quite the contrary. And I would prefer to walk home than have to spend more time in your presence."

He allowed her words to whip about him like a lash. Yes, perhaps it was better this way after all. He had hurt her enough. She was right. He was no gentleman. He would have set her up in a way of life that would have killed her spirit. And now he had allowed her to sacrifice her conscience when he might have offered his name as well as his body. She was right. It was better that she had seen the truth and had come to hate him. Perhaps she would suffer less.

"I shall not inflict my company on you, ma'am," he said, making her his most elegant bow. "Allow me to escort you to my carriage. It will convey you home."

They walked side by side and in silence down the stairs, past the impassive servant who opened the door for them, and out to his waiting carriage. He handed her inside and waited for her to settle her dress about her, clasp her hands in her lap, and stare straight ahead with pale, set face. He hesitated, decided to say nothing, and closed the door quietly. He watched as the carriage disappeared down the street. And then he went back inside the house and upstairs to fling himself diagonally across the rumpled bed, his face buried in the pillow that still bore the imprint of her head.

He had always treated with some amusement the ridiculous poetic idea of a heart breaking with love. He did not feel at all amused at this precise moment.

Clara Sullivan had been thin and pale and unable to walk when Harriet had worked for her. She had suffered a lengthy, debilitating illness during the years she had spent in India with her father, an illness that had killed her mother there. She had married Frederick Sullivan, knowing that he was a mere fortune hunter, because she was lonely and twenty-six years old, and because he was, so she had told Harriet, beautiful.

When she came down the steps outside the house at Ebury Court to greet Harriet as soon as the latter alighted from the carriage Sir Clive had insisted she travel in, it was almost hard to realize that she was the same Clara. Slim, but no longer thin, elegant, her cheeks tinged with healthy color, her dark hair short and wavy, her dark eyes shining, she looked almost beautiful and certainly happy. She hugged Harriet tightly and bent to exclaim over Susan's prettiness and to admire her new doll.

And Frederick Sullivan, who had come out with her, still darkly and quite devastatingly handsome, was greeting her with what seemed like a smile of genuine welcome. He looked now, Harriet thought, like a potential lady-killer who had decided that perhaps it was more satisfactory to kill only one lady—with love. It was Freddie, dissolute gambler and wastrel, who had somehow convinced Clara that she could walk again, who had somehow brought joy into the life of a lonely woman. And who somehow seemed to have fallen in love with her in the process.

He kissed Harriet's cheek as he shook her hand. "Harriet," he said, "you are looking remarkably smart. Slaying the poor male population of London by the score, I would not doubt."

"Modesty forces me to admit, Mr. Sullivan," she said, "that it has been by the dozen, not the score."

He offered her his arm as Clara took Susan by the hand. "Now before we set one foot inside the house," he said, "let's have done with this Mr. Sullivan nonsense once and for all, shall we? My name is Freddie. A rather disreputable-sounding name, perhaps, but you must blame my parents for that."

"Freddie," she said, smiling and blushing.

"We must take Susan up to see the boys, Freddie," Clara said. She turned to Harriet as they entered the house. "Kevin may still be sleeping, but we promised Paul that he could come down when Susan arrived. He wore Freddie ragged this morning by positively refusing to get down off his pony's back when our ride was over. They stayed out for longer than an hour after I had brought Kevin inside."

"Ah, one escaped convict," Frederick said as a very dark, wiry little boy came streaking down the stairs toward them. "And one distraught nurse left behind in the nursery, I would not doubt."

Harriet could feel herself relaxing. It felt so good, so very good, to have left London and the past month behind her. So very good.

Paul wanted to go outside. Without a moment's delay. So did Susan. Frederick sighed, chuckled, bent to swing his son up onto one shoulder, looked down into Susan's wistful face, stooped down again and lifted her more gently to his free shoulder, and retraced his footsteps down the stairs.

Clara linked her arm through Harriet's. "Will you mind if we do not join you immediately, Freddie?" she called after his retreating back. "I want to hear all about London and the Season. Have you had great success, Harriet? I am sure you must have. You have not lost one iota of your beauty since I first knew you, and now you add great elegance to it. Have you met anyone special? I do hope you have. I know Lord Wingham was special to you, but as I keep saying to Freddie, I do hope you will soon find someone with whom you can spend the rest of your life in happiness. Someone just like Freddie." She laughed.

"Well," Harriet said, "I have had two offers of marriage, one of them very eligible indeed. But it is too soon yet. Too soon after Godfrey. I have been content merely to enjoy myself. And I have certainly done that." She smiled brightly as they entered the drawing room and Clara rang for tea.

"Have you?" Clara looked at her closely. "I am glad, Harriet." She hesitated. "Freddie says that Tenby has been in town." Clara had been fully aware of her painful infatuation with Lord Archibald Vinney six years before.

"Yes," Harriet said, still smiling. "I have seen him, Clara, and even danced with him once or twice. He has just become betrothed to Lady Phyllis Reeder, the Earl of Barthorpe's daughter."

"Yes, she would be," Clara said. "He was always very high in the instep. There was no—leftover-feeling there, Harriet?"

"Oh, goodness no." Harriet laughed. "He is still as handsome as ever. But fortunately I am older and wiser, and being married to Godfrey taught me that there is far more to look for in a relationship than good looks." She sighed. "I wish Godfrey had lived longer. He was not an old man."

Clara smiled her sympathy. "He gave you Susan," she said. "She is quite delightful, Harriet, and so like you that it is almost comical. I sometimes envy you your daughter except when I remember how weak with love and pride I am over my sons. They are both going to be as handsome as Freddie. Did you know that Julia and Daniel have had another boy? Daniel was quite upset, apparently, when he knew there was a third on the way."

"I called on her yesterday morning," Harriet said. "He is positively fat, Clara, and quite adorable. And Lord Beaconswood did not look at all upset. He had that look—oh, that look I remember on Godfrey's face when Susan was born." She settled gratefully into a conversation about children.

The Duke of Tenby got up early on Friday morning so that he could ride in the park and give his horse its head without endangering anyone's life but his own. He should pen some apology, he had been telling himself since the afternoon before. He should write to her and apologize for everything, particularly for his harsh and unfair words of the afternoon. And yet he could not write. The fairest treatment he could afford her was to honor her good-bye, to leave her strictly alone. It was better if she thought him an utter scoundrel, who could not even beg her pardon for insults given.

Had it been rape? He had been haunted by the possibility. She had said no. But she had told him it was not easy, and he had felt the control she had tried to keep imposed on herself. He had deliberately broken through that control and turned her no into a yes. A temporary yes. Did that constitute rape? A yes reluctantly given? A yes that he had known in his heart was really no? She had released him of that charge, at least, but he was not sure he could release himself.

He was to accompany Phyllis and her parents and his grandmother to a garden party that afternoon. Before then he must come to terms with himself or at the very least retreat safely behind his customary mask. He must. He owed it to his future wife to appear to be glad of her company.

Perhaps he could redeem himself somewhat in his own eyes if he could at least treat his fiancée with the proper respect and perhaps even affection. He must cultivate affection for her.

He resolutely put Harriet out of his mind, or at least as far back in his mind as he could force her.

Both his grandmother and his aunt were in the breakfast room when he arrived home. His grandmother was often up early. His aunt claimed to have been driven up by cramps in her legs.

"Dear Archibald," she said as he bent to kiss her cheek. "I always had a weakness for gentlemen in their riding clothes. They always look at their most virile then."

"Sophie!" the duchess said, shocked, while the duke chuckled.

He opened his letters—mostly invitations and notes of congratulation—after exchanging greetings with the two ladies. There was nothing of great importance, he thought, scanning them quickly. Until he came to the bottom of the pile and found a whole letter to be read. He glanced down at the signature. "Phyllis." He raised his eyebrows and read.

His grandmother was explaining something loudly to his aunt when he raised his head. She turned and looked inquiringly at him.

"You look as if you had seen a ghost, Archibald," his aunt said.

"Lady Phyllis wrote this last evening," he said. "She was going to leave a similar note for her father to read this morning. She was eloping with Lockhart last night. Poor girl. Her reputation may never recover from the scandal."

His grandmother stared at him, her expression wooden.

"Well, bless the girl," Lady Sophia said. "She doesn't need society, Archibald. All she needs is that pleasant young man and his place in the country. Scandal won't harm them there."

The duke looked keenly at her. "What have you done, Aunt?" he asked.

"Eh?" she said. "Don't whisper, Archibald. Some people are willing to take advice. Some people don't mind benefiting from the wisdom of their elders. I want you to take me

to see my little pet this afternoon. I have missed her pretty
face all week. No one to talk to. Is someone going to bring
me more coffee?"

A footman hurried forward.

The duke folded the letter carefully and set it down beside his plate. He felt numb. Too numb to feel relief.

"Well," his grandmother said, "I was obviously sadly
mistaken, Tenby. The breeding was not there after all. But
it was extremely naughty of her to allow matters to go so
far. I suppose you are happy about it?"

He did not answer.

"I suppose your first thought is of that other woman," she
said. "I'll not have it, Tenby."

"And I'll not have the matter discussed now, Grandmama," he said, looking her steadily in the eye. "I have
some thinking to do. When I have done it, perhaps I shall
consult you. It is still my hope and my intention to keep my
promises to you."

"But not with that woman," she said.

"I shall consult you, Grandmama," he said, "when I have
had time to think." He hesitated. "*That woman* is Lady
Wingham. A lady, Grandmama."

"I suppose," she said stiffly, her back very straight, "I
have some thinking to do too, Tenby. I have always wanted
your happiness. You must know that I have always wanted
that."

His tone softened. "We will talk later, Grandmama," he
said. He raised his voice. "I shall escort you to Sir Clive
Forbes's after luncheon, Aunt Sophie. And come there half
an hour later to bring you home again."

Lady Sophia sipped her coffee and said nothing.

Old fiend, the duke thought. Wonderful old fiend.

16

The Duke of Tenby drove his curricle to Ebury Court in Kent on Monday, having fought with himself all weekend—with what he owed Harriet, with personal inclination, with what he owed his position. His aunt, of course, had urged that he throw caution to the wind. She had not even waited until they returned home from their call at Sir Clive Forbes's and their discovery that Harriet had gone away. He doubted that Lady Forbes would have told him where she had gone—the woman had looked at him rather severely. But she had told his aunt.

"You have to go after her, Archibald dear," his aunt had said when they were in the carriage again. "You are free again, after all, and you do love the gel, after all."

"And that is all that matters, Aunt?" he asked. "Love?"

"Unfortunately no," she said after he had had to repeat his question. "One cannot be quite foolish. One cannot live on love. But if it comes to a choice between love and duty and choosing love will not bring disaster, then that is what one should choose. Would marrying my dear little Lady Wingham bring disaster into your life, Archibald?"

By no means. But perhaps marriage to him would bring disaster into hers. He was no gentleman. He was a man without honor. She did not want to see him again. Except that he suspected she was deeply hurt. He suspected that she loved him.

"Did you give this same advice to Lady Phyllis?" he asked loudly.

"She behaved foolishly," his aunt said. "An elopement is not good even if they do intend to live quietly in the country. But perhaps she meant to be caught, Archibald. Once she had written to you and sent the letter, it would not matter, would it? Perhaps she has persuaded her mama and papa to let her have the man she wants. He is the heir to a barony, you know."

She was proved quite correct. When the Earl of Barthorpe, much embarrassed, called soon after the duke's return home with his aunt, it was to inform his grace that Lady Phyllis had returned to the country with her mother and would in all probability marry the Honorable Mr. David Lockhart on or soon after her twenty-first birthday.

The duchess remained silent until Saturday afternoon, when she came into the library, where her grandson had been sitting all day, and sat down on the chair opposite his.

"She is gone into the country, then?" she said.

"With the countess," he said. "It is better for her than an elopement. Life would have been difficult for her. Even a broken engagement will not be easy."

"I did not mean Lady Phyllis," his grandmother said.

His hand played with a paperweight on the desk before him. "She has gone into Kent," he said. "Freddie Sullivan's wife is her friend."

"And you intend to go after her?" she asked. "You intend to marry her, Tenby?"

"What makes you think I would consider such a thing?" he asked.

"She is an unusually beautiful woman," she said. "And charming and modest with it. I have seen the way you look at her, Tenby. And the way she looks at you too, though she is far more well bred about it than you."

"Six years ago," he said, "I would have asked her to marry me. But I was called to Grandpapa's deathbed instead."

"It is an infatuation of long standing, then," she said.

"A *love* of long standing," he said softly, glancing up at her. She looked at her sternest and most straight-backed.

"I learned very young," she said, "that there are things in life very much more important than love, Tenby. Love, like self, must always be placed last. I learned early not to look for happiness in life and to despise those who make it a life's aim. I have asked myself yesterday and today what my life has accomplished, what to me is the most precious product of my life. I have thought of my parents, of early— friends, of your grandfather, of your father, of you. Maybe it is because you are last on the list, the one still present in my old age. Who knows? But I have been led to the conclusion that nothing and nobody in my life has meant more to me than you."

"Grandmama," he said, distressed, and waited for the burden of his duty to be rested squarely on his shoulders once more.

"It is because I love you, boy," she said, looking sterner than ever. "I have never thought about it because love is unimportant. But when I thought about it yesterday and today, I realized that it is true and that it hurts my heart a little. Love does hurt. I remember that from a long time ago. I want to die, Tenby, knowing that you are happy, knowing that love has been set high among the priorities of your life. I would like to see your heir before I die. But it is more important to see you happy."

She looked at him as if she had just delivered the sourest lecture of her life. She had looked just this way when he had been caught at the age of twelve romping with a group of village boys. First her lecture on what he owed his position and then his grandfather's cane.

"Grandmama," he said again, his hand closing about the paperweight.

"If she will make you happy," she said. "If Lady Wingham will make you happy, Tenby, then I will gladly become the dowager duchess in order that she may have my title. And I will love the girl. I believe she is lovable. And I will expect her to be delivered of a boy sometime next spring. The sooner the better. You will not have me with you forever. And your mother needs a grandchild."

"Grandmama," he said, "she may not have me."

She got to her feet and stood very erect before him. "As the Duke of Tenby," she said, "it is your duty to secure your line. If Lady Wingham is the duchess you want, you will see to it that she has you. Without nonsense and without delay."

Her sudden and unexpected consent in some ways made

his decision more difficult. Through a combination of strictness and an affection they seemed not to have been aware of, his grandparents had ruled his life since he was eleven years old. It was true that he had lived a life of some independence since his majority and had tasted all the pleasures that young manhood had to offer. But his grandparents would not frown at that. A man of his rank and fortune was expected to sow wild oats. It was part of growing up. In important matters, he had always been obedient to his training.

Now, in these few days, he felt that he had finally reached full manhood. By a stroke of sheer good fortune, he had been freed from the sort of life he had been prepared for and would have hated and would perhaps have passed on to his own children. He had been given the gift of freedom, the gift of a second chance. He did not want to rebel for the sake of rebelling. But he wanted to take charge of his own life, make his own decision about his future, be a worthy Duke of Tenby in his own way.

It complicated matters somehow to know that his grandmother had given her blessing to the course he leaned toward. If he was going to go after Harriet to try to persuade her to have him despite his shabby treatment of her throughout their acquaintance, he wanted it to be because that was what he had decided he wanted to do. On the other hand, of course, it would be good to know that he would not be hurting his grandmother.

Ultimately, of course, he knew that he really had no choice. The alternative to not going after Harriet was misery pure and simple. And it would be no temporary thing. He had loved her for six years. He still loved her. He would always love her. In the end he stopped torturing himself with indecision when the decision had surely been made before he had started. Surely as soon as he had read Phyllis's letter he had known that he would offer himself to Harriet if she would have him.

He drove his curricle to Ebury Court on Monday, more nervous than he had felt in his life.

There were people outside the house, he could see as he drove up the driveway. A man and two children, he saw as he drew nearer. It would be Freddie and his sons. This would make things a little easier. He would not have to make a formal entry into the house alone. He grinned at his friend as he jumped down from the curricle and handed the ribbons to a groom who had come running up from the stables. Freddie was strolling toward him in his shirtsleeves, his hair windblown. It still seemed strange to see Freddie, of all people, domesticated.

They shook hands heartily.

"Archie," Frederick said, laughing. "Looking as usual as if you had just stepped off Bond Street. You have decided to call on old friends at last, have you? It's about time. I hear congratulations are in order."

"Yes." The duke grinned again. He felt a strong urge to prolong this conversation. "I have just been freed from an irksome betrothal. You behold a free man again, Freddie, my boy."

His friend laughed and slapped him on the shoulder. "Double congratulations," he said. "This is more than a fleeting visit, then, Arch? Good. Clara will be delighted to see you. And you can help me with the cricket lessons."

The duke looked toward the two children, one with a cricket bat, the other bowling. At the same moment the ball shattered the wickets as the batter ineffectually sawed at the air with the bat. Freddie's older boy cheered with triumph and threw himself backward onto the grass. The batter burst into tears.

"Oh, oh," Frederick said.

"You have produced a little blond and I did not know of it, Freddie?" the duke asked, reaching for his quizzing glass as he walked toward the children with his friend.

And then the little girl turned, a look of abject misery on her face, and gazed up imploringly at Freddie. "I can't hit it," she wailed. "It's no good. I can't hit it."

Large green eyes. Rumpled golden-blond curls. A perfect little miniature of Harriet. Oh, God. The duke released his hold on the handle of his quizzing glass as Freddie stooped down on his haunches and ruffled the child's hair with one hand. He suddenly felt a million miles away from Harriet. He had thought he knew her. He had thought so when he had known nothing about a central—surely *the* central—fact of her life. Her marriage had been fruitful. She had this little child to give love and meaning to her life.

And then he saw from the corner of one eye that Freddie and these two children had not come out of doors alone. He turned to watch Clara Sullivan approach across the lawn with Harriet, Freddie's baby toddling along between them, holding to a hand of each. His heart felt rather as if it were trying to pound its way right out of his chest. He bowed to both ladies and took Clara's hand to raise to his lips.

"I have come to impose upon your hospitality for a day or two, ma'am," he said. "If you will have me."

"If we will have you," she said. "How foolish, your grace, when Freddie is forever inviting you here. You know Harriet, Lady Wingham, of course."

He looked into her eyes for the first time. "How are you, ma'am?" he asked. "You have a beautiful daughter. I did not know of her existence."

"It would be easy not to," Clara said, "when one is in London and attending the activities of the Season. Children tend to become confined to the nursery."

"I always spent the mornings with Susan," Harriet said quietly, "And an hour or more of the evenings. My daughter is more important than anyone else in my life." Her face was pale, her eyes and her voice defiant.

Their attention was distracted. Freddie was still murmuring comforting things to Susan and coaxing her to take the bat in her hands again. His son had other ideas.

"*You* take the bat, Papa," he said. "It's fun when you bat. Send *her* inside to play with Kevin. She's just a girl. Girls are a nuisance and don't know anything."

"Oh," Clara said as the duke reached for his quizzing glass again.

"I'll take her for a walk," Harriet said quickly. "I am quite sure she really is spoiling the game."

Frederick had stood up. "Paul, my lad," he said, beckoning with one finger, "you and I are going to take a little stroll together into the house before coming back to play—

with Susan. Come along." He reached out a hand, which his son took, looking considerably subdued.

Harriet was upset. "What is he going to do?" she asked.

"Give Paul a spanking," Clara said. "My heart bleeds a little every time it has to happen, but I no longer try to stop it as I did at first. Freddie gives our boys tons of love, but they must learn not to be brats. No, Harriet, you must not feel responsible. Even my palm itched at that dreadful discourtesy. My son will not talk about other children in that way—even at the age of five."

The duke strolled toward the little girl, who was disconsolately scuffing the grass with one soiled shoe. "The bat won't seem to hit the ball?" he asked.

"No. It's a silly game anyway," she said. "I don't like it."

"What I always found," he said, "was that I had to stop thinking of the wickets behind my bat as simply pieces of wood."

She darted a look up at him with green eyes that seemed very familiar. "But they *are* wood," she said. "Look. And they keep falling down."

He went down on his haunches before her. Before the child Harriet had borne. The child she loved more than anyone else in life. Susan. "Name someone you love," he said.

She looked at him curiously. "Mama," she said.

"Good," he said. "Now someone else."

She thought. "My new doll," she said. "The one Aunt Amanda and Uncle Clive gave me."

"And one more," he said.

She thought for a while longer. "Uncle Freddie," she said.

"Splendid." He turned her, his hands on the tiny, fragile little waist, and indicated the wickets. "The middle one is Mama. The one on this side is your doll and the one on the other side is Uncle Freddie."

She giggled.

"Your job," he said, "is to protect them with your bat so that they do not get hurt and fall over. It used to work wonderfully for me. My mama and my grandmama and my dog rarely got hurt. I protected them."

She turned to look into his face with Harriet's candid,

trusting eyes. "But the ball won't hit the bat," she said, and her eyes filled with tears again. "Mama will get hurt."

"It's all in the timing," he said. "If you swing at the ball as soon as the bowler releases it, your bat is around and useless by the time the ball comes flying past. On the other hand, if you wait until the ball is level with you and then swing, the wickets are down before the bat is properly in motion. The secret is to swing at just the right moment."

She sighed, caught sight of his quizzing glass, and touched its jeweled handle with one small finger. "It's pretty," she said.

"Thank you." He smiled. "I shall let you peer through it the first time you hit the ball. Let me throw you a few practice balls. For the moment the wickets are blocks of wood again. Agreed?"

"I can't hit it," she warned him. "You are going to get cross, like Paul."

"Try me," he said gravely, getting to his feet and holding out the small bat toward her. She sighed again and took it.

The first time he bowled the ball to her, slowly and gently, she demolished a portion of Freddie's immaculate lawn and the wickets shattered.

"That always happens the first time during a practice," he said. "Next time hold the bat firm and lean into the ball. It will give you a feel for when exactly it arrives."

She trapped his next ball and left the wickets intact behind her. She knocked them down when she jumped up and down, squealing in delight. "Mama," she called. "Did you see? Did you see?"

The duke laughed.

"Yes, indeed I did," Harriet said, and he realized that she was still standing there. Clara was following behind the baby, who was running across the grass, his legs wide apart.

"Here come Paul and Uncle Freddie," the duke said, hiding a rueful smile at the nonchalant look on the boy's face. It was a well-remembered look from his own boyhood experience, a look that tried to tell the world that his stinging rear end was really nothing at all. "Maybe Paul will bowl and Uncle Freddie will field while I help you with the bat.

Those wickets are Mama and your doll and Uncle Freddie now."

"Not my doll," she said, pointing to the nearest wicket. "You. Who are you?"

"Tenby," he said. "Now we will certainly have to be sure to put up a good defense."

Paul marched forward. "I apologize, Susan," he said handsomely. "I can't hit the ball very well either unless Papa bowls slowly to me, and I'm not even a girl."

Freddie closed his eyes briefly.

"You are to bowl," Susan said, "and Uncle Freddie is to stand over there. Tenby is going to help me with the bat." She raised her voice. "Watch me, Mama. Watch me, Aunt Clara."

The duke exchanged grins with Freddie.

"Be prepared to chase after a six, Freddie, my lad," the duke said, standing behind Susan and setting his hands lightly over hers on the handle of the bat. "Right. Have at it, Paul, my boy. A nice overarm fast one straight at the center wicket."

They all had tea together in the nursery. In the few days she had been at Ebury Court, Harriet had learned that that was a daily ritual, abandoned only with the greatest reluctance, according to Clara, when they had visitors who did not have children. Today it was easy to avoid awkwardness by playing with the baby, building him a tower of wooden bricks in one corner of the room until he decided to knock it down and she had to start again. Freddie wrestled on the floor with Paul while Clara poured tea. Susan, inexplicably and embarrassingly, had set her favorite book beneath her arm, squeezed onto the chair beside the duke, and handed him the book. Harriet wondered how he was enjoying reading it to her and whether he was reading the wolf's part to Susan's satisfaction. She heard a deep and menacing growl even as she thought it. Susan, she saw at a glance, was holding his quizzing glass to her eye.

In her room later, having washed and changed and combed her hair after a couple of hours out-of-doors in a healthy breeze, Harriet wondered if she was going to be able to go downstairs to dinner. There would be no children. Just the four of them. Two couples. Clara, Freddie, herself, and—Lady Phyllis Reeder's betrothed. She wondered if he had known she was there when he decided to pay a call on his friend. Surely not. Surely he wanted to see her as little as she wanted to see him. Unless he was stalking her, tormenting her. It was not easy, perhaps, for someone of his rank to give up a possession—that was all she had ever been to him—until he was fully ready to do so.

She hated to think that he had come to torment her. She wanted to believe that she had been wrong when she had accused him of being without honor. She wanted to believe that their quarrel had brought out the worst in both of them and in no way represented the persons they really were when rational.

She hated to think that he now knew about Susan. Why she had been reluctant for him to know, she was not sure. Except perhaps in keeping part of herself from him she had thought to keep her identity, to save herself from becoming submerged entirely in her love for him. Now she felt utterly defenseless. And he had played with Susan, showing a humor and a patience that she would not have expected, though she had glimpsed it with Lord Mingay's children at Barthorpe Hall. He had read the story to Susan three times in a row, repeating the wolf's part over and over each time he came to it and Susan had demanded more.

Good heavens, Harriet thought, feeling quite sick, he was going to make as good a father as Freddie was. To her children. Lady Phyllis's children. She fought the tears that wanted to flow. She fought even harder and bit upon her upper lip when a tap came at her dressing-room door and Clara opened it and peeped around it.

"Are you ready?" she asked. "Good. We will go down together."

Harriet shook he head. "I—I don't feel very well," she said, "or very hungry. Too much fresh air, I suppose. It was rather windy, was it not? I believe I will stay here if you don't mind, Clara."

"But you are dressed," Clara said. She came inside after a pause and closed the door quietly behind her. "It is no coincidence, is it? I told Freddie it was no coincidence, and he said of course it was not."

"What is no coincidence?" Harriet took refuge in ignorance.

"Did he tell you," Clara asked, "that his betrothal is ended? His fiancée eloped with someone else, or tried to."

With Mr. David Lockhart. Oh, dear God. "No," she said, "he did not tell me. Why should he?" But she felt the telltale color creep up her cheeks.

"Harriet." Clara came across the room toward her and knelt in front of her. She took her hands in a firm clasp. "Oh, Harriet dear, it did not fade during all those years, did it?"

"I—'' Harriet drew a deep breath. "No."

"And he has come pursuing you here?" Clara said. "Just as he did before? Has he been making you improper proposals again? Shall I have Freddie send him away? He will if I tell him you are being harassed, even though Tenby is his friend. I'll not have you upset in my own home, Harriet."

Harriet looked at their hands. "Perhaps it is me you should send away," she said. "I was his mistress for almost a month, Clara. But no longer. I ended it last week."

"Oh, Harriet." Clara squeezed her hands more tightly. "Oh, my poor dear. He is quite unscrupulous where women are concerned. I'll have Freddie ask him to leave."

"No," Harriet said. She swallowed. "Don't do that. I ran six years ago—back to Bath rather than go with you and Freddie to London and perhaps have to see him again. And I ran last week rather than risk having to see him every time I went to another entertainment. I am going to stop running and stop avoiding him. I have to learn to live with the fact that he inhabits the same world as I and that sometimes—when we are both in London or when we are both here or in Bath—we move in the same circles. I am going to learn to see him just like any other man."

"Oh, Harriet." Clara set her head to one side.

"I am," Harriet said firmly. "I am going to fall out of love with him if it takes the rest of my lifetime to do it."

She got to her feet and Clara rose also. "Let's go down to dinner. I am starved."

Clara laughed despite the look of continued sympathy in her eyes. "I like your spirit," she said. "And he is a gentleman, after all. He will not harm you in our home, Harriet. He was very good with Susan."

"I don't want him near Susan," Harriet said, marching rather belligerently toward the door and opening it. "Susan was Godfrey's. And she is mine. I don't want her smiling at him and carrying her books for him to read." She stopped suddenly and looked back at Clara. For a moment she had to bite her lip again. "I should have chosen a new father for her when I was in London. She needs a father so badly, Clara. Telling her how Godfrey used to play with her is no substitute for having a father to play with her now."

Clara tutted. "Susan will have a new father soon enough," she said, "and you a husband, Harriet. It will happen, dear. I promise." She linked her arm through Harriet's and moved her in the direction of the staircase.

17

He was almost reluctant to get her alone. Perhaps it was that he did not know quite how to approach her. Or that he was afraid of rejection. One never knew with Harriet. One could certainly not count on her jumping at the chance to become a duchess.

He did not press matters during the evening. He was content to have Freddie and Clara as chaperons and to draw some wry amusement from the fact that although Harriet was not silent, she conversed exclusively with them and did not once look him in the eye. She made polite noises whenever he called on her to confirm some observation he had made about London and the Season or else pretended not to hear him at all.

He was content to look at her, golden in contrast to the very dark coloring of both Clara and Freddie; dainty, elegant, refined, beautiful. He was content to look at her with longing and cautious hope and a certain fear.

Obviously his looks were as transparent as they had been at St. James's Square and at Barthorpe Hall.

"Well, Archie," Frederick said when the ladies had left them alone and retired to bed. He handed his friend a glass of brandy and settled comfortably in a chair with his own. "To what do we owe the pleasure?"

"Of my company?" the duke asked. "Does there have to be a reason? Is not the call of an old friendship enough?"

"Let's be blunt." Frederick chuckled. "Clara is concerned about your intentions toward Harriet. They were somewhat base a number of years ago, I seem to remember."

"Do I have to have any intentions?" the duke asked.

"Could it not be pure chance that has brought us both here at the same time?"

"You have been undressing her with your eyes all evening," Frederick said. "And liking what you see, Arch."

The duke set down his glass on the table beside him. "I think not, Freddie," he said quietly. "I believe you insult the lady by suggesting that she invites such impertinence."

"This is interesting." Frederick hooked one leg over the arm of his chair. "Very interesting indeed. Perhaps we should move on to other topics of conversation before I find myself with an engagement to meet you at dawn. Clara would not be amused. I will say this, though, Archie. A leg shackle is not at all bad. In fact, I would not free myself of mine if I were offered all the inducements the world has to offer. You would enjoy one too, my lad—with the right woman, of course." He chuckled.

The duke did not press the matter the following morning, either. They were all to ride out together—the children too. Paul was mounted on his own pony and preened himself when the duke leveled his quizzing glass at him and complimented him on his seat. Freddie had the baby up before him. Susan was to ride with her mother. Harriet mounted first and then reached down for a groom to lift the child up.

"It would be best if she rode up here with me, ma'am," the duke said, moving his horse over beside hers. "Your sidesaddle will make holding her difficult."

She stiffened but did not look at him. "We will manage perfectly well, I thank you, your grace," she said.

"Susan," he said, looking down at the child, pretty in a green velvet riding habit and jaunty little feathered hat, "the choice will be yours. Would you prefer to ride on your mother's sorry hack or on this splendid black stallion? I shall not try to influence your decision."

She looked from her mother to him, from her mother's horse to his. And then looked up at her mother and pointed at his horse. "May I, Mama?"

It was a mistake, he knew. Harriet rode out of the stable-yard without a word, her back rivaling his grandmother's for dignified straightness. He bent down without the groom's assistance and lifted her daughter to sit before his saddle. She settled there and looked primly about her. So like Harriet that he wanted to laugh.

"He is splendid," she said. "I am going to have one just like him when I grow up."

"Are you?" he said. "All the young men will come flocking to see such a dashing horsewoman."

But she was too young to be interested in the prospect. "Do the wolf again," she said.

He tucked one arm about her as he guided his horse after the others with his free hand on the reins, and growled ferociously.

She laughed with delight. "Again," she said.

"Actually," he said, feeling anger bristle from every pore of Harriet's body as she rode ahead of them, "I believe wolves howl." But he growled again into the little girl's ear. Freddie must have said something to amuse the baby. He was shrieking with laughter.

They rode for an hour. Harriet stayed ahead the whole time, talking determinedly first with Clara and then with Freddie. He had made a mistake, the duke thought again. He should have allowed her to take Susan, even though it would have been awkward to do so when she was riding sidesaddle.

By the time luncheon was finished the rain that had threatened all morning was coming down in a fine and gloomy drizzle. It was not a great atmosphere in which to force the issue, the duke thought. He would have much preferred bright sunshine. But he could not put off the moment any longer. If he did, he might lose his nerve altogether. Or he might feel obliged to leave. Now was the time. Later in the afternoon they would be playing with the children again and taking tea with them.

But he could not find Harriet, though he wandered about the house and even tapped on her dressing-room door and peered about the door of the nursery. Clara was in there, singing a lullaby to the baby, whose head was nestled on her shoulder, while the other two children were doing something at a table with the nurse. But there was no sign of Harriet.

Freddie was in the library. "Ah, there you are," he said

when the duke appeared. "Do you fancy a game of billiards, Archie? It looks as if our spell of glorious weather is finally over."

"I am looking for Harriet," the duke said.

"Are you?" Frederick said. "*Harriet*, Archie? Not Lady Wingham?"

"Have you seen her?" the duke asked.

"Yes, actually," Frederick said.

The duke frowned. "Well?"

Frederick ran the fingers of one hand through his hair. "The thing is, Arch," he said, "I have to ask you what your intentions are."

"What the devil are my intentions to you?" The duke's frown had become thunderous.

"Clara will have my head if I allow you to harass her friend," Frederick said. "Actually she would not be averse to my asking you to leave, old boy. For myself, I am Harriet's host and owe her my protection."

"Well, the devil," the duke said. "You have grown damnably respectable, Freddie."

"Guilty as charged," his friend said. "The fact as I understand it, Arch, my boy, is that she gave you your walking papers sometime last week. I can't have you propositioning her again on my property—or on Clara's property, to be strictly accurate."

"Damn you, Freddie," the duke said. "I am aiming for a leg shackle if it is any of your business. Where is she?"

Frederick grinned. "Under the circumstances," he said, "Clara would kill me for *not* telling you. Go to it, Arch. Are you sure your grandmother won't organize a firing squad when she finds out? Unclench those damned fists. Do you know where the summerhouse is?"

"Yes," the duke said.

"She was headed there," Frederick said. "So that she would not accidentally run into you, Arch. So that she could have some peace and quiet. Maybe she won't mind being disturbed for a marriage offer, though."

The door shut with a click before he had quite finished the last sentence. He chuckled and went upstairs to his wife's sitting room to await her return from the nursery.

* * *

The damp had not yet penetrated to the summerhouse. Or the chill, though she had brought a shawl with her and held it about her shoulders now for comfort. The large glass windows of the octagonal summerhouse seemed to have trapped the heat of the sun for the last several weeks and had not yet let it go.

She had brought a book with her, but it lay unopened on the bench beside her. She sat with closed eyes, her head back against the glass of one of the windows. The gloom and the drizzle were appropriate. They matched her mood. Susan was enjoying herself. She liked playing with Paul—most of the time—and she liked fussing over Kevin too. Freddie, who with his man's energy was willing to play endless physical games, had become one of her favorite people. And someone else too since yesterday. Harriet swallowed. She hated him. If he had come by coincidence, he should have left as soon as he knew she was there too. If he had come by design, he was despicable. Yet Susan liked him.

She wished she could go back to just a week ago. A week and a day. Viscount Sotheby was a kind and courteous gentleman. He would have made a good father to Susan, and that was what Susan needed desperately. She needed a father to give her a sense of total security. And he would have made a good husband. He would have given companionship, affection, dependability—all those things she had lost when Godfrey died and ached to have again.

"Godfrey." She wiped away a tear with one hand.

Viscount Sotheby had said that he would remain one of her admirers, that perhaps at some future time he would renew his offer. Perhaps if she went back to London now, he would renew it before the end of the Season. Perhaps he would. But she let go of her plans before they could even begin to develop in her mind. She had been able to be a good wife to Godfrey even though she had never been able to give him her whole heart, because she had had her honor to offer him. She no longer had that to offer any man.

She must return to Bath. If he intended to stay, she must

leave soon. Tomorrow, perhaps. Susan would be upset, but they would have to go.

And then the summerhouse door opened hurriedly and someone rushed inside and closed it again. Harriet turned her head and opened her eyes. And closed them and turned her head back again. Of course. Freddie was his friend. And she had told Freddie where she was going in case Susan should need her. Or had she told him for another reason? She could no longer be sure of her motives.

"Ugh!" the Duke of Tenby said. "I have probably ruined a perfectly good pair of Hessians and one of Weston's most costly coats. The weather has a distinct resemblance to pea soup."

"Go away," she said. "I do not want you here. I do not want you in my life, your grace."

"Don't you, Harriet?" he asked. "Will you at least allow me to dry off a little and catch my breath?"

"Why have you come?" she asked. "To torment me?"

"What a strange reason that would be," he said. "Did you know that my betrothal has been shattered, Harriet? It seems that Phyllis tried to elope with one of her father's neighbors, a man so dull and insignificant that I cannot even recall his face. Lowering, is it not?"

"Perhaps," she said, "she loves him."

"Undoubtedly she must," he said, "else she would not have risked reputation and fortune in order to run off with him when she might have had me, would she?"

"I am glad for her," she said. "I would not wish you on anyone, your grace."

"What a splendid setdown," he said. "It is a shame it has to be wasted on an audience of one, Harriet. I don't believe I have ever heard a better."

"And so," she said, "your motive for coming here is clear. There is no impediment to our renewing our affair. Now that there is no question of adultery I can have no further scruples. And it was agreed that we meet twice each week until the end of the Season for an hour and a half of physical pleasure. You have come to claim what remains of that time. And perhaps longer than that if you are not sated with me by then. It seems there will be no summer wedding after all. Unless you have someone else in your sights already."

"It *was* a pleasure, Harriet," he said, his voice caressing her. "You must admit that."

She opened her eyes again and looked at him. He was sitting quite close to her. His eyes looked very silver in the dullness of the afternoon light. "Yes," she said. "And that is all that matters, is it not? Gratification of the body's cravings. It equates happiness."

"*Would* you be my mistress again?" he asked softly.

She closed her eyes once more. Though the question was expected, she had not expected the wave of longing that it brought with it. She almost believed the words she had just spoken in bitterness. She could have him again with just one little word. She could have his arms, his kisses, his body. The illusion of love. For a short while longer. Perhaps even for not so short a while.

"No," she said.

"Why not, Harriet?" She felt his knuckle caress the back of her hand, but he withdrew it before she could move her hand away.

"Because it brought me no happiness," she said. "Because it was wrong."

"Being in my arms brings you no happiness?" he said. "I am sorry."

"It was wrong," she said. "What we gave—and took— should be given and taken only within marriage. It is wrong when it is done for its own sake. I cannot do it again, Ar—, y-your grace. It will always be on my conscience that I once put pleasure before morality."

"Why did you do so?" he asked. "You took me by surprise, I must confess."

She opened her eyes once more and looked at him. He was seated sideways, one elbow on the back of the bench that extended right about the perimeter of the room. "I always wanted you," she said. "This year I thought that because I was a widow and you were still unmarried, I would have you and no one would be harmed. I was mistaken. I was harmed. It was wrong. That room. What we did there.

It was devoid of everything but—itself. I have been very unhappy."

"Have you, Harriet?" There was depth suddenly to his eyes, a depth that frightened her. She closed her eyes again and pressed her head back against the glass. "I have been too."

Unhappy? Did he know what happiness and unhappiness were? Did he know anything but getting his own way or not getting his own way?

"Because you did not finish what you started last Thursday?" she asked. "Because I will not sleep with you ever again? You will find someone else. There must be any number of women of *ton* who would gladly lie in your bed, and hordes of women in the theaters who would be delighted to be in your employ."

"Do you mean to hurt when you speak thus, Harriet?" he asked. "If you do, you succeed admirably."

"I don't think you know what it is to be hurt," she said. "Except perhaps in your pride. This must be a black week for you. Rejected by both your betrothed and your mistress."

"Perhaps," he said, "I should answer the question you began with. My reason for coming. I came to beg your pardon, Harriet."

"For what?" she asked. "You did nothing that was not done with my consent. You were right on Thursday. I wanted you. I wanted you to force yourself on me so that lying with a betrothed man would not be on my conscience."

"You are incurably honest," he said. "But it was not just that, Harriet. I have come to beg your pardon for six years ago." She turned her head to look at him. "I knew that in addition to being a virgin you were a total innocent. I knew that as a parson's daughter your moral values were dear to you. But I wanted you and I thought I could have you and I convinced myself that what I had to offer you by way of money and jewels and security for your future justified the offers I made you. They did not. I would have your forgiveness if you feel you can give it."

He had taken her completely by surprise. She swallowed. "Thank you," she said. "Oh, thank you. Yes."

"One burden gone," he said. "It has been a burden, Harriet. I thank you, my dear. And this year."

"This year I was no longer the things you said," she replied quickly. "And this year I consented. You need not have this year on your conscience."

"This year you seduced me," he said. "I ask your pardon for giving in to seduction, Harriet."

She stared at him, stupefied.

"You did," he said. "At Kew you offered me *carte blanche*."

"I did not." She was not sure whether the words had forced themselves past her lips or not.

"If you think back very carefully to the conversation we had there," he said, "I think you will be forced to admit, Harriet, that you offered to be my mistress when I had asked no such thing of you."

Could it be true? She could not sort her thoughts into order to remember that afternoon clearly, but she could remember thinking that she should have waited for him to speak first, to make his intentions clear. But she could also remember his beginning that part of their conversation by telling her that he wanted her.

"You were not going to ask me to be your mistress?" she said.

"No."

She leapt to her feet, horrified. She spread her hands over her face. If only a great hole would open at her feet, she thought, she would gladly jump into it.

"Are you feeling mortified?" he asked. "You behold before you a seduced man, Harriet. Or you would behold him if you would turn around and uncover your eyes."

"Go away," she said. "Please go away."

"I must beg your pardon," he said. She did not realize he had stood up until she felt his hands on her shoulders, turning her. She buried her face against him, her hands still over it. One of his hands stroked over the back of her head. "I accepted your offer because it seemed easier, Harriet. I could have what I wanted—or what I thought I wanted—

with no sacrifices, no commitment. But you were right a few moments ago. The whole thing was wrong because it was devoid of everything but physical pleasure. Well, not exactly, perhaps, but neither of us could admit to more than that. But there was no future, only a series of beddings with the hope that eventually we would both have had enough and would be content to part. That is all I have ever known with a woman before, you see."

"Please go away," she said.

"Forgive me," he said, "for cowardice, Harriet? And for degrading and hurting you."

"You did not degrade me," she said. "I did that all by myself. And you did not hurt me. I—I have not been hurt."

"I hope you are lying," he said quietly.

She lifted her head at last, setting her hands just below his shoulders. "You told me you wanted me," she said. "If you were not going to offer me *carte blanche*, what then?"

"I was going to ask you to marry me."

Her stomach lurched. "I don't believe you," she said.

"You see what happens when you start lying yourself?" he said. "Pretty soon you believe everyone else is lying too."

"I still don't believe you," she said.

He tutted."I was going to ask you six years ago too," he said. "I was going to seek you out a third time, Harriet. But my grandfather fell ill and died and suddenly I was Tenby and had all the responsibilities that went along with the title and became several notches higher in the instep. So I did not go. And I never asked Freddie about you. I did not know you had married. Or that you had become a mother."

"You would not have been allowed to marry me," she said, fixing her eyes on the single diamond that was pinned to his neckcloth.

"There would have been all hell to pay," he said.

"Well, then." She felt inexplicably hurt. "You had a lucky escape. And this year too if you speak the truth about Kew. I gave you what you wanted free of charge."

"Except that it was not what I wanted," he said.

"I'm sorry," she said, trying to move away from him. "I told you at the start that I lacked experience. I had known only an elderly and sickly husband, who gave me love in plenty but none of your e-expertise."

"You see?" he said, his voice so low that it was more like a caress than spoken words. "It was not what I wanted, Harriet. I wanted to give you love in plenty. Instead I gave you sexual expertise. And we both know where and with whom I learned that."

"Do-on't." Her voice was a wail as she buried her face again. "Don't, Archie. You do not know how vulnerable I am. My heart is already breaking. Don't destroy me."

"Why is it breaking?" he asked. "Tell me. Put it into words."

"You know very well," she said, pounding the sides of her fists twice against his chest. "Don't torment me. You know very well."

"I hope so," he said. "Will you let me make amends for two abortive attempts, Harriet? Will you marry me, my love?"

The endearment more than the offer turned her weak at the knees. "The duchess—" she said.

"—sent me here with her blessing," he said. "I was coming anyway, Harriet, but I was glad when she approved. She will love you dearly for the rest of her life, you know, if you will but present me with a boy within the year."

"Oh, Archie." Her breath was going as well as her knees.

"I will love you for the rest of my life even if you never do," he said. "Or if you present me with ten daughters instead. Will you marry me?"

"Susan—"

"—is in a fair way to capturing my heart," he said. "She has all her mother's wiles. I don't stand a chance. And I do believe that if I can learn to howl like a wolf instead of growling like a hound, I may be able to capture her heart too. Will you let me try? Will you let me be a father to her, Harriet? Will you marry me?"

"Archie," she said.

"Yes, love?"

But she could only repeat his name.

"You have become dreadfully inarticulate," he said. "Shall I kiss you while you think of something to say?"

"Archie," she said.

"I usually babble when I am nervous," he said. "Though I do not remember being nervous with anyone but you, Harriet. It is not at all manly, and definitely not ducal. I'm going to kiss you."

She lifted her face to his and closed her eyes as his mouth came down on hers, open. Her knees had gone and her breath. Her wits followed suit, and she clung to him, her arms about his neck, her mouth opening to the push of his tongue. Finally all her defenses went, completely, without a trace, beyond recall.

And then the silver eyes were looking down into hers. "It is very flattering for a man to see such vacancy in the eyes of the woman he has just kissed," he said. "Shall I be quite unscrupulous and press the advantage? Will you marry me?"

"Yes," she said.

"Yes, I should press the advantage?" He raised his eyebrows.

She smiled at him. "Archie," she said, "you are foolish sometimes."

He gazed into her eyes, and she could see that at some time during that kiss all his defenses had come down too. She could see vulnerability, yearning, and something else in them.

"I love you," she said. "I have always loved you."

"Ah," he said, "confession time at last. I lust after you, Harriet. I always have. I did not realize until I had satisfied that lust that I craved far more. You have created a hunger in me that only you will be able to satisfy until my dying day. It is a hunger for love. To receive it. And to give it."

"Archie," she said.

"Next week," he said. "Special license. We have to start working on that boy without further delay, Harriet. Or on those ten girls. Or on all eleven if you wish. Ah, my love, you will never know quite what that blush does to my heartbeat."

"Perhaps," she said, "we should go back to the house and tell Susan. And Clara and Freddie."

"And back to London to tell my grandmother and Aunt

Sophie," he said. "We had better prepare to have all the breath squeezed from our bodies by Aunt Sophie and probably every bone ground to powder too. The mind cringes from the prospect. But none of it can be done in the immediate future, Harriet. My boots and my coat will be damaged beyond redemption if they are taken out into this rain again. It looks as if it might stop—in about an hour's time, would you say? About teatime? What can we do to while away a tedious hour, do you suppose?"

She laughed and rested her forehead against him again. "I cannot imagine," she said. "But I am sure you will think of something, Archie."

"I have a mind to find out what it is like to, ah, unite us when it is more than just a physical thing," he said. "When it is done for love as well as for pleasure. Would you care to oblige me? It is something that cannot be done alone, after all."

"Archie," she said.

He tutted. "Inarticulate again?" he said. "May I take that one word as assent? I am going to take it as assent. Lift your face to me again, love, and let us get started. An hour does not seem so long a time, does it?"

She lifted her face.

"Ah, my sweet little blusher," he said, looking closely and fondly into her face before covering her mouth with his once more.